WHERE DEATH DELIGHTS

The Crowner John Series by Bernard Knight

THE SANCTUARY SEEKER
THE POISONED CHALICE
CROWNER'S QUEST
THE AWFUL SECRET
THE TINNER'S CORPSE
THE GRIM REAPER
FEAR IN THE FOREST
THE WITCH HUNTER
FIGURE OF HATE
THE ELIXIR OF DEATH
THE NOBLE OUTLAW
THE MANOR OF DEATH
CROWNER ROYAL
A PLAGUE OF HERETICS

WHERE DEATH DELIGHTS

A forensic mystery of the nineteen-fifties

Bernard Knight

severn House

This first world edition published 2010
in Great Britain and in the USA by
SEVERN HOUSE PUBLISHERS LTD of
9–15 High Street, Sutton, Surrey, England, SM1 1DF.
Trade paperback edition published
in Great Britain and the USA 2010 by
SEVERN HOUSE PUBLISHERS LTD

British Library Cataloguing in Publication Data

Knight, Bernard.
  Where Death Delights.
  1. Forensic pathologists–Fiction. 2. Wye, River, Valley
  (Wales and England)–Fiction. 3. Detective and mystery
  stories.
  I. Title
  823.9'14-dc22

ISBN-13: 978-0-7278-6874-9   (cased)
ISBN-13: 978-1-84751-222-2   (trade paper)

All Severn House titles are printed on acid-free paper.

Severn House Publishers support The Forest Stewardship Council [FSC],
the leading international forest certification organisation. All our titles that
are printed on Greenpeace-approved FSC-certified paper carry the FSC logo.

Mixed Sources
Product group from well-managed
forests and other controlled sources
www.fsc.org Cert no. SA-COC-1565
© 1996 Forest Stewardship Council
FSC

Typeset by Palimpsest Book Production Ltd.,
Grangemouth, Stirlingshire, Scotland.
Printed and bound in Great Britain by
MPG Books Ltd., Bodmin, Cornwall.

ACKNOWLEDGEMENTS

I would like to thank fellow crime writers Brian Innes and Michael Jecks for information on forensic chemistry, document examination and weapons; Judge John Prosser QC for some advice on legal history; Dr Wayne Jones of Linköping University, Sweden, and Professor Derrick Pounder of Dundee University for historical data on toxicological analysis – and Peter Haig and Jeremy Wills of Molyslip Atlantic Ltd for information on lubrication additives. Any errors are due to my misinterpretation of their kind assistance.

AUTHOR'S NOTE

In this tale of crime and detection, you will find no mention of CSI, DNA, SOCOS, PCA, PCR, PACE, CPS, HOLMES, FME or any of the endless forensic acronyms, as the action is deliberately placed in 1955. This was the year the author first became a pathologist and is a blatant piece of nostalgia, though the era has now become very popular in books, radio and television, possibly as a form of escapism.

To write an authentic crime novel nowadays, one has to defer to Health and Safety Regulations, Crime Scene Managers, Team Initiatives, Mission Statements, Human Tissue Act, Data Protection Act, Home Office Directives and all the depressing panoply of the bureaucratic Nanny State and political correctness.

Maybe our overcrowded world now needs these Orwellian strictures, but the stress levels were far less fifty years ago, when a trilby-wearing detective inspector in a belted raincoat could lean against the autopsy table with a fag and a mug of Typhoo Tips and chat to the pathologist about last Saturday's game!

Though the geography is authentic, considerable trouble has been taken to make all the characters and situations totally fictitious.

'Taceant colloquia, effugiat risus. Hic locus est ubi mors gaudet succurrere vitae . . .'

'Let conversation cease, let laughter flee. This is the place where death delights to help the living'

Inscription on the marble wall of the City of New York Chief Medical Examiner's Office and Morgue

PROLOGUE
The Welsh Marches – May 1955

A small lorry was perched on the rim of the wide concrete bowl. Two hundred yards across, it sat in the green countryside like a giant saucer. Fields sloped down on one side and woods rose on the other. The purple mass of the Black Mountains loomed on the horizon, beyond the fertile undulations of the borderland between England and Wales. Away on the left, the Skirrid could be seen, its profile split by the earthquake said to have occurred on the day of the Crucifixion.

Three men sat in the cab of the Austin one-tonner, squeezed together in the comfortable manner of workmen who have a legitimate reason to do nothing and still get paid for it. The driver had a copy of the *News Chronicle* spread over the steering wheel, while the older man in the middle was marking a folded copy of the *Sporting Times* with the stub of a pencil. On the nearside, the youngest member of the trio, an acne-scarred youth waiting to be called-up for National Service, stared down into the bowl of the small reservoir, where the steel-grey surface reflected the clouds.

'They're a 'ell of long time coming, in't they?' he complained in a nasal version of a Forest of Dean accent.

The driver raised his head from his paper. 'You did tell 'em it was urgent, din't you?'

'Course I did! But the copper on the other end was as thick as two short planks. I hope he passed it on, after me walking best part of mile to the bloody phone box.'

As if to allay his concern, there was the sound of an engine labouring up the steep slope of the lane from the main road and a moment later, a black Ford Consul, with a 'Police' sign on the roof, appeared through the open gateway on the other side of the reservoir. Reluctantly, the Water Board men climbed out and leaned against the back of the truck,

which was filled with barrows, spades and the other imple-
ments of their trade. They waited impassively for the car to
come up the ramp on to the circular apron. A uniformed
inspector and a large man in plain clothes emerged and
walked towards them, looking down at the water below.

'What's all this, then?' boomed the inspector, in the time-
honoured greeting of policemen everywhere. He was a thin
man with a lined face and a bushy moustache, almost certainly
ex-RAF, thought the youth.

The driver stepped a pace forward, touching a finger to
the peak of his flat cap. 'I'm the foreman, Ted Reynolds. I
sent the lad to phone you when we found this stuff.' He
pointed the finger away from the water, towards the bushes
that filled the area between the concrete and the perimeter
fence twenty yards away. The man in the tweed suit and a
trilby with a turned-down brim introduced himself as PC
Christie, the coroner's officer. The five of them walked the
few paces to the edge of the rim and stared across the water
to the distant hills.

'What exactly is this place?' asked Christie.

'An old holding reservoir, gives a head of pressure down
to the villages round Pontrilas and Grosmont,' responded the
foreman. 'We come up now and then to clean the sluices
and check the inlet valves.'

'Best show us what you've found,' grunted the inspector.

Ted Reynolds turned and led the way across the concrete
into the rough ground beyond, filled with saplings and bram-
bles. The lad hung well behind, not too keen on a reunion
with what he had discovered two hours ago. Reynolds halted
behind a scraggy elder bush, then bent and pointed down
with a calloused forefinger.

'Yer 'tis, I reckon there's more under the surface,' he
prophesied, poking at a brown object with a piece of twig.
The inspector and the coroner's officer squatted one each
side of him, staring down at the thing projecting from a drift
of last autumn's leaves.

'The lad came over here for a pee,' explained the foreman.
'Then he called us to have a look.'

He beckoned to the young labourer, who reluctantly came
nearer.

'I thought it was some old dead sheep, but when I kicked at it, it looked different,' he muttered.

The foreman gave it another prod with his stick. 'I used to work in an abattoir, so I know what the top end of a thigh bone looks like. But this ain't no cow nor sheep – it's yooman!'

The inspector took the twig from him and carefully scraped away some of the damp leaf mould from around the knob which projected above the surface, revealing a discoloured bone that went down into the soil.

Then he looked up and spoke to the coroner's officer.

'John, what d'you want to do about this? Call in CID or deal with it like a sudden death?'

Christie was a calm, avuncular man who looked and dressed like a prosperous farmer. He rubbed his chin thoughtfully.

'Better tell the DI, I suppose. Let him have a look at it and then get the remains taken to the County Hospital in Hereford. They can deal with them there, unless anything naughty turns up and we have to call in the Home Office chap.'

He turned to the Water Board foreman. 'Don't touch anything, and make sure nobody else comes near until we get another officer up here.'

Reynolds nodded, glad of an excuse to postpone working for another hour or so. The two policemen went back to their car, where the inspector radioed to get a local constable to stand guard until the CID appeared. Then with a wave to the workers, he made a cautious three-point turn on the concrete and vanished in the direction of Monmouth.

ONE
The Wye Valley – June 1955

'If I'd realized that setting up house was as hellish as this, I'd have stayed in bloody Singapore!'

He staggered through the office door with a large cardboard box and dumped the heavy typewriter on a new desk, whose five-ply top creaked ominously.

'Stop complaining, Richard! We've broken the back of it now.'

He stifled the obvious retort about breaking his own back and dropped into the swivel chair behind the desk, wiping the sweat from his face with a large khaki handkerchief. It was very warm and the confines of the Wye Valley seemed to hold in the summer heat, even though he should be used to it, having lived in the tropics for the past thirteen years. Looking across at Angela Bray, he almost resented how cool and fresh she looked in a yellow summer dress. His business partner sat at a table, checking lists of laboratory equipment, ticking off delivery notes against her own inventory of what they needed. The rest of the room and the one next door, which was to be their main laboratory, were piled with crates and cardboard boxes, most carrying labels bearing the name of suppliers in Cardiff and Bristol.

'All we need now are some clients, or it'll soon be overdraft time!' he muttered, thinking of their rapidly dwindling bank balance.

Angela slapped down her pencil and glared at Richard Pryor. 'Come on, Richard, the coroner has promised you regular post-mortems in Chepstow and Monmouth. And you've got those medical school lectures in Bristol, so that's a good start. We agreed that it would take us at least a year to break even.'

Her level-headed pragmatism was a counterpoint to his swinging moods, for she was always calm and self-possessed whatever the crisis. Pryor sometimes thought of her as the 'ice maiden', except that the thick mane of brown hair that framed her handsome face was hardly that of some Nordic beauty.

'That's the last of the stuff from the car,' he announced, his good humour returning. 'So I'll start shifting some of this stuff into the lab.'

He climbed to his feet and took off the jacket of his crumpled linen suit, which like all his clothes, was a legacy of more than a decade in the Far East. Before next winter, he reflected wryly, he would have to get something warmer.

Angela looked up briefly from her papers.

'Sian will be back soon, she can tell you where some of the things go. Then she can start putting the reagent bottles and apparatus in the right places.'

He humped a dozen boxes into the next room, which had been his late aunt's dining room but which now was lined with white Formica-topped kitchen units, a large wooden table standing in the bay window. With the last carton in his arms, he stopped in front of Angela.

'Where d'you want this microscope?'

She tapped her lists together and stood up, almost as tall as Pryor.

'I'll come and see, shall I? You'll be using it as well, once we get some histology going.' They spent the next hour in their new laboratory, unpacking boxes and starting to fill cupboards with bottles of chemicals and strangely shaped bits of glass. Even though it was not yet mid-morning, the old mansion was already stifling in the hot June day and Angela Bray mentally added a couple of electric fans to her next list of purchases.

'Where's that damned girl?' asked Richard eventually. 'I hope she's going to be reliable.'

Sian Lloyd, their new laboratory technician-cum-secretary had offered to stop off at the post office to get a supply of stamps and a wireless licence.

Angela sighed. 'She has to get a bus from Chepstow, then walk up from the village. Give her a break, Richard, she doesn't have a car like us.'

'Talking of a break, we could do with our elevenses.'

He looked hopefully at his partner, who steadfastly ignored

his hint that she should assume some domestic duties. 'There's no milk' she said. 'But if you want black Nescafé, feel free to make it.'

'I thought Jimmy was bringing us some groceries and things.'

'He is, but after shaking a couple of bottles of milk around on that motorbike of his, it will probably be butter by the time he gets here.'

Pryor had inherited Jimmy Jenkins along with the house that Aunt Gladys had left him in her will. He had been her gardener, odd-job man and part-time driver and when Richard had appeared as the new owner, he had materialized again and taken up his old duties virtually by default. Richard had to admit that though at first he had suspected the man was something of an idle scrounger, the house and four acres needed the attention that a pathologist and a forensic scientist were in no position to provide.

Thirst drove him to the old-fashioned kitchen that lay at the back of the big Victorian house, and in the rattling old Kelvinator fridge he found a flagon of local cider. Taking a couple of glasses back to the office, which had once been his late uncle's study, he put them on the table and sat down opposite Angela, who had gone back to check something on her equipment lists.

Abstractly, she murmured some thanks, still immersed in her papers. When she got to the bottom of the last page, she looked up at her partner and caught him staring out of the French window at the distant trees on the English side of the valley. Covertly, she studied his profile and decided again that he was not a bad-looking chap, in a stringy sort of way. Forty-four years old, he had that lean, sinewy appearance, often seen in men who had spent many years in the East. Though not a frequent cinema-goer, she was reminded of actors like Stewart Granger or Michael Rennie with their 'big white hunter' look, a similarity which Richard Pryor unconsciously reinforced with his belted safari suits with button-down pockets. He suddenly came out of his reverie and his deep-set brown eyes fixed her with a worried gaze.

'Do you think we've done the right thing? Both giving up good jobs to take a leap in the dark like this?'

'We've been through this before, Richard,' she said patiently. 'We agreed that we'd give it two years. If it doesn't pan out then, both of us are well enough established to go back to what we did before.'

Angela took a sip of her cider and shuddered slightly at the acrid flavour.

'People with our qualifications and experience are not going to starve, you know, even if we have to join the brain drain to the States or Australia.'

Dr Angela Bray had been a forensic scientist at the Metropolitan Police Laboratory in London and Richard Glanville Pryor was formerly the Professor of Forensic Medicine in the University of Singapore.

She had become increasingly frustrated by public service bureaucracy and the lack of any foreseeable advancement in the system, whilst Pryor had been offered a generous 'golden handshake' after nine years in the university, who wished to appoint a local Chinese in his place. He could have stayed on, but the size of the financial inducement, coupled with a weariness with the tropics and a yearning for his native Wales, tipped the scales.

He and Angela had met the previous year at an International Forensic Science Congress in Edinburgh. After discovering a mutual desire to make a radical change in their professional lives, they decided to combine their talents by setting up a private partnership to offer forensic expertise to anyone who needed it. Angela's decision was reinforced by the prospect of living in the beautiful Wye Valley on the Welsh border, as she had fond memories of holidays in the valley. There was little to keep her in London, so now it was crunch time, to see if their ambitious venture would succeed.

Richard had been living in the house for over a month and Angela had moved down a fortnight earlier, after burning her boats by selling her flat in Blackheath. One thing they had not fully foreseen was that their professional partnership was going to be less of a problem than their personal lives. Though Garth House was a large place with five bedrooms, it was not proving easy to share the accommodation, especially as it possessed only one bathroom.

Angela had made it quite clear from the outset that their

relationship was purely professional – she had no intention of becoming housekeeper, cook or surrogate wife. The obvious answer was for her to find somewhere to live nearby, but this seemed ridiculous with such a large house available, especially as their finances were already stretched. After spending the first few nights in a bed and breakfast in Tintern Parva, the nearest village, Angela rebelled at the ongoing cost and inconvenience.

'I'm moving in to the middle bedroom,' she announced, arriving with her cases in the back of her white Renault Dauphine. 'The village gossips can call me the scarlet woman from London if they like, but it's crazy to leave a big house like this half empty. As soon as we can afford it, we'll divide it properly into two flats.'

Garth House now belonged to both of them, as they had set up a limited company for their venture, he putting in the house and Angela the proceeds of the sale of her flat. As the courteous Richard had lugged her cases upstairs, he had wondered how this was going to work out. Were there locks on the bedroom doors, for instance?

'But I'm not cooking or cleaning, remember,' she called up after him. 'We'll have to camp out for a bit, until we sort out some more permanent arrangement.'

So far, their lifestyle had been spartan, with Shredded Wheat and Typhoo Tips for breakfast, a sandwich lunch and usually something from a tin as supper. Sometimes they splashed out on an evening meal in a café at Chepstow or Monmouth, the towns at each end of the famous winding valley with its steep, wooded sides. Aunt Gladys had died at eighty-six in a nursing home, leaving the house furnished. Though much of it was old and worn, they had kept the better pieces to kit out some of the bedrooms. The downstairs rooms, apart from the kitchen and one turned into a communal lounge, were given over to the needs of their practice. As well as the office, there was a large laboratory and a workroom each for Angela and himself, together with a toilet at the end of the corridor that led back from the central hall. A preparation room and wash-up for apparatus occupied the former scullery and what had been a huge pantry was now to be a storeroom.

As they finished their drinks, there was a throaty roar from outside as a motorcycle climbed the steep drive from the main road below and swung around the back of the house to the yard behind. Here there was a coach-house with space for two cars underneath a large loft that Angela had her eye on for an extension to the laboratory. With a final noisy revving, the engine of the Royal Enfield died and moments later the rider and his passenger marched into the office.

'Jimmy saw me at the bus stop and gave me a lift,' announced their sole professional employee. Sian Lloyd was a lively, ebullient blonde of twenty-four, small and shapely, with a snub nose and blue eyes. Not a girl to be pushed around, she gazed out at the world defiantly, speaking her mind on anything that concerned her – and some things that did not. Sian came from a working-class family, her father a welder in a local engineering works, a shop steward and fervent socialist, some of which had rubbed off on his daughter. She was fully qualified, having passed all the examinations giving her Fellowship of the Institute of Medical Laboratory Technology, and she had already started on an external degree in biochemistry.

'Here's the licence – and the stamps.' She placed an envelope on the table in front of Angela. 'Jimmy's left the groceries in the kitchen.'

Behind her, their odd-job man touched a finger to the greasy cap in which he seemed to have been born. Richard wondered if he even wore it to bed.

'Got all the stuff on the list, Miss Angela – and I saw some nice-looking sausages in Emery's shop, so I brought you half a pound.'

Jenkins was a broad, powerful man with a short neck and long arms. The fanciful Richard wondered if he had a touch of gorilla in him, after seeing his hairy arms and chest when he was clearing some of the neglected area behind the house. Jimmy, who appeared to be about fifty, had a wide, weather-beaten face with a broken nose and a permanent grin, which exposed irregular teeth yellowed by years of smoking Woodbines. On the rare occasions when he lifted his cap to scratch his head, he revealed stubbly grey hair that stuck up like a scrubbing brush.

'Goin' to rain tonight, no doubt about it,' declared Jimmy. 'So I'll get out and trim that hedge down by the front gate while it's still dry.'

Unless Richard gave him some definite task, he seemed to decide for himself what jobs he would do, but in spite of earlier misgivings, his employer had to admit that Jimmy seemed a good worker.

Angela took Sian into the laboratory to carry on sorting out the new equipment, while Richard walked down the corridor from the hall to the room at the back of the house which he had earmarked for his own. His medical books and journals were piled on the floor and he began stacking them on the bookcases that lined one wall. It had been a library-cum-smoking room in the distant days when Uncle Arthur had been alive.

Angela's room was the former drawing room in the front of the house. Like the lab, it had a magnificent view across the valley, with the River Wye meandering at the bottom and steep tree-covered slopes opposite. The large bay window matched the one across in the laboratory, and only Pryor's sense of chivalry prevented him being a little envious of Angela's domain.

It was Wednesday, but there was nothing else for him to do until the following Monday, when he was to start carrying out post-mortems for the coroner at the small public mortuaries in the area – assuming there were any customers that day. Though he wished no one any ill will, he trusted that the mortality statistics would ensure that there be some sudden deaths, suicides and accidents, as this would be almost their only financial income until their reputation spread and business came in from further afield. Thanks to a professional contact in Bristol University, he had been offered twenty lectures a year to medical students. The salary was derisory, but it gave him a nominal academic appointment and hopefully widened his medico-legal contacts which could lead to work from police, lawyers and doctors in the area.

As he hefted up heavy textbooks on to the shelves, he thought that the last time he had opened any of them was six thousand miles away, in the island city at the bottom of the Malay peninsula. He had enjoyed his years in Singapore, but with the Empire rapidly shrinking, it was time to move on, especially when the university had been so generous in wanting to get rid of him.

As he ruminated about his life in the tropics – and his failed marriage – he heard the distant ringing of the telephone on a table in the hall. Pryor had already asked the GPO to put extensions in the office and the two doctors' rooms, but it would be weeks before they got around to it. He started towards it, but his new employee had beaten him to it.

'There's a call for you, Prof!' said Sian, speaking as excitedly as if the call was from Mars. 'It's some solicitor, maybe he's got some work for us.'

Sian Lloyd had already identified strongly with the venture and was agog that maybe someone wanted their expertise. Pryor hurried into the hall and picked up the heavy black phone. A carefully measured voice answered his 'hello'.

'This is Edward Lethbridge, of Lethbridge, Moody and Savage. We are solicitors in Lydney and I wondered if you could help us?'

Richard felt his own frisson of excitement at this possibility of their first case. 'I'm sure we can, Mr Lethbridge. We have hardly opened for business yet, but I'm sure that we can do something for you. How did you hear of us so soon?'

'The coroner, Doctor Meredith, gave us your name and telephone number. I've known him for years, as we have occasional dealings in the coroner's court. This is a little difficult to explain over the telephone, so I wonder whether you could call at my office.'

Only too anxious to follow up this invitation, Richard arranged to meet Edward Lethbridge in Lydney that afternoon. Sian hurried in to the laboratory to tell Angela and start putting more bottles in place in case they were needed for this new development. The biologist was more restrained in her reaction.

'He probably wants us to do a paternity blood test in some family dispute,' she said evenly, 'Still, it's all grist to the mill, and we certainly can do with the money.'

*   *   *

It was not a paternity test, but was hardly a serial-killer case either, as the pathologist discovered later that day. He drove the ten miles to Lydney in his five-year-old Humber Hawk, the Severn estuary visible down on the right of the A48, which took most of the traffic from England into South Wales. It was a busy road, far too narrow, tortuous and built-up for the volume of traffic it had to bear, thought Pryor. With the rapid increase in manufacturing and trade generally since the war had ended, the infrastructure of the country was proving woefully inadequate. Big lorries lumbered past him almost in convoy and those in front held him up, many of the old trucks of pre-war vintage belching fumes from their worn engines. A decade after VE and VJ days, things were improving rapidly, but there was still a long way to go.

Lydney was a small industrial town, with a branch railway going up into the Forest of Dean to the few remaining coal mines that lurked in that strange and historic region. Richard drove into the long main street and eventually found Lethbridge, Moody and Savage above a building society office in the main street.

A middle-aged secretary showed him into a gloomy room where the senior partner of the firm with such a threatening name was waiting for him. Edward Lethbridge looked a typical provincial solicitor. He was a thin, desiccated man in a faded pinstripe suit, steel-rimmed glasses perched on his long nose. After a limp handshake and after a few platitudes about the hot weather, he came straight to the point.

'We have a client who lives in Newnham, a few miles up the river from here. She's an elderly lady by the name of Agnes Oldfield. We have done some work for her in recent years, as her nephew Anthony vanished three years ago and we have made strenuous efforts to trace him.'

The lawyer sank his chin to his chest so that he could look at Pryor over his glasses.

'Last week, she read an account in the local paper of an inquest held by Dr Meredith on some human remains found near a reservoir up beyond Abergavenny. She is convinced that they belong to Anthony.'

Richard was rather at a loss. 'If there was an inquest, then surely that settled it?'

Lethbridge smiled a secret smile, and shook his head.

'The verdict was that the deceased was an Albert Barnes, but my client wishes to dispute this.'

'Ah, a matter of identity. What do you want me to do? Review the papers, then examine the remains?'

The solicitor steepled his fingers, elbows on his desk, an old mahogany relic which looked as if it been bought by his great-grandfather.

'The papers, certainly. However, there is a difficulty,' he added ruefully. 'The body, or what was left of it, was buried a fortnight ago.'

Richard felt deflated. Once a corpse was in the ground, he knew that it was a devil of a job to get permission to dig it up again.

'The coroner has been good enough to release the inquest proceedings to me, as I persuaded him that Mrs Oldfield was a sufficiently interested party to allow her solicitor to have access to them.'

He opened a drawer in the cavernous desk and slid a thin folder across to the professor. 'If you would care to take these away and study them, perhaps you could come up with some suggestions – even if it is only confirmation that Mrs Oldfield is barking up the wrong tree.'

Pryor took the file and opened it briefly to riffle through a few flimsy pages.

'Is there anything else you can tell me about the matter?' he asked hopefully.

Edward Lethbridge shook his head. 'Not really, doctor. If you decide to look into the case, then I suggest you talk to the lady herself. I would be happy to make an appointment for you. And there is, of course, Trevor Mitchell.'

'Who's Trevor Mitchell?' asked the mystified pathologist.

'A former detective superintendent who has set up as a private enquiry agent. He lives in St Brievals, not far from you. He does some work for me occasionally and I recommended him to Mrs Oldfield some time ago, to look into her nephew's disappearance.'

After a rather diffident conversation about an hourly fee rate, Richard left, clutching the papers. He treated himself to a pot of tea and a Chelsea bun at a nearby café, resisting the temptation to open the file on the stained gingham-patterned oilcloth that covered the table. For a moment, he thought nostalgically of the eating house in River Valley Road in Singapore, where he used to call in for the best *nasi goreng* in the Colony, a savoury fried rice with which no Gloucestershire bun could hope to compete.

He drove slowly back to Chepstow in his comfortable saloon, which he had bought second-hand as soon as he arrived back in Britain. Driving down Castleford Hill, the steep gradient to the famous iron bridge over the swirling Wye, he looked up at the great castle on its crag above the river, one of the first the Normans had built to subdue the local Welsh. Though born in Merthyr Tydfil, he knew this area quite well, having stayed with his aunt many times, both as a schoolboy and later when a medical student in Cardiff. His years in the East had not diminished his love for his native Wales and he found that to be back again among these hills, valleys and castles was immensely satisfying. As the traffic lights on the bridge turned green, he patted the lawyer's file on the seat alongside him, confident that this was the start of a new era in his life.

He drove complacently up through the winding streets of Chepstow and on to the valley road past the racecourse, relishing the breeze that came through the open window, as he looked down on the impressive ruins of Tintern Abbey, a mile or so down the valley from home, as he now termed it.

Back at Garth House, he passed Jimmy hacking away at the hedge, stripped to his waist in the heat. Parking the Humber in the open coach house alongside Angela's smaller car, he walked to the back door and into the kitchen, calling for his partner as he went.

'We've got a job, Angela! Got a moment?'

They sat at the table in the office and Richard opened the buff folder to display a few sheets of handwritten notes, together with a couple of official forms and several newspaper cuttings. Sian had sidled up to the door, unable to resist eavesdropping on their very first case, anxious to be accepted as part of the team. To her a professor was a very august person and she was determined to give Richard the

respect he was due, but not to be intimidated. Anyway, she
rather fancied him, this lean, tanned man from the East, a
fact which Angela had already noticed.

Pryor explained to Angela the general outline offered by
Edward Lethbridge and then began scanning the documents,
before passing them to Angela. There was silence for ten
minutes, until they had digested the relatively meagre information that was on offer.

'This Mrs Barnes seems to have it all sewn up,' commented
Angela. 'I wonder why Widow Oldfield is so intent on proving
it was her nephew?'

'The solicitor hinted that she was keen on his money, as
it seems she was his only surviving relative,' said Richard.
'He was forty-five when he disappeared and was apparently
very well-heeled from money left him by his parents. Unless
she can get a declaration that he's dead, she can never get
probate and hopefully inherit.'

Typically, Angela wanted to rehearse the facts methodic-
ally. 'The post-mortem report is a bit sketchy, but it seems
that what was recovered was over half a skeleton, but minus
the skull.'

'The most useful part is missing, as far as identity goes,'
agreed Pryor. 'No head, so no teeth to examine.'

'Why wouldn't it have a head? Animals?'

The pathologist nodded. 'It must have been lying for
several years out in the countryside, by the sound of it.
Predators, especially foxes, but also dogs, rats and even
badgers, would have made a mess of it in that time. A lot
of the other bones were missing, too.'

'Did they have any idea of how long it had been there?'
asked Angela.

'The report says that the bones still had remnants of liga-
ments and tendons, which fits in with a couple of years since
death – no way of being exact about that, in spite of the
claims by writers of detective novels!'

'Who's this doctor who did the post-mortem?'

'A pathologist in Hereford County Hospital, a Dr Marek.
By the name, he must be Polish. Not a forensic chap, but
the police were obviously satisfied that there was nothing
suspicious about the death.'

He shuffled the pages about on the table and picked up the single page of the autopsy report. 'As you say, not very detailed, but seems sound enough given the little there was to work with.'

'So why did the coroner reckon it was this Albert Barnes?' said Sian.

'When the local paper announced the finding of the remains, this Mrs Barnes from Ledbury went to the police and said it might be her husband. She had reported him missing four years earlier, but he never turned up. The wife said he often used to go walking and sometimes fishing in that area. The police showed her a ring and a wristwatch that was still with the remains and she was adamant that they were his.'

'Did the bones fit with what was known of this man Barnes, I wonder?' asked Angela.

Pryor looked again at the post-mortem report, turning it over, but failing to find any more written on the back. 'It just says "typically male pelvis and limb bones consistent with a man more than twenty five years of age and of average height".'

Sian looked unimpressed.

'Most men are older than twenty-five and of average height,' she commented. 'Doesn't help much.'

'If you had the bones, especially the femora, you could calculate his height, couldn't you?' asked Angela.

Richard nodded, but made a face expressing caution.

'To within an inch or so either way, but as there's no record of Albert Barnes's height, apart from his wife saying he was "average", it doesn't help a lot. And anyway, the bones are six feet down in some cemetery.'

'The inquest report is short and sweet as well,' observed Angela. 'The police offered no evidence of foul play, there were no injuries on the skeleton – not that that means much without a head.'

'It was the wife's definite identification of the wedding ring and the watch that clinched it with the coroner. That was fair enough, he had no reason to disbelieve her.' Pryor threw the paper down on to the table.

'So your old coroner pal Brian Meredith declared it was

Albert Barnes and brought in an open verdict,' concluded Angela.

'Hardly an "old pal"! Until last month, I hadn't seen him since before the war, when we were students together in Cardiff. I'd heard he'd gone into general practice in Monmouth and become the local coroner as well.'

Richard Pryor and Brian Meredith had qualified in 1936, but their paths had then diverged. Richard had taken up pathology and in 1940 been called up into the Royal Army Medical Corps. He had spent most of the war in Egypt and Ceylon, but when Singapore was liberated in 1945, he had been posted to the laboratory of the British Military Hospital there, ending his service with the rank of major. When 'demobbed' after the war, he had taken local release and stayed on as a civilian pathologist in the General Hospital, dealing with coroner's and police cases. This post carried an additional appointment in the university medical school to teach forensic medicine.

'So what happens now?' asked Sian, disappointed that their first case seemed a bit of a damp squib. 'Sounds as if this Mrs Barnes has got a cast-iron case.'

'We've not got the remains, so I can't even try for a blood group, even if we knew what group Albert was,' said Angela.

Richard nodded disconsolately. 'Without the damned bones, we're stumped!'

There was a cough from the doorway behind them and turning, they saw Jimmy James standing there, his sweating body stripped to the waist, an open bottle of beer clutched in one hand.

'Doc, just tell me where they're buried and I'll dig the buggers up for you tonight!'

TWO

Richard declined to take up Jenkins' offer – in fact, his handyman's apparent readiness to break the law so blatantly gave him something else to worry about.

'That bloody man might turn out to be a liability,' he growled to Angela later that day. Sian had left to catch her bus home at five o'clock and the two principals were sitting in the kitchen, eating a scratch 'high tea' of Fray Bentos corned beef and a salad, followed by a tin of peaches with Carnation tinned milk. The sausages were being kept for a late supper.

'I don't think he was serious,' countered Angela. 'You have to take anything Jimmy says with a large pinch of salt!'

Pryor shrugged as he finished his dessert. He then took the dishes to the big Belfast sink in the corner. 'I admit he works hard outside, but I wish he'd keep his nose out of our business.'

Angela went across to the gas stove and lit the burner under the aluminium kettle, then used the same match to light a cigarette. 'I must try to give these things up,' she said, pushing the packet of Kensitas back into the pocket of her white coat. 'I needed them with all the stress of living and working in London, but down here in this peaceful country-side, I should be able to kick the habit.'

Her tone rather suggested that 'peaceful countryside' was code for 'deadly dull rural backwater' and Richard was suddenly aware of how little he really knew about his new business partner. He had heard on the gossip network that flourishes amongst the small world of forensic specialists, that she had never been married but had had a traumatic breakdown of an engagement to a senior police officer in London. He also knew she came from a rather 'posh' family background in the Home Counties. Her parents ran a stud farm in Berkshire and she had been educated at a well-known boarding school, hence her well-modulated Thames Valley accent.

Quite different from his own, he thought ruefully. Though years abroad had blunted his Welsh accent, he was a product of a secondary school in a very different 'valley', that of the Taff near Merthyr. His parents were still there, his father having retired a few years earlier from an exhausting general practice in Aberfan.

His reverie was broken by Angela sitting down again after filling the brown teapot and bringing it to the table.

'So what's the next move over our first and only case?' she asked, pouring the strong liquid into a couple of cups. Even though they were virtually camping out, her sense of propriety had made her fill a small jug with milk. The pint bottle from the village shop, the cardboard top already pecked by ardent sparrows, remained in the fridge. As Richard added his customary two spoonfuls of sugar, he ruminated about Mrs Barnes's bones – or should it be Mrs Oldfield's bones?

'I'll have to talk to this lady in Newnham, I suppose,' he said. 'Get her story first-hand and see if she can add anything that could help establish identity. Maybe she'll say he had a wooden leg!' he added facetiously.

Though Angela was not without a sense of humour, she was already learning to ignore her partner's frequent whimsies.

'What about this private detective fellow?' she asked. 'I'm always a bit wary of them, I imagine a chap in a dirty rain-coat taking snaps of a co-respondent through bedroom windows.'

Pryor grinned, his lean face revealing a good set of white teeth.

'Don't forget the brown trilby pulled down over his eyes!' He took a sip of the hot tea, before continuing. 'But seriously, this man Mitchell sounds OK. Lethbridge said he was a detective super in the Gloucestershire force until a year or two ago. He was in the Division that covered the Forest of Dean, so he must know a lot about the area across the river.'

'You'd better have a word with him as well,' suggested Angela. 'You never know, perhaps he can pass a bit of work our way, and vice versa,' she added practically.

As it turned out, the pathologist met Trevor Mitchell very soon, for next morning Pryor rang the solicitor in Lydney,

who after a few phone calls, made arrangements for him to
see Mitchell that morning and to go on to interview Mrs
Oldfield afterwards.

Leaving Angela and Sian to continue stocking the laboratory, he took the Humber up the valley for a short distance,
past the hamlet of Llandogo, and across the river bridge. A
side road took the heavy black car up a steep lane with sharp
bends that climbed the English side of the valley, with superb
views in all directions. At the top was the ancient village of
St Brievals, which had been the medieval capital of the Forest
of Dean and still had a castle to prove it. He stopped outside
the Norman church to ask a lady for directions and was sent
down a nearby lane to a thatched cottage whose picture should
have been on a box of chocolates, even down to the roses
around the door. A rap on the panels brought an almost
immediate response, being opened by a large man wearing
bib-and-brace brown overalls, looking like a carpenter or
a plumber.

He held out his hand and pumped Richard's vigorously.

'Come in, Doctor, come in! Excuse the rig-out, but I've
just come in from my workshop.'

As he led the way into a low living room, with blackened
beams in the ceiling, Pryor saw that Mitchell was a powerful
man just past fifty, with a thickset body and cropped iron-
grey hair. His face reminded Richard of a bulldog, the
Churchillian features looking as if they had been crushed
from above downwards.

Mitchell piloted the doctor to a deep armchair, covered in
flowery chintz like the rest of the three-piece suite. The room
was like a film set of an English country cottage, with half-
panelled walls, a large stone fireplace and numerous pictures
of rural scenes. It even had a glass case containing a stuffed
otter sitting on a dresser filled with blue and white china.

'You'll have some coffee, Doctor?' asked the investigator,
in a tone that seemed to rule out any refusal. He went to a
door at the back and in a deep bass voice roared out instructions to someone in the nether regions.

Then he came back and dropped heavily on to a settee
opposite.

'I understand that old Eddie Lethbridge put you on to this,' he began. 'A dry old stick, but he's sound enough, not like some of these slick lawyers in the city.'

Pryor nodded. 'So far, there doesn't seem much to go on. I hope this lady isn't wasting her money on a wild goose chase.'

Trevor Mitchell grinned, his stern face lighting up for a moment. 'She's not short of a few bob, is Agnes – though she's keen to add a lot more to it from her nephew's money. I've benefited from making a couple of similar goose chases for her in the last couple of years.'

'D'you think there's anything in this one?'

Mitchell shrugged his wide shoulders, from which his head seemed to rise without any neck.

'No reason why it shouldn't be. This Anthony fellow did just vanish over three years ago, so he has to be somewhere!'

'But this Mrs Barnes seems to have it sewn up, with this ring and the watch.'

The former detective pursed his lips. 'It's only her word that says they belonged to him. There's no corroboration from anyone else, she's got no one to confirm it.'

They were interrupted by the kitchen door opening and a small lady entered carrying a tray. She was a wisp of a woman, with fair hair coiled in a roll around her head. Wearing a floral pinafore that almost matched the loose covers of the furniture, she gave Richard a smile from her elfin face as she set down the tray of coffee and biscuits on a small table between the two men.

'This is my good wife, Doctor!' announced Trevor. 'Mary, this is the professor from Singapore we've been hearing about. Come to live in Garth House, down in the valley.'

'I hope you'll be very happy there, Professor,' said Mary Mitchell. 'I knew your aunt slightly, she sometimes used to come up here to church whist drives.'

With another smile, she went back to her kitchen, leaving her husband to hand a plate of Crawfords Rich Tea biscuits to his visitor.

'So do I call you "Doctor" or "Professor"?' he demanded.

'"Doctor" will do, thanks,' answered Pryor. 'I held a university chair for a short time, but that was a long way from here. It always seems daft for men to hang on to their military rank long after they've packed it in. I suppose I could equally call myself "Major", but it would sound silly.'

After a biscuit and a few sips, they got down to business.

'I'm going to see Mrs Oldfield after I leave here,' said Pryor. 'Anything I should know before I meet her?'

'Bit of an old snob, is Agnes,' confided Mitchell. 'She's not seventy yet, but seems older, a real hangover from Edwardian days. Speaks her mind, and damn the consequences!'

'So why does she think these remains are those of her nephew, this Anthony chap?'

Mitchell grinned again, which lightened his forbidding features. 'She thinks every set of bones found within fifty miles of here must be his! This is the third time I've gone poking into other deaths – but they had cast-iron identities. At least this one is a bit more open to doubt.'

He drank down his coffee and replaced the cup in its saucer.

'Anthony had plenty of money, as he and his father ran a factory in Swindon during the war, making some bits for aircraft. His parents died some years ago, but he didn't need to work again, so he enjoyed himself.'

'How old was he, then?' asked Richard, taking another biscuit.

'Forty-five when last seen three years ago. He used to do a lot of hill walking in the Black Mountains and the Brecon Beacons – he was keen on fishing as well. He lived in a private hotel in Cheltenham, but latterly came to stay with his aunt, to be nearer the hills, she said. Apparently, he was also dotty about archaeology, and used to visit ancient places both here and abroad.'

'And you didn't find any trace of him from the time he vanished?'

Mitchell shook his head. 'He wasn't classed as a missing person for a long time after that. He used to just push off whenever he felt like it without telling anyone, as he had no other relatives. It was only when she hadn't heard a word from him for over a year that she began to wonder if he was dead. That's when she hired me, but what could I do?'

'So he could be living in Nepal or camping in the Mexican jungle?' said Richard.

'It's possible, but Mrs Oldfield won't have it! She reckons he's dead, but until it's proved or he stays missing for seven years, she can't collect. He intended leaving everything to her, according to Agnes – and the solicitor confirmed it to me.'

Richard took another biscuit and opened the file that the lawyer had given him the previous day.

'According to this, the remains found near the reservoir were those of a man in middle age, of about average height and build. Not very helpful, as that fits about half the male population of Britain! Was there anything about the two missing men that wouldn't fit that description?'

The former detective shook his head.

'Of course, I've only been dealing with Anthony Oldfield, the Barnes angle is new to me. But Anthony, from what his aunt says and the photos I've seen, was a pretty ordinary-looking bloke, a bit on the lanky side perhaps.'

'Has the solicitor asked you to look into the Barnes side of things on Mrs Oldfield's behalf?' asked the pathologist.

Trevor Mitchell nodded. 'Yes, he told me that she wanted me to cooperate with you. She's dead keen on winning this one, her nephew must have a lot of family money tucked away and she wants it.'

Pryor looked pleased at this. 'I'm glad we can work together on this. As a doctor, it's a bit difficult for me to go knocking on doors and asking questions.'

Mitchell's face screwed up even more as a quizzical expression spread across his face.

'What sort of questions, Doc?'

'Well, anything noticeable about this Albert Barnes, which would be inconsistent with what's described in this post-mortem report, little though that is.'

Mitchell thought for a moment. 'Like a hunchback or club foot, you mean?'

'That sort of thing – but we wouldn't get that from his wife, who sounds as keen as our client on proving that the remains were that of her relative.'

'But we might get something from a neighbour, perhaps.'

The pathologist nodded. 'At least they wouldn't be biased witnesses. It's a long shot, but we've got little else to go on.'

'And of course, we haven't got the bones any more, they're buried,' added Mitchell.

Pryor nodded. 'Without getting a sight of those, I can't see we can go much further.' He finished his coffee and stood up.

'I said I'd be at Newnham by eleven o'clock. Mustn't keep the lady waiting, especially as she sounds like an old-fashioned stickler for good behaviour. I'll see if there's any more medical details I can get from her. A pity we've got no head.'

'At the moment, we've got nothing at all, Doc,' said Mitchell, accompanying him to the door. 'I'll make arrangements to see Mrs Barnes to get her end of the story. She won't be thrilled to see me, if she realizes that I'm trying to throw doubt on the coroner's findings.'

Asking his host to thank his wife for the coffee, Richard made his way to his car, where he sat and pulled out a dog-eared book of AA road maps that had belonged to his father. Though he knew the area fairly well, from holidays with his aunt before the war, he needed to check on the route to Newnham, which was on the other side of the forest, on the main A48 to Gloucester. His finger traced out the road up to Coleford, then across to Cinderford and down an unclassified road to Newnham, which lay right on the river. Richard recalled it was one of the best places to see the famous Severn Bore, another memory from his student days.

He set off, window down in the rising heat and drove across the forest, through the most heavily wooded part of the Royal Forest that had provided England with so many ships in centuries gone by. In midsummer, the foliage was still fresh and green, quite different from the deep, lush colours of the jungle and rubber trees with which he had become so familiar during his years in the Far East. However, today the temperature was almost as great, a freak heatwave for June – but it was a dry heat, not the suffocating damp-ness of the tropics.

The road took him past the seventeenth-century Speech House in the middle of the forest, where the Verderers still held their Court every forty days, as they had done since the time of King Canute. Richard had learned these nuggets of

local history during his pre-war holiday tours with Uncle
Arthur in his old Morris Ten saloon.

As he came down the last lap of the journey into Newnham,
the panorama of the narrowing river estuary lay below him,
spread out like a map. The town had one main street which
was the A48 trunk road, running downhill, then turning
towards the river bank. When his small side road met the
main one, he followed Trevor Mitchell's directions and turned
up into a narrow service lane that ran in front of a row of
old houses. He remembered the brick clock tower in the
middle of the town and the sixteenth-century Victoria Hotel
at the top of the main street, but his attention was on the
names outside the tall terraced houses on his right.

Crawling in bottom gear, he soon spotted 'Meadowlane'
cut into a slate plaque at the side of a heavy front door. There
was only one other car parked in this section of the road and
he pulled up behind it and went to ring the bell.

It was answered by a short woman in a long linen apron,
with a frilled mob cap on her grey curls. For a moment,
Richard thought he had strayed into a stage production of a
Regency play, but the woman smiled and pulled the door
open wide.

'Doctor Pryor? You are expected, please come in.'

He went into a rather gloomy hallway, unsure whether or
not this was Mrs Oldfield, though she did not tally with Trevor
Mitchell's description. The house smelled of mothballs and
furniture polish.

'Mrs Oldfield is in the drawing room,' said his guide,
clarifying matters and indicating an inner door on the left
of the hall. The servant, for that was what he decided she
must be, tapped on the panels, opened it and stood aside
for him to enter, calling out in a strong Gloucester accent,
'Dr Pryor, ma'am!'

In the high-ceilinged room, its bay window looking down
on the main street, he saw another elderly lady in a high-
backed chair, one hand on a silver-headed ebony stick. She
sat erect, her plain dark dress closed at the throat by a large
cameo brooch. Her face was long and lined, set in a severe
expression, under a swept-back mass of white hair, gathered
in a bun at the back.

For a moment, he thought of Queen Victoria, though she was really nothing like the pictures he had seen of the old Empress – perhaps it was the stern expression and the gimlet-sharp eyes that regarded him.

'Excuse me not rising to greet you, Professor,' she said in a surprisingly melodious voice. 'But I suffer from severe arthritis. Please be seated.' As she waved her cane to indicate a similar chair opposite, he saw that all her finger joints were badly distorted.

As he made some polite greeting and subsided into the chair, Agnes Oldfield waved her wand at the old servant, who was still hovering in the doorway.

'You may serve coffee now, Lucas,' she commanded grandly and the woman vanished. Even though it was less than an hour since taking coffee with Mitchell, Pryor felt it unwise to decline, even if the draconian old lady had allowed it.

Obviously her code of conduct demanded some light conversation before they got down to business.

'I understand you have not long returned from living in the East, Professor,' she began. Again, he desisted from explaining that he preferred being called 'Doctor' and gave a quick resume of his recent life.

'You were in the Army?' she demanded.

'A major in the Royal Army Medical Corps,' he admitted.

Agnes Oldfield gave a delicate sniff. 'My late husband was a colonel in the Hussars. We lived in India for a time, you know.'

Pryor again felt that he was playing a bit-part in some Oscar Wilde comedy, but the moment passed as Lucas came in with a tray of coffee, immaculately served in thin china amid a profusion of solid silver jugs, basins and spoons. They waited while the maid went through the ritual of moving small tables, pouring coffee and setting one at the side of the lady of the house, before giving Richard his cup. Then she proffered a plate of thin ginger biscuits and quietly left the room.

'My solicitor has explained the problem, I take it, Professor,' she began, fixing him with a beady eye.

'I feel sure that this tragedy involved my nephew Anthony and that the coroner was in error with his verdict.'

Richard placed his cup back on the saucer, half-afraid of chipping the delicate china.

'I understand perfectly, Mrs Oldfield. The problem is the lack of evidence to work with. I hoped that perhaps you could – well, fill in some of the gaps, as it were.'

He almost said 'put some flesh on the bones' but that would have been a slip of the tongue that he knew this severe lady would not appreciate.

'What do you need to know?' she asked, lifting her own cup with some difficulty.

'Can you give me some better details of his physical appearance, for a start? His exact height, build and any old injuries or serious illnesses, for instance.'

She frowned and sipped her coffee as she considered this.

'I've told Edward Lethbridge all I know,' she replied. 'I can't tell you his exact height, he was perhaps a little taller than you, say five feet ten inches. He was rather slim, because he was such an active man, always walking or climbing somewhere.'

'Did he ever have any serious falls doing that? Had a fracture of an arm or leg, perhaps?'

'Not that I was aware of, no. Though he was away for months at a time, before the war and since, even going abroad to the Alps or the Middle East or somewhere.'

Aware that he was getting nowhere fast, Pryor tried another tack.

'Do you know if he was ever admitted to hospital for anything – I'm thinking of the possibility of obtaining X-rays, for example.'

'What could they tell you, Professor?' she demanded.

'If we could compare them with the actual bones, we might find a match?'

He refrained from saying that they were more likely to exclude a match than confirm it, thinking she would not want to hear the pessimistic side – but she was ahead of him.

'But you don't have the actual bones, do you?' she snapped.

Pryor sighed, she had a sharp mind, but an abrasive manner, as Trevor had warned.

'Not yet, but we need more facts to support an application for them to be re-examined.'

'An exhumation, you mean? Would that be necessary, I would prefer poor Anthony to be left in peace.'

She had obviously already made up her mind about the identity. Richard turned up his hands in a gesture of despair.

'Without a better examination, there would be no hope of overturning the verdict.'

Agnes Oldfield pondered this for a moment and Pryor could almost hear the cash register ringing in her head as she weighed an exhumation against an inheritance.

'Very well, if it is the only way,' she announced regally. 'How can that be arranged?'

Richard shook his head. 'It's not that easy, I'm afraid. We have nothing to go on from your end, so to speak. Your nephew vanished three years ago, but there is not the slightest evidence that he is dead. Before we can even approach the coroner about an exhumation, it would have to be shown that those remains were not those of Albert Barnes. That would be to rectify the coroner's verdict, not to replace it with your contention that the remains were those of your nephew – that would have to be a separate exercise. Mr Mitchell is investigating this possibility even as we speak.'

He thought it useful to emphasize how her minions were getting on with the job.

There was nothing more that he could extract from Mrs Oldfield, though he spent a few minutes getting a better idea of how her nephew had vanished. It seemed that in June 1952, he had checked out of his private hotel in Cheltenham with all his belongings and arrived at his aunt's house in Newnham, saying that he wanted to stay with her until he found another hotel or a flat in Bath, where he fancied living for a time. After a few weeks, he set off with a suitcase, saying he was going to stay a few days in Bath to look around – and never came back.

'I never heard another word from him,' she said finally.

Feeling that further poking into these matters was a job for Mitchell, rather than a forensic pathologist, Pryor rose to his feet, saying that everything possible would be done and that she would be kept informed – hopefully by Edward Lethbridge, he told himself.

After a perfunctory shake of a crippled hand, he took his

leave and Lucas let him out into the street, which felt light and warm after the gloomy interior of the old house.

He drove home through Blakeney and Lydney and arrived at Garth House about twelve thirty. Deciding he could face no more corned beef or egg-and-bacon for lunch, he recklessly invited Angela out for a meal.

'It's Friday, so let's celebrate having survived our first week!' he said gaily. Angela was already beginning to recognize his swings of mood and today he was obviously upbeat, so she went along with it.

Sian always brought sandwiches, to which she added an apple and a bottle of Tizer, so leaving her to man the telephone, Richard ushered his colleague into the Humber and drove off down the valley towards Chepstow. None of the local pubs offered anything but drink and crisps, apart from the large hotel opposite the abbey, so he was aiming for a small café-cum-restaurant he knew of in the main street of the ancient town near the mouth of the Wye.

'What's brought this on, partner?' asked Angela, reclining in the passenger seat, which was much more comfortable than her little Renault.

'We've got to talk about organizing the house better than at present,' said Richard. 'So look on this as a business lunch and charge it against expenses.'

'Expenses! We haven't got any income yet to charge it against,' she said scornfully, but secretly she was pleased to be pampered a little, even if it was probably only for a plaice and chips.

They parked in the town, the ruins of the huge brooding castle above them on the edge of its cliff over the swirling river. The restaurant was little more than a large shop, with a dozen tables and a counter with a huge hissing coffee machine alongside a glass case displaying an assortment of cakes. However, to Angela's surprise, they were presented with a typed menu card which offered fresh salmon, steak and kidney pie, gammon or cold ham, all with either chips or three vegetables.

'I still can't get used to so much food becoming available,' she said. 'You were out of it for years, gorging in Malaya with your fried rice and prawn curries. It's hardly any time since we finished with ration books here!'

She settled for salmon and new potatoes, while Richard went for the steak and kidney. The place had no licence, so they drank water until it was time for a coffee.

'Now then, madam, we've got a lot to discuss,' said Richard firmly, after they had finished apple tart and custard and were on a second cup of coffee.

'Domestic or professional?' she asked.

'Both, because one affects the other,' he replied.

'We can't go on pigging it in Garth House, we'd be better off camping in a tent in the garden. We need a decent meal at least once a day and someone to keep the place clean and generally look after us.'

The scientist nodded. 'I don't disagree with you, Richard. But how are we going to pay for it?'

'I've still got a few quid left from my golden handshake and I'm sure we'll soon be picking up some more work. If it comes to the crunch, we can take out a small mortgage on the house.'

In spite of her resolution, Angela took her Kensitas from her handbag and lit up. 'First and last today,' she declared. 'But what are you thinking of doing?'

She recognized that one of his intense moods was coming on, which she applauded, except she knew it tended to fade away fairly quickly, unless she badgered him.

'We need some sort of housekeeper, who can clean the place up and do a bit of cooking. Somebody local, who can come in each day, not a live-in servant like that old biddy has in Newnham.'

He had described his morning's activities to her during the drive down from Garth House.

'It would be good if she could type as well,' added Angela. He looked at her suspiciously for a second, wondering if she was being sarcastic, but she was serious.

'Look, we thought Sian might be able to type the reports, as well as work in the lab,' said Angela. 'But have you seen her trying to use that typewriter? I can do better with two fingers.'

'I thought she had been to a secretarial college in Newport?' he objected.

'For two months after she left school, that's all,' said

Angela. 'She hated it, she told me, that's why she got a job in a hospital lab.'

'OK, so we need someone who can cook, clean and type! A bit of a tall order out here in the sticks, isn't it?'

'It was your idea, Richard. We can only try, as like you, I'm fed up with living out of tins and making my own bed. Thank God there's a good laundry service in Chepstow.'

He gave her a brilliant smile, making her think that he wasn't such a bad looking fellow after all, with that wavy brown hair. A pity about those awful safari suits, though.

'Right, I'll see what we can do. Maybe Jimmy will know someone, he probably knows every single person between here and Monmouth.'

Angela looked doubtful. 'God knows what sort of people he knows – probably find us a gypsy who can only cook hedgehogs!'

'Who cares, as long as she can type!' he said facetiously.

They both burst out laughing, almost euphoric with a sudden realization of how much of a task they had taken on with their new venture.

In the car on the way back, she told him that while he was out that morning, she had had a phone call from a solicitor in Newport wanting to arrange a blood test in a disputed paternity case.

'A doctor in the Royal Gwent Hospital recommended us,' she said. 'He was in your year in medical school in Cardiff.'

Richard was delighted at some new business coming in already. 'Who the hell would that be, I wonder? How did he know I was here?'

'Your pal the coroner, it seems. He's spreading the word around, thank God.'

'Have you got all the necessary stuff for your serology yet?' he asked, as Garth House came into view.

'Yes, it's all under control. Though we'll need a new fridge to keep the sera and other things in, especially in this weather. We can't put everything in that old relic in the kitchen, alongside our food.'

Encouraged by the prospect of cases and income, Angela went off with Sian to continue their blitz on the laboratory shelves and cupboards, while Pryor went outside to look for

Jimmy Jenkins. The land belonging to Garth House sloped up fairly steeply from the main road towards the dense woodland beyond. The house was built in the lower part, within fifty yards of the road below. There was a patch of kitchen garden near the house, just behind the outhouses, but the rest of the four acres was rough grass and bushes, neglected since his aunt and uncle had died.

'Only good for a few sheep, that is,' said Jimmy, leaning on his hoe, with which he had been weeding between a few rows of beetroot, runner beans and carrots. He wore his usual baggy corduroy trousers, but his plaid shirt was hanging on a nearby bush, exposing his barrel-shaped chest to the hot sun.

'I've got plans to start a vineyard there eventually,' declared Richard. It was one of his recent fantasies to plant vines on the south-east facing slope and make his own wine.

Jimmy looked at him from under his poke cap as if he was mad. 'You'd be better off with a few sheep. Grow your own meat, boss, not bloody wine!'

Jimmy drank only beer, at least a couple of pints a day down at the Three Horseshoes in Tintern and his tone suggested that he thought wine was a drink fit only for 'nancy boys', as he called them.

Pryor was in too good a mood to argue, so he raised the matter of a domestic help, explaining that they needed someone part-time to do a bit of cleaning and cooking.

'Do you know anybody around here who might be interested?' he asked his handyman.

Jimmy pushed up the back of his long-suffering cap to scratch his head with a dirty forefinger.

'Mebbe I do, must give it a bit of thought, Doc,' he said slowly. 'An' you could put a card in the post office, they got a board for free adverts there.'

Having said his piece, he started vigorously attacking the weeds with his hoe, so Richard left Jimmy to his task and went indoors, thinking that he might well take the man's advice and put a small advertisement in the local post office.

THREE

At the time that Sian Lloyd was painstakingly tapping out Richard's dictation of the advertisement, Trevor Mitchell was parking his car in Ledbury, a small market town between Hereford and Malvern. He had telephoned Edward Lethbridge as soon as the pathologist had left his cottage and by noon, had had a call back to say that Mrs Molly Barnes was willing to talk to him that afternoon.

'She sounded very reluctant,' the solicitor said. 'But I pointed out that the coroner had agreed and that as it was an open verdict, the case could be reopened if he was not satisfied.'

Mitchell thought that this smacked of mild blackmail, but he kept his feelings to himself and agreed to meet the lady at her home in Ledbury at two thirty. He parked his Wolseley 6/80 in the High Street, finding a free space near the half-timbered Market Hall and walked up The Homend, a continuation of the main street. A quick enquiry from a passer-by directed him into a side road, where he found Molly Barnes's small semi-detached house, probably of nineteen-twenty vintage. The brass knocker on the front door was answered by a short, wiry woman with a combative expression already on her face. If he looked like a bulldog, then she resembled a rather irritable Yorkshire terrier. In her forties, she had spiky brown hair that stood out untidily from her head. Mrs Barnes wore a faded floral pinafore and clutched a dust pan and brush in her hands.

'You're the enquiry man, I suppose,' she said ungraciously. 'You're early, but you'd better come in, I suppose.'

Putting down the pan, she showed him into a front parlour where three gaudy china ducks were flying in formation above a tiled fireplace and a 'cherry boy' ornament stood on a table in the bay window. She waved him to one of the armchairs of a moquette three-piece suite that was made long before the war began and sat opposite, perched on the edge of the settee, tensing herself to defend her rights.

'Now what's all this?' she demanded. 'The coroner held an inquest and his officer gave me a death certificate.'

Mitchell, with thirty years' experience of interviewing people, decided to tread softly with Molly Barnes.

'Another lady has claimed that the remains might be that of her nephew, who disappeared around the same time,' he said carefully.

'Has she got a ring and wristwatch to prove it?' asked Mrs Barnes, pugnaciously.

'It would help your case a lot if you had some other evidence to confirm the identity of your husband,' replied Mitchell gently.

'I don't have a case!' she retorted. 'My case was settled by the coroner, it's this other woman who's got to come up with something better!'

The former detective sighed quietly, recognizing a sharp-witted character who was not going to be trodden on.

'What I mean is, did your husband have any physical characteristics that would help to confirm that it was really him? Had he ever broken an arm or a leg, for example?'

The feisty little woman scowled at him. 'I thought there had been a post-mortem to look into all that?' she countered. 'But no, he had had nothing like that. Came all through the war in the Rifle Brigade without a scratch, he did!'

Trevor felt he was getting nowhere, fast.

'Tell me about the last day, when he went missing,' he asked.

'He just went off one Saturday morning on his bike, going fishing as usual. Mad keen on fishing, he was.'

'Did he say where he was going?'

'No, only that it was over Hereford way. I never took much interest in his fishing.' She sniffed as if that was a pastime beneath her contempt.

'Obviously, he would have had his rods and things with him?'

'Of course he would – he had a long canvas bag slung on his back, the rods came to pieces to fit in.'

Mitchell enquired about his health and if Albert Barnes

had had any heart trouble that might explain a sudden collapse.

'He had a terrible cough sometimes – he smoked too much. But I never heard he had a bad heart.'

'Did he go to his doctor at all? Have any X-rays?'

She shook her head emphatically. 'Fit as a fiddle, my Albert. He had to be in his job, he worked on the railway, humping heavy tools about.'

Trevor was running out of questions and had one last shot in his locker.

'Could I see the watch and the ring, please?' he asked.

Molly Barnes looked at him suspiciously. 'What would you want to look at them for?' she demanded. 'The police and the coroner had them for over a week.'

'Just to tie up any loose ends,' he answered humbly. 'I have to look as if I'm earning my fee,' he added in an attempt to lighten her mood.

Muttering under her breath, she went out and he heard her going upstairs. A few minutes later she returned with an old Cadbury's chocolate box with a faded picture on the lid looking very much like his own cottage in St Brievals. Opening it, she sorted through a tangle of bead necklaces, brooches and shiny buttons and retrieved a gold ring and a steel-cased wristwatch without any strap.

'The coroner's officer told me the strap had rotted away,' she volunteered, as she handed them over.

'This was his wedding ring, I presume?'

'Yes, my Albert always wore it,' she said bleakly.

'Which year were you married?' he asked idly.

'Nineteen forty-one, in the war. He was on a week's embarkation leave, before going to Egypt.'

Mitchell held the narrow band between his finger and thumb, squinting at it briefly. 'What about the watch? Where did he get that, d'you know?'

The widow shrugged her thin shoulders. 'I don't know, he brought it back when he was demobbed at the end of the war. Picked it up in Germany perhaps, he was posted there later on. He said you could buy anything there with a packet of fags.'

The watch had a black dial with the famous logo above

the word 'Omega'. In tiny letters at the bottom, it said 'Swiss Made'. There was nothing written on the plain metal of the back.

'So how did you know that this ring and the watch belonged to your husband?' he asked, handing them back.

'I just did!' she snapped. 'I've been looking at them every day for the past nine years, since he came home from the army.'

'But one gold ring looks much the same as any other,' pointed out Mitchell. 'And this watch isn't particularly unusual.'

The woman slammed the lid down on the chocolate box.

'I tell you I knew them! I knew every scratch and mark on that watch,' she spat angrily. 'You're just trying to make me out to be a liar, you should be ashamed of yourself.'

She jumped out of her chair and went to hold the door open.

'I think you'd better go, I've got nothing else to say to you. I'm going to complain to my solicitor.'

Trevor had had a similar threat a hundred times in his career in the police, but hauled himself to his feet and meekly left the house, thanking her civilly for her help before she slammed the front door on him.

On the pavement outside, he took out a small notebook and made a very short entry, before walking back to his car.

On Monday morning, the coroner's officer in Monmouth telephoned to say that there were two cases for post-mortem. Richard happily agreed to come up straight away to begin his new career in one of the local mortuaries. Sian and Angela shared in his satisfaction and even went to the back door to wave him off, as he drove out of the yard and down the steep drive, to turn left up the winding valley.

'Looks like a schoolboy who's been promised a new football!' said the technician, with an apparent wisdom beyond her years. As they went back into the house, Angela had to agree with her.

'He's blissfully happy at the prospect of cutting up a couple of corpses! But good luck to him, it was a big step to go solo like this. We need all the work we can get.'

Richard drove up the twists and turns of the famous valley, where British tourism had really begun in the eighteenth century when rich people began taking boat trips down from Ross to Chepstow.

When he arrived at Monmouth, he followed the directions to the mortuary given by the coroner's officer. Though he was a serving police constable, it was several years since he had worn a uniform, as he was permanently seconded to be the coroner's right-hand man. His directions sounded ominous, but from the few cases Pryor had done before the war, he was not surprised at the location of public mortuaries. The local authorities had an obligation to provide such a facility and although some larger hospitals hired out their mortuaries to the coroner, most of these other places were pretty low on the list of priorities of the cash-strapped councils.

As he suspected, when the Humber nosed its way through the high wooden gates to which John Christie had directed him, Richard found himself in a municipal refuse depot. It had rained hard during the night and the large yard was inches deep in dirty mud, which a rubbish truck was slowly churning into even worse mire.

There were several shabby buildings around the yard, including a large open garage for council vehicles, a pound for stray dogs and a blockhouse which still bore a faded wartime sign declaring it to be a 'Gas Decontamination Centre'.

Several other council trucks were parked there and as he weaved his way past them, he wound the window down to ask a man in oily dungarees for directions to the mortuary. The council worker, whose drooping cigarette appeared to be welded to his lower lip, pointed past the dog pound, from which a furious barking was shattering the peace of Monmouth.

'Jus' round the corner, mate,' he advised. 'Can't miss it, looks like a gents' lavatory.'

His description was perfect, as when the pathologist parked around the corner, he saw an oblong building of dirty brick, with a flat concrete roof. It was pierced by some narrow windows high up on the wall and at one end there was a set of double doors which had last been painted green about the time Neville Chamberlain returned from Munich.

Pryor stepped out into the grimy slush of the yard and got his square doctor's bag from the boot of his car.

There was no bell push on the door, so he hammered on it with his knuckles. One half was soon opened and he was greeted by a large man in a greenish tweed suit. He wore a shirt with a small check pattern and a woven wool tie. On his head was a matching tweed trilby, which only needed a few fish hooks in the band to make him the complete country-man. He had a craggy face with a square jaw, his big nose set between deep-set brown eyes. He introduced himself as John Christie, the coroner's officer.

'Welcome, Doctor, welcome!' greeted Christie effusively, holding out his hand. 'Nice to have a pathologist up here again, since Doctor Saunders retired. All our cases have had to go down to Newport, costs a lot more in undertaker's fees.'

He led the way into the building, which consisted of two dismal rooms. The one just inside the doors held the body store, an eight-foot high metal cabinet which, from the three labels stuck on its door, was a triple-tier refrigerator of doubtful antiquity. The rest of the space contained a battered desk to hold the mortuary register and several trolleys for moving coffins and bodies.

'The "pee emm" room is through here, sir,' said Christie, in a booming voice that suggested that he had been at least a warrant officer during the war. He pushed open another pair of doors into the other half of the building. Richard was half expecting to see a large slab of slate as the autopsy table, as he had once seen in Bridgend, but was relieved to find a porcelain version on a central pillar. There was very little else in there, just a large white sink with one cold-water tap, a sloping draining board and a gas water heater above it. A small table stood against one wall, with a glass cupboard above it containing bottles of formalin and disinfectants.

'Doctor Saunders always did his organ-cutting on this,' explained John Christie, indicating a contraption standing on the autopsy table. It looked like the tray that invalids take their meals on in bed, a large board with four legs to stand across the lower half of the corpse.

Pryor looked around the rest of the chamber which hopefully was to be his regular place of work. The usual paraphernalia of a morgue was there, mops and buckets standing in a corner, a butcher's scales hanging over the draining board and several pairs of grubby Wellington boots under the table. A few red rubber aprons with chains around the neck and waist, hung from hooks on the wall.

'There's no mortuary attendant, then?' he asked tentatively.

The officer shook his head. 'Not enough work to warrant the expense, says the council. We've got one down in Chepstow, though. Here one of the chaps in the depot sees bodies in and out for the undertakers.'

'So I have to do all the donkey work myself?' hazarded Richard. Maybe this wasn't going to be such a windfall after all, he thought.

The policeman's rugged face cracked into a grin.

'Don't worry, Doctor, I'll give you a hand. I'll sew up and clean down – and take off the skull when you need it.'

He was as good as his word, too. While the pathologist put on boots and a rubber apron, then took his instruments from his black bag, the coroner's officer had trundled a body in from the fridge, sliding it off the trolley on to the table and placing a wooden block under the head. He wore no apron and his green trilby stayed firmly on his head throughout the whole proceedings.

Before Pryor began his examination, Christie produced some papers from his breast pocket and laid them on the table.

'This first gent is a sudden death, sir. Collapsed in the pub, probably just heard that the price of beer had gone up,' he added heartily. 'Seventy-one years old, history of chest pains, but hasn't seen a doctor for a month, so had to be reported to us.'

'What's the other one?' asked Pryor.

'Probably an overdose, there'll be an inquest on her. Lady of sixty-five, lives alone. History of depression, not seen for three days. Found dead in bed, empty bottle of Seconal on the floor, but we don't know how many were left in it. I'm chasing the prescription date today.'

'Have to have an analysis on that one,' said Richard. An extra fee and some work for Sian in the laboratory, he thought.

Both autopsies went off smoothly and he took his samples for analysis into bottles he carried in his capacious case, which had three large drawers stuffed with equipment. He had had it made to his own design in Singapore and the sight and feel of it made him aware again of how much life had changed in a few short months.

Christie was busy with a sacking needle and twine, restoring both bodies to a remarkable degree of normality, given the primitive facilities. Richard was secretly amazed at how the officer did everything so calmly and efficiently in his tweed suit and hat, without getting a single drop of blood on himself. He seemed to be able to work from a distance, bending over and reaching far out with his long arms. His only concession to hygiene was the wearing of a thick pair of household rubber gloves.

Pryor washed his hands under the trickle from the gas heater, using soap kept in a Player's glass ashtray. There was a clean towel on the table, God knows from where, he thought. As he dried his hands, the busy officer asked about his report.

'How d'you want to do it, Doctor? I used to jot down a few notes for Doctor Saunders and he'd add a conclusion and sign it. The coroner seemed satisfied with that, just in longhand.'

The new broom shook his head. 'No, I'll just make a few notes myself, then I'll dictate a report back at the office and have it typed up, then post it to you.'

He hoped Sian was up to the task, if they started getting more than a few cases at a time. As he leaned over the table to write some notes on a pad taken from his case, he heard John Christie dragging the second corpse on to a trolley.

'I'll put them away when you've gone, Doc,' he said.

'Business to be done now.' He approached the table, pulling a wallet from his jacket and then laying four one-pound notes alongside Richard's notebook.

'The going rate is two guineas a case, sir. I don't know what happens in Singapore, but here there's been a long tradition that the coroner's officer gets the shillings off the guineas.'

Pryor recalled that in the few coroner's autopsies he had done before going to the Forces, the same regime had operated, though then he hadn't got the pounds, they went to the senior pathologist!

'The coroner said he'd like you to call in on him, if you've the time, sir,' said the officer, as he saw him to the outer door.

Richard knew where his old college friend had his surgery, as he had called on him soon after he arrived at Garth House, unashamedly touting for any work that was going. Brian Meredith was almost exactly the same age, but had escaped being called up during the war, due to poor sight, which required him to wear spectacles with lenses like the bottom of milk bottles. He was a surgeon's son from Cardiff and had been in general practice since soon after qualifying, most of it in Monmouth. Well connected, with one brother a barrister and the other a solicitor, he had been appointed a couple of years ago as the coroner for East Monmouthshire.

Richard left the council yard and drove around the back of the small town, remembering that it was famous for being the birthplace of King Henry V and home of Charles Rolls of Rolls Royce, the first Briton to die in an aircraft crash.

'I wonder if he had a post-mortem?' he murmured, as he looked for the cream-painted building that housed Meredith's family practice. Spotting it in the road behind the ancient Monmouth School, he pulled into a paved space in front and went into the waiting room, causing a doorbell to jangle as if it was a shop.

Morning surgery was over and the row of hard chairs around the walls was bereft of patients. An inner door opened and Brian's moon face peered out, his heavy glasses giving him the appearance of a benign owl. When he saw who it was, he advanced with hand outstretched. He was as unlike the lean, tanned man from Singapore as could be imagined. Short, portly and starting to go bald, he looked ten years older than Richard, but there was an air of benign prosperity about him that told of years of a settled lifestyle.

'Richard, nice to see you again. How did the first day go?' They chatted their way back into his consulting room where the GP sat his old friend down in the patient's chair. After the inevitable reminiscences about their student days, they got down to business.

'If you're happy with the arrangements, Richard, you are welcome to take on the cases in Monmouth and Chepstow. Since Dr Saunders retired, we've had to send them either to Newport or Hereford, both of which are outside my jurisdiction.'

Pryor was keen to confirm his agreement to this and also thanked Meredith for putting him on to the solicitor in Lydney.

'I wondered why those remains from the reservoir went up to Hereford?' he remarked.

The coroner nodded. 'There was no one here to deal with them. Mind you, if there'd been anything even slightly suspicious, I'd have had to send them to Cardiff, as Dr Marek in Hereford makes no claim to having any forensic expertise. It'll be useful having you in the area, I must say.'

Pryor saw a chance to get his feet more firmly under the table.

'I'd be more than happy to help in that direction, but I've got no official standing with the police or the Home Office.'

Brian Meredith tapped the side of his nose, reminding Richard of Jimmy Jenkins's habit. 'I may be able to put a word about here and there, Richard. You're too good a prize not to be used around South Wales.'

Emboldened by the extra four pounds in his wallet, Pryor suggested that as it was almost lunchtime, he might treat his friend to a meal somewhere. Meredith lived a couple of miles outside Monmouth – 'a doctor should never live in his practice premises, if he wants any peace' was his favourite saying. He accepted the offer of lunch and took Richard to one of the best hotels near the town centre. As he looked at the prices on the menu, the pathologist felt his wallet getting lighter by the minute, but he reckoned it was worth it if Brian could pull a few strings for him.

'How did you get on with old Lethbridge and this bone business?' asked the coroner, over their rather tough steaks.

'The lady in Newnham is dead set on upsetting your verdict,' answered Richard. 'She's got a private investigator looking into it, as well.'

'Trevor Mitchell? He's a good man, I met him a few times when he was still in the CID across the border. Any chance that I'm going to have to eat my words?'

Pryor shrugged. 'Not so far, but I'm waiting to hear from Mitchell as to what he found when he interviewed Mrs Barnes.'

'She was a tough little bird, spoke her mind at the inquest!' said Meredith. 'It seems she wants to get married again and urgently needs a declaration that her husband is dead.'

The conversation veered towards more personal matters until they finished their meal, when Pryor manfully paid up at the till and walked back to the surgery with Meredith.

'I'll have to call you up to an inquest sometime on that lady with the overdose,' said the coroner as they entered his forecourt.

'We'll run an analysis to make sure it was that Seconal,' said Richard, as he unlocked his car. 'You should have the result in a day or two, along with the post-mortem reports on both cases.'

Meredith's pale eyebrows rose on his chubby face.

'That's a welcome change!' he admitted. 'The forensic lab in Cardiff usually takes at least a couple of weeks!'

They shook hands and Pryor climbed into his car and shut the door. He was about to start the engine, when the coroner came to the window, which Richard wound down.

'It completely slipped my mind, I almost forgot to ask you,' said Meredith. 'My barrister brother, who's in chambers in Swansea, rang me last night to see if I could recommend someone to give a sound pathological opinion. I don't know what it's all about, but I said that there was no need to go looking up in London, as you were on the doorstep, so to speak.'

Suddenly feeling that his outlay on a good lunch seemed to be proving worthwhile, Pryor happily nodded his assent. 'So what shall I do about it, Brian?'

The other doctor pulled a prescription pad from his side pocket and scribbled a telephone number on the back.

As he handed the sheet through the window, he told Richard to speak directly to his brother Peter to find out more.

'Best of luck with the new venture,' he said as he waved

goodbye. 'There should be some more work for you at the Chepstow mortuary later this week.'

Feeling buoyant with these harbingers of future work, Richard let in the clutch and drove off, back down the valley that he already thought of as home.

FOUR

It had been agreed that Sian need not come in on Saturdays unless there was something urgent going on, so when Richard returned with his samples on Friday afternoon, she busily began setting up her equipment for barbiturate analysis, with the promise to 'get cracking' first thing on Monday morning. Her enthusiasm was infectious, as she was almost ecstatic at having 'her first case', as she put it. Even the usually impassive Angela was smiling benignly at Richard's news of more work and both the women were itching to know what the barrister in Swansea would have to say.

However, they had to wait over the weekend for it, as Pryor's attempt to phone the chambers in Swansea where the coroner's brother was based, produced only a message from a clerk that Peter Meredith had left for the weekend, but that he would get him to return the call on Monday.

The weather had cooled down but was still pleasant and with little else to occupy him over the fallow two days, Richard looked forward to 'striding his own broad acres', as he liked to think of his bit of land, as well as sorting out his office and his room upstairs. He was not by nature a very tidy person, unlike Angela who was almost obsessive about 'a place for everything and everything in its place', as his grandmother used to say. However, he made an effort, buoyed up by the hope that an increasing workload would make this the last chance he had of getting really organized. His workroom was on a back corner of the house, behind the room used for an office, and he had plans to have a doorway knocked through to save having to walk around the corridor and into the hall to get into the office.

After another scratch meal with Angela in the kitchen – this time more salad and a tin of John West salmon, followed by cheese and biscuits – he percolated some Kardomah coffee and took it into the 'staff lounge', as they grandly called it.

This was the room between Angela's office and the kitchen, entered by a door at the foot of the stairs.

Angela was relaxing in one of the large armchairs, part of the three-piece suite they had retained from his aunt's furniture. The room was much as the old lady had left it, with a good, but faded carpet on the floor, a large sideboard against one wall and a stone Minster fireplace on the other.

'Should be cosy enough in the winter,' she said, as she poured coffee into two mugs on the small table in the centre. 'As long as we can afford the coal! Heating this house will cost a fortune.'

'I should think we could get wood easily enough around here, the whole valley is a forest,' replied Richard, full of optimism today. 'I'll have to ask Jimmy, he'll probably offer to cut down someone's trees for us!'

They listened to the six o'clock news on the massive Marconi radiogram that had been part of the furnishings, but the details of the national rail strike and the disaster at the Le Mans motor race in which a crashed Mercedes had killed over eighty people, were too depressing and they switched it off.

'No trains, but I think I'll drive up to Berkshire in the morning to visit my parents,' announced Angela. 'I need to bring down some more of my things I've left with them since I left the flat.'

'At least you can get a decent meal when you're home,' suggested Richard. 'I wonder if we'll get any replies from that advertisement?'

'Hardly likely in a place as small as Tintern Parva,' replied Angela. 'I think you'll have to put it in the local Monmouthshire paper to get any hope of a response.'

It turned out that she was wrong about this, for later that evening as she was sitting upstairs her room, enjoying the view of the sunlit valley through the bay window, she heard the distant ringing of their solitary telephone in the hall below.

It stopped after a few rings and a few moments later, there was a tentative tap on her door.

'Are you decent?' came Richard's voice. Even in the short time they had inhabited the house, they had both become meticulous about respecting each other's space and he

normally kept well clear of Angela's territory. The bathroom
was a problem and he was determined to hive off part of the
spare bedroom behind his, to have a second one constructed.

She went to the door and invited him in, motioning him
to another chair opposite hers in the bay window. Because
of the wonderful view, she used this front room as her lounge,
again with remnants of the original furniture pressed into
use. Her bedroom was the one behind and another project
they had in mind was a connecting door, to save her having
to go out on to the landing each time she wished to move
from one room to the other.

'I heard the phone, was that more business for us?'

He shook his head and gave her one of his impish grins.

'Guess what? That was a reply to our card in the post
office. It's only been there a few hours!'

She leaned forward, as surprised as he had been.

'Good God? Who was it, someone from the village?'

'Yep, a lady called Moira Davison, lives just down the
valley on the main road.'

'Moira Davison? Sounds Scottish, maybe all she can cook
is haggis!' said Angela, facetiously.

'She didn't sound Scottish, she had a slight local accent.
Said she can cook, but her main talent is secretarial work.'

Angela looked dubious. 'Can she make beds and clean the
house as well, I wonder?'

Richard shrugged. 'We'll find out on Monday. I suggested
she came up here to see us in the afternoon. Hopefully, I'll
be down in Chepstow mortuary in the morning.'

They discussed the economics of the matter and decided
to see if she would come for five days at four pounds a week,
given that she seemed suitable.

'What about income tax, national insurance and all that?'
asked Angela, as ever the practical one of the pair.

'I'll have to ask my accountant about that – when I get
one,' he said vaguely. 'Until then, we can slip her a few quid
on the quiet.'

Having committed themselves to the black economy, they
had to wait until Monday to see what Mrs Moira Davison
was like.

*   *   *

Left alone on Saturday morning, after Angela had left for Berkshire, Pryor decided to wash his car in the back yard, using a hosepipe, sponge and chamois leather.

He was very fond of the Humber, a handsome black saloon for which his father had stumped up the cost. Though five years old, it was as good as new and a great improvement on the pre-war Morris Ten he had had in Singapore. The car had survived the Japanese occupation but had been rapidly succumbing to rust in that humid climate.

When he had finished, he made himself a bacon and egg fry-up in the kitchen, washed down with a bottle of beer from Hancock's brewery in Cardiff.

He fervently hoped that the 'Scottish woman' as Angela persisted in calling her, would want the job, as he was already fed up with this 'indoor camping', especially after the luxury of a houseboy and an amah in the house in Singapore. In fact, the thought of Angela relaxing after a good lunch at her parent's place, made him suddenly decide to follow her example. Locking up, he drove off on a ninety-minute journey to Merthyr and arrived at his parents' house in Cefn Coed in time for tea.

Though he had stayed with them after returning from Singapore, while waiting for Garth House to become available, they were delighted to see him. During his long years abroad, he had only managed two visits home and it was now pleasant for them to have him in the next county. By seven o'clock, he was slumped in an armchair, replete after a massive meal that his mother had cooked, telling them all the details of this first week in the new venture. His father had helped with the burden of financing it, buying him the car and a new binocular microscope, as well as some other equipment, so he was happy that his son seemed confident that this rather risky endeavour was going to succeed.

As the evening wore on, he gave in to his mother's persuasion and decided to spend the night there, sleeping in his old room, where he had grown up until he went to university. After a morning lie-in and a large Sunday lunch, he drove back home and arrived around four o'clock. As he went into the large empty house, he was surprised to find

that he missed Angela's presence and was looking forward
to her coming back that evening.

Sian had laboriously typed his two post-mortem reports
before leaving on Friday and he went to his room at the back
of the house to check through them. He signed the one which
concluded that the cause of death was 'myocardial infarction
due to coronary thrombosis', but that relating to the woman
would have to wait until Sian did her analysis for barbiturates.

He was looking at the reports, typed on plain foolscap
paper, and was contemplating having standard forms printed
with their partnership names at the top, when he heard the
phone ringing. It was in the hall, just outside his room and
he answered to find that it was the coroner's brother, Peter
Meredith.

After some polite introductions, the Swansea barrister
explained that he was involved only as a 'go-between' and
the person seeking advice was a professional friend of his,
Leonard Massey, QC, of the Middle Temple.

What Meredith had to say only strengthened the suspense,
as Richard related with relish when Angela returned soon
afterwards. He sat her in the staff lounge and brought in a
tray of tea and biscuits from the kitchen.

'A Queen's Counsel looking for a pathologist down here
in the sticks?' she exclaimed. 'But why? They're coming out
of the woodwork in London – Keith Simpson, Francis Camps,
Donald Teare!'

After years in the big city, she knew all about the forensic
scene there, but Richard shook his head as he poured her a
cup of tea.

'This isn't to do with one of his trials up there,' he said.
'This is personal, for the dead woman involved is his daughter.
It seems that he wants a second autopsy – and the first one
was done in Swansea.'

His partner raised her elegant eyebrows. 'So what was
wrong with the first one? How did she die, anyway?'

Pryor offered her the plate of Peek Frean's shortcakes, and
took one himself after she declined.

'Peter Meredith didn't know much about it himself, but
said that it was reported to the coroner and that it was said
to be a drowning in the sea.'

'So where do we go from here?' asked Angela, sipping her tea.

'I told Meredith that I was happy to give any help I could, so he's ringing his QC pal with our phone number. He should be contacting me tomorrow to give me more information.'

'Roll on tomorrow!' said the scientist gaily. 'This could be the start of something big, as they say in Hollywood! Getting the lawyers to put your name about will do us no harm at all. Tomorrow might be a memorable day, especially if the Scottish lady comes up trumps!'

It was to be an eventful day, one way and another.

Sian was in early and with Angela supervising, set about the barbiturate analysis. Though the scientist was primarily a biologist, an expert in blood, semen and anything botanical or zoological that had a forensic angle, she had been about the Metropolitan Police Laboratory for so many years that many of the other techniques had rubbed off on her. Sian had worked mainly in the clinical chemistry section of her hospital laboratory and had been studying for an external degree in biochemistry for the past year, going on half-day release to the Technical College, a practice which her new employers had willingly agreed to continue.

While they worked away together, Richard had a call from John Christie to say that there were two more post-mortems waiting at the Chepstow mortuary, so by ten o'clock, he was down in the ancient town sited just above the point where the Wye emptied into the Severn.

Though the mortuary was in yet another council yard, it was slightly more modern and a little larger, with a small office for the attendant partitioned off from the outer room. This worthy was a small man, with a very large, bald head and prominent projecting ears like jug handles. He advanced on Richard to solemnly shake hands, his almost childlike features wreathed in smiles.

'I'm Solomon Evans, doctor – everyone calls me Solly.'

In spite of his smooth, guileless face, Richard thought he must have been about fifty, and it soon became apparent that he was a little backward, except when it came to collecting his tip for each post-mortem. John Christie, who had arrived before Richard, gave him a conspiratorial wink over Solly's head.

'This chap does the best skull-sawing you ever came across, doctor,' he said, which caused the little man to give a beaming smile.

The two cases were already in the post-mortem room, which was a little more elaborate than Monmouth, with a long metal draining board attached to the sink and a proper wash-hand basin. There was even a small desk for writing notes and an electric heater fixed high on the wall.

The coroner's officer related the histories, one of which was a body recovered from the river, the other was another sudden collapse in the street. By the time Pryor had dealt with the examination of the bodily organs of the latter, Solly had opened the scalp and with a handsaw, meticulously removed the calvarium, the bowel-shaped top of the skull. This exposed the dura, the thick membrane over the brain.

'Never seen him accidentally cut through that, in all the times I've been here,' said Christie, giving Pryor another wink.

'If I ever damage that, I'll not take my tip from you, Doctor,' promised the little man solemnly.

The presumed drowning took longer to deal with, as the pathologist found no classical signs, which was not unusual, especially as from the state of the body, it must have been in the water for several days. However, there was no other obvious cause of death, but Pryor collected blood and urine samples, as well as some tissue blocks in small pots of formaldehyde, to take back to Garth House.

The deceased had been identified as a fifty-year-old man from the town, last seen outside a public house on the previous Wednesday night, in an advanced state of inebriation.

'He was a well-known drunk, Doctor,' said Christie.

'Been run over twice when he was in his cups, and I reckon this time he wandered down to the quayside and fell in. Been washing up and down with the tide ever since, until he got caught in an old tree trunk.'

Richard finished his work, washed his hands and made some notes, then did the financial business with the coroner's officer, handing over an additional half-crown per case to Solly. He was back at the house in time for lunch, such as it was, but before that, he handed over his samples to the two women.

'We need a blood and urine alcohol and perhaps you'd have a look for diatoms, Angela? There was too much post-mortem change to be definite about drowning.'

The biologist held up the pots containing the lung tissue.

'There's a lot of argument in the journals about whether the diatom test is reliable, but we'll give it a try again,' she said dubiously.

Sian was itching to break into the conversation. 'Stacks of barbiturate in that lady, Doctor Pryor!' she said proudly. 'The system worked fine on our first try-out, the report's on your desk.'

Richard was careful to congratulate the young woman, as he wanted to encourage her keenness and she went off beaming, anxious to set up her Widmark system for alcohol analysis.

'Any calls from that chap in London?' he asked Angela, as they made their way to the kitchen to rustle up something to eat.

'Nothing so far – nor any sign of the Scottish lady,' as she persisted in calling the potential applicant.

'We did say in the afternoon, so let's keep our fingers crossed,' said Richard, as he rooted in the old fridge.

Pushing aside a sealed box of blood-grouping sera, he pulled out a bowl of tomatoes, a washed lettuce and a cucumber, while Angela put plates, cutlery and mugs on the table.

'I have visions of her as a big, fat woman with a double chin and her hair rolled into a head band, like they did during the war,' she said.

'I don't give a damn what she looks like as long as she can clean, make beds and cook something,' replied Pryor. 'I wonder if she can make Chinese fried rice?' he added, wistfully.

Sian came in with her tin box of sandwiches and a bottle of Corona orangeade, a change from her usual Tizer. Angela opened a tin of Spam, which they ate with salad and some fresh bread from the village bakery, followed by part of a Lyon's Swiss roll. Just as they were finishing and thinking of making tea, the phone rang outside.

'Perhaps that's him!' exclaimed Sian, whom Angela had told about the mysterious Swansea case. Richard hurried out and was gone for about five minutes, leaving the two women waiting impatiently for news.

He returned and sat down in maddeningly slow motion.

'Well, was it him?' demanded Angela.

'Yep, we've got another job, by the looks of it. It will mean a bit of travelling.'

He gave them the gist of his conversation with Leonard Massey, whose married daughter had been found dead in the sea off a rocky part of the Gower coast over a week ago. She had been swimming alone and was presumed to have drowned, which was confirmed by a coroner's post-mortem.

'An inquest was opened a couple of days later and a burial order issued, the full inquest to take place at a later date,' said Pryor.

'So where do we come into it?' asked Angela.

'Massey wants a second post-mortem, as he's not satisfied with the circumstances. He was a bit cagey about telling me more on the phone, but he's coming down to Swansea tomorrow to see the coroner and suggests I meet him there afterwards for a conference.'

'Business is looking up!' commented Angela. 'I had a call this morning from a solicitor in Bristol wanting two more paternity tests.'

A distant knock on the front door reverberated through the empty hall and Sian jumped up to answer it.

'Probably your new Scottish charlady,' she said as she left the room.

'Better see her in the office, hadn't we?' suggested Richard. By the time they reached the door opposite, Sian had let the new arrival in and led her down to the waiting pair, who took her into the office.

Richard introduced himself and the other two women and settled her on to one of the three hard chairs in the sparsely furnished room. He glanced across at Angela and a lift of his eyebrows conveyed his feelings. Far from being the fat, motherly figure she had anticipated, Moira Davison was an attractive brunette of about thirty, her slim figure neatly dressed in a cream summer suit over a pale blue blouse, the long slim skirt suggestive of the current 'H-line' fashion. Her black hair was cut in a page-boy style with a straight fringe above her blue eyes.

'That was a quick response to my rather amateurish advert!' began Richard, wanting to keep the interview informal.

Moira Davison smiled, lighting up her almost elfin features. 'I happened to be in the shop soon after Mr Follet put the card in his window,' she replied. 'It was a sudden impulse, I'm afraid, but I'm quite serious about it. It's time that I got on with my life again.'

Angela took up this rather cryptic remark.

'I presume it's "Mrs" Davison? So why do you want to work here? I assume you're local, as you saw the advert in the post office.'

Moira nodded. 'I'm a neighbour, really. I live in the second house down, just around the bend between here and the village. I lost my husband three years ago and I've been rather withdrawn since then. But as I say, it's time to pull myself together now and I felt this might the stimulus I've been waiting for.'

She sat primly on the hard chair, holding a cream handbag on her lap, with a pair of light gloves resting on top. Richard liked the fact that she had taken the trouble to dress and behave professionally when seeking a job, even though she lived virtually next door.

He explained the set-up at Garth House and their need for someone who would help both with the office work and with keeping the establishment afloat from the point of view of food and creature comforts.

'Quite honestly, I'm not very domesticated,' admitted Angela. 'We can't go on living out of tins and on fry-ups!'

'I take it you can cook something better than that?' added Richard, almost wistfully.

Mrs Davison gave another smile. 'I think so, my mother was a very good cook and she taught me a lot. I managed to feed my late husband for a few years without him complaining!'

They both were reluctant to ask about her married life, but she seemed to sense this.

'Keith was an industrial chemist, working in a factory in

Lydney. Three years ago there was a explosion and he was killed.'

She seemed quite composed about the tragedy and went on to volunteer some more relevant information.

'I was brought up in Chepstow and after leaving school, did a year in a secretarial college in Newport. Then I went to work in a solicitor's office until we moved here about seven years ago, so I can type and do the usual office routines, like filing and simple accounting.'

Angela caught Richard's eye and got a slight nod in reply. 'Sounds just what we need,' she said. 'I know my partner is more concerned with his creature comforts, but your office skills would be welcome, especially as you used to work in a solicitor's office.'

'I know many of the lawyers in this area, from having to phone and write to them,' agreed the brunette. 'I'd love to have the chance of a trial period, if that would suit you.'

They got down to more details of just what they wanted her to do, the hours required and the salary. Richard called Sian back in to meet Moira and he could see from her covert amusement that she felt as he did about Angela's hopelessly wrong forecast of what 'the Scottish lady' would be like.

'We've also got another staff member,' said Richard. 'Mr Jenkins does the garden and odd jobs, but I expect you already know of him?'

Moira laughed. 'Jimmy Jenkins? Everybody for miles knows Jimmy. I heard that he had attached himself to you, just as he did for your aunt. Jimmy's fine, as long as you keep him on a short lead and don't let him talk you into anything daft!'

They soon agreed on terms for a month's trial, Moira coming from nine until four o'clock, five days a week.

'I'll make a cooked lunch every day, then put something ready for your supper,' she suggested. 'Weekends are a bit more difficult, but we'll work something out.'

Moira saw no reason why she shouldn't start next day and they gave her a quick tour of the house to get an idea what she was letting herself in for. Richard saw her to the front door and even offered to drive her home, but she said it was barely five minutes walk away.

'Well what do think of that?' he asked, when he came back to the others in the office.

'Watch yourself, doctor, a pretty widow like that will wrap you round her little finger!' warned Sian, with a grin. 'But if she can type better than me, I'm all for it!'

He turned to Angela. 'What about you, will she do?'

The biologist tapped her chin thoughtfully with a long forefinger.

'She seems just what we need, but the proof of the pudding is in the eating – perhaps literally here. Let's see how the first month goes.'

Privately, her instincts were rather similar to Sian's. The woman was too damned good-looking for her liking, with such an impressionable fellow like Richard around. Though Angela had no designs whatever on her partner, there was an almost primeval hint of competition when a new attractive woman came on the scene.

Her ruminations were cut short by the telephone ringing again and after answering it, Sian returned to tell Pryor that the Lydney solicitor was on the line.

'Doctor, I've had a talk with Trevor Mitchell,' announced the dry voice of Edward Lethbridge. 'He's been up to Ledbury to see Mrs Barnes. In fact, he said he's been back to the town to have a nose around and he thinks there's possibly some grounds for doubting her positive identification of her husband's remains.'

Richard was intrigued by Mitchell's quick results.

'How much doubt must there be before the coroner might consider an exhumation?' he asked the lawyer. 'Because without that, I can't really do anything for you.'

'We will need a lot more than Mitchell's suspicions. I wanted to ask you if you think looking at Albert Barnes's medical notes would be of any possible help?'

Richard frowned at the telephone. 'I didn't know he had any medical records. It's the first I've heard of them.'

'No, his wife saw fit to forget to mention them. He had an accident at work a few years ago, according to one of his friends that Mitchell tracked down in a Ledbury public house. He worked as a platelayer on the railway and was knocked down by a wagon during shunting. Nothing very serious, but enough to send him to Hereford County Hospital for a night.'

Pryor considered this for a moment.

'I'm not sure what we might learn from them, depends on what injuries he had. But unless we look, we'll never know.'

'Exactly, but of course we'd need his wife's consent to have a view of them.'

'Would she give it, d'you think?' asked Pryor.

'She probably wouldn't want to, but it would look fishy if she refused. Anyway, that's my concern, I just wanted to know if you thought it worth the trouble.'

'Yes, I'm sure it would be. But what did Trevor Mitchell find that raised these doubts?'

'I think he'd better explain himself, Doctor. As you know, he lives not far from you and he suggested he called to talk to you about it later today.'

Things were certainly livening up, thought Richard, as he went back to the laboratory, where both women were now busy with their tasks. Angela was squatting on a stool in front of their fume cupboard, a big glass cabinet with a sliding door in the front like a sash window. An extractor fan sucked noxious fumes out through a vent into the old chimney, which was just as well, as she was carefully pouring concentrated nitric acid into a small beaker containing bits of lung from the Chepstow drowning. Evil yellow fumes were wreathing up towards the fan, which would become worse when she began heating the horrid mixture over a Bunsen burner.

Pryor stood behind her and told her of the call from Lethbridge.

'Trevor Mitchell's coming over sometime today. It'll be good for you to meet him, he might well bring more trade our way.'

He wandered over towards Sian's side of the room, where she had her chemical and analytical equipment.

Though what she was being asked to do in a forensic context was different to the hospital routines to which she had been accustomed, the techniques of handling materials and instruments were similar. With Angela's help and a good selection of technical manuals on the shelf, they could get by for now, though anything complex would have to be sent away, down to the nearest Home Office Forensic Science laboratory in Cardiff or off to some specialist commercial outfit.

'I'm running that blood and urine you brought in, for alcohol,' she explained. 'Angela said she had a call from a defence lawyer wanting a urine sample tested in a road traffic case, so maybe we can work up some business in that direction?'

He nodded, wishing that the government would get on with bringing in a fixed maximum blood level for drivers, rather than relying on clinical testing by police surgeons of ability to drive. Apart from issues of road safety, it would be healthy for his bank balance, as many arrested drivers would want a second analysis as a check.

Feeling at a loose end – and rather redundant with the two women working away at something to which he couldn't contribute – he went to his room and started to read the most recent issue of the *British Medical Journal*.

It was four o'clock before Mitchell arrived and this co-incided nicely with a tea break. After introducing him to his colleagues and showing him the laboratory, they sat in the staff room over Typhoo Tips and Peek Freans, while the former detective superintendent told them about his findings in Ledbury.

'The story was bit "iffy" from the start,' he said.

'Molly Barnes said her husband was a keen fisherman, but the chaps I spoke to in the pub said they'd never heard of him going fishing.'

'There was no fishing rod found near the body?' asked Angela.

'No, and what's more, there's no fishing allowed in that reservoir. So if Albert went there, it was for something else.'

'How is he supposed to have got there?' asked Sian, deter-mined not to be left out of the team.

'On his pushbike, that's something his pals in the Red Lion confirmed,' said Trevor. 'He was a keen cyclist, appar-ently. Often at weekends, he used to go off on his own into the country, probably to get away from his wife!'

'But the bike has never been found?' asked Angela.

'No, but it's not easy to identify cycles, maybe a long way from home – and they get pinched all the time.'

'Perhaps he had a lady friend somewhere and he's done a runner with her,' suggested Richard.

'With a sharp-mouthed wife like Molly, I wouldn't be surprised – though he didn't take any of his clothes or possessions, according to her.'

'If you can believe anything she says,' muttered Sian, darkly. She had already decided the wife was guilty.

'What else has raised your suspicions?' asked Pryor.

'I had a quick look at that wedding ring that she showed me so reluctantly. When I got home, I checked the hall marks, it was assayed in Birmingham in 1931, which is a bit odd, as they weren't married until 1941.'

'I'll bet she'll have an answer for that,' said Sian. 'She'll say it was second-hand, they couldn't afford a new one.'

Mitchell nodded. 'Or say they had to get wed quickly when he was on leave during the war. But it's still odd, like the wristwatch.'

'What about it?' asked Angela.

'It was an expensive one, an Omega. His missus spun me some tale about him getting it during the war in Germany for a packet of Woodbines.'

'Is there a problem about that?' asked Angela.

Trevor emptied his cup and Sian poured him another.

'I called in at a jeweller's when I was in Gloucester this morning. I showed him a photo of the watch that was taken for the coroner's inquest. The jeweller said that model wasn't made until 1950, so the story about getting it in the war was phoney. It's worth a fair bit of money, too, though I don't think Mrs B realizes that. Albert was only a railway worker, so where did he get a valuable Omega?'

'It's suspicious, but doesn't sink her story,' said Richard. 'The ring could have been second-hand – and he may have got the watch by some underhand means and not wanted to tell her. Perhaps he stole it or won it in a poker game?'

The former police officer nodded reluctantly. 'I suppose so. But why didn't she tell me that he had been to hospital, when I asked her about his health? I spoke to his mates in the pub and they recalled that he had been hit by something at work and had concussion and a leg injury.'

'Edward Lethbridge wants me to have a look at his hospital notes,' said Pryor. 'I'm not sure that they can help, but you never know.'

'Lethbridge is going to have a word with Brian Meredith, but I can't see him doing anything about an exhumation unless we come up with something a good bit stronger.'

'Do you know where the remains are buried?' asked Pryor.

'In the council cemetery at Ledbury. They've only been down a few weeks.'

Sian listened with fascination. This was better than a hospital lab, with its endless routine blood sugars, ureas and fractional test meals. She never thought she'd hear someone ask 'Do you know where the remains are buried?'

As Mitchell was leaving, Richard speculated on what Agnes Oldfield would make of the developments.

'She'll be proclaiming to the world that it was her nephew, jumping the gun before we've got any further,' replied Trevor. 'I hope Lethbridge will keep it to himself for now, but I suppose he'll have to prove to her that he's earning the fee she's paying him.'

He drove off in the direction of St Brievals and left Pryor wondering what the next day might bring – hopefully, a decent meal prepared by their new employee. Then the memory of the trim and elegant Moira with her big blue eyes and black fringe momentarily overshadowed his obsession with his stomach.

FIVE

As Richard Pryor drove along the A48 towards Swansea the next afternoon, he decided that lunch had definitely been a success. Moira Davison had explained apologetically that she had had little time to be adventurous with the menu, as she had needed to get supplies in from the limited range in the village shop and to get organized in the kitchen, finding out where things were kept. However, gammon, chips and peas had gone down very well, with a milky rice pudding to follow. He also decided that Moira was as efficient as she was attractive and hoped that her typing and office skills were going to be as good as her cooking.

Now he was on his way to meet the London lawyer, Leonard Massey, in the chambers of the coroner's brother. As he passed through Pyle and reached Margam, he came within sight of the great new steel works at Port Talbot and he began remembering the route quite clearly. In his student days before the war, he used to go down to the Gower Coast on his motorcycle, a modest Excelsior two-stroke, which was a pig to start, but good once it got going. 'The Gower', as it was universally known, was a twenty-mile peninsula jutting westwards from Swansea, with one of the most beautiful coastlines in Wales. High cliffs, long beaches of golden sand, and a spine of unspoiled green hills made it one of the most popular targets for trippers and holidaymakers. Yet by the sound of it, that very attraction had caused the death of Massey's daughter, if she had drowned along what could be a dangerous coast.

The Humber purred along through the heavily built-up industrial areas of Briton Ferry, Neath, Skewen and Morriston. He passed an oil refinery, tinplate and spelter works, forges and foundries until the last few dismal miles of old ribbon settlement took him into the town centre, virtually destroyed during the blitzes and rebuilt in the cheapest style of tasteless architecture of the austere post-war years.

The address he had been given was in Walter Road, which rose from the town centre along the flank of the hills that backed Swansea Bay, likened by some poet to the Bay of Naples, its five-mile curve of sand stretching round to Mumbles Head with its prominent lighthouse.

Walter Road led to the more upmarket suburbs of the town and was a mixture of smart shops, schools and large old houses, many given over to the premises of doctors and lawyers. He drove slowly, scanning the street numbers and found a parking space not far from the tall Edwardian house that was his destination. In the porch, a long board listed the barristers who inhabited the place, one near the top being Peter Meredith.

The front ground-floor room was the clerk's office and he was conducted from there by a smart young lady to a room on the first floor, where Peter Meredith met him at the door with an effusive greeting and a vigorous handshake.

'Great to meet you, Doctor – my brother has often spoken of you, especially since you came back from foreign parts!'

He was an older, thinner version of Brian Meredith, in fact he was almost gaunt, but Richard put that down to the restless energy with which he seemed to be imbued, both in speaking and in moving about. He led the way into the large room, which was a typical lawyer's den, with a large leather-covered desk and walls lined with shelves groaning under the weight of legal texts and law reports. Another man was sitting in front of the desk, who rose to shake hands as Peter introduced them.

'This is my old friend Leonard Massey, Doctor. We did our pupillage together in London. I'm sorry we have to meet in these sad circumstances.'

Richard sat in the other seat in front of the desk as Meredith went around to his own chair and indicated a tray in front of him. 'We've just had this delivered, I'm sure you could do with a cup after your journey.'

As he fussed with a coffee pot and a milk jug, Leonard Massey addressed himself to the pathologist.

'It's very good of you to come down like this, Doctor Pryor. I know some of the London people, of course, especially Keith

Simpson, but it would be so much easier to deal with an expert on his home soil, so to speak.'

Massey was in his fifties, a heavily-built man of rather sombre appearance. Faultlessly dressed in a dark suit, he wore a spotted bow tie and had thick black eyebrows that turned up at the ends. Pryor thought that he was like a stage version of a successful QC, grave, ponderous and with a 'presence' that tended to dominate any company.

As Peter Meredith passed over a cup of coffee, Richard admitted that so far, he knew virtually nothing of the circumstances or how he might be able to help.

Massey nodded regally and launched into a detailed explanation of the problem.

'This concerns my only daughter, Linda, who was twenty-eight years old. She was married to Michael Prentice about five years ago and they lived at Pennard, near Bishopston, a few miles west of Swansea.'

Richard knew the village from some of his student jaunts, years before.

'Michael was originally an industrial engineer, though he had hardly ever become involved in the technical side.'

The barrister said this with a hint of scorn and Richard sensed that Leonard's son-in-law was not exactly his favourite person.

'He made his money – quite a lot of it, it seems – from various entrepreneurial ventures, mainly around the motor industry, as he was passionate about high-performance cars.'

Pryor was beginning to wonder how this connected with the need for a forensic pathologist, but the lawyer soon reached the crux of the story.

'When my daughter first married him, they lived near Slough, where he was a partner in a firm which was making electronic ignition systems, but then he formed a consortium to develop some other revolutionary ideas to do with engines. I don't exactly know what it was, but they set up a small Research and Development unit and a pilot factory on an industrial estate somewhere near Swansea.'

'Very generous terms were being offered by the local councils to attract business,' cut in Peter Meredith. 'Five years' holiday from rent and rates.'

'Anyway, they moved here eighteen months ago and bought a nice house very near the sea. Then two weeks ago, we had a panic message from Michael to say that Linda had vanished from the house while he was at the factory. The next day, her body was recovered from the sea by the coastguards.'

His voice did not break, but it became wooden, as if he was forcing restraint on his feelings.

'She often went swimming in the sea,' offered Peter, helpfully covering up his friend's emotions. 'The house was virtually on top of the cliffs at Pennard.'

'Obviously the death was referred to the local coroner and he ordered a post-mortem, which confirmed drowning as the cause of death.' Massey had recovered his poise now and spoke in a brisk courtroom manner.

'My wife and I were devastated, of course. We came down and tried to help Michael in making all the necessary arrangements, though he seemed to have it all under control. The funeral was actually set for tomorrow, but it's had to be postponed.'

Richard waited silently for the punchline.

'Last Thursday, I had a phone call at home from an old girlfriend of Linda's, who was in boarding school with her. She lives in Reading and before my daughter left Slough, they saw a lot of each other. They've kept in touch and seemed quite close.'

He paused to take a mouthful of coffee.

'This friend, Marjorie Elphington, had been in France and only arrived home on Thursday, to hear from another schoolfriend that Linda had drowned. She rang me straight away, because she had had several letters from Linda in the past few months, saying how unhappy she was and that Michael wanted a divorce because he had taken up with another woman.'

Pryor began to see where the story was taking them.

'You knew nothing of this?' he asked.

The barrister shook his head ponderously. 'Not an inkling! But since her marriage, Linda had grown more and more distant from us, especially since they moved to Wales. We didn't see her that often – to tell you the truth, neither my wife nor myself were all that keen on her husband.

All he seemed interested in was making a fast buck, as they say!'

Richard began to wonder if he had driven almost eighty miles because of a father's dislike of the man who had stolen his daughter, but there was more.

'Marjorie was particularly worried by Linda's last letter, about a fortnight earlier,' said Massey in sombre tones. 'She said that Michael was becoming abusive because she refused to even contemplate a divorce and several times had actually shaken and punched her during flaming rows.'

'And you think he may have something to do with her death?' concluded Pryor.

Leonard Massey shrugged. 'It may sound far-fetched, but I wouldn't put it past the chap. And I can't rest without at least making every effort to prove that it didn't happen that way.'

Richard thought for a moment. 'You say that the post-mortem confirmed drowning as the cause of death? Nothing else found?'

Massey took a thin briefcase from the floor besides his chair and handed Pryor a sheet of paper. 'I saw the coroner on Friday and I copied out the relevant parts of the report he had from his pathologist. He seemed quite satisfied that it was drowning.'

Richard quickly scanned the few handwritten paragraphs.

'There were some abrasions and bruises recorded, scattered over the body,' he observed.

Massey nodded. 'He explained those by the body being tossed around in the tide for perhaps more than a day. The body was seen by a fisherman at the foot of the cliffs and it was recovered by the coastguards, who said it was in a deep gully between sharp rocks, which could easily have caused those marks.'

Peter Meredith, who had been listening intently to the others, wanted to clarify the time scale.

'You said she went missing on a Tuesday night – at least, that's when her husband said he returned home to find the house empty. And then her body was found on Thursday morning?'

Massey nodded. 'He didn't report her missing until the

next evening, because he admits they had some marital problems and he thought she had just up and left him.

'But when he had no message from her after twenty-four hours, he rang the police – especially as he says that he found that her handbag and almost all her clothes were still there.'

'Was she in the habit of going off alone to swim?' asked Pryor.

'Yes, that was true enough. She loved swimming and she loved that coast, she was very happy to move down there from the Home Counties.'

There was another silence as the three men thought about the possibilities.

'So what's the situation at the moment?' asked Richard.

Leonard Massey moved into his courtroom mode again. 'I want to be absolutely sure that there's no sign of any foul play, Doctor Pryor! I've spoken to the coroner and in the circumstances, he has no objection to a private post-mortem examination.'

'How does the husband feel about that?' enquired Meredith.

'He has no choice in the matter,' replied Massey, brusquely. 'The inquest has not been held, so the coroner still has full jurisdiction. If the possibility of a non-accidental cause exists, then he is entitled – indeed, he should be obliged – to take all measures to confirm or exclude it.'

There seemed no answer to this, so Pryor confined himself to practicalities.

'Where was the first autopsy carried out – and by whom?' he enquired.

'In the public mortuary – a rather primitive place, I'm afraid. It's in Swansea itself, though the coroner who's dealing with the matter is in Gowerton, a few miles away. The doctor was a retired pathologist who still does coroner's work. A Doctor O'Malley, I believe.'

He delved into his black leather case once more and handed Richard another sheet of paper.

'These are the phone numbers of the coroner's officer and of the undertaker and my own contact details. You are more used to making these arrangements, so perhaps I could leave it with you. I will naturally be responsible for your usual fee and expenses.'

Pryor stood up and shook hands with the other two men.

'I will have to offer this Dr O'Malley the courtesy of attending,' he explained. 'It will probably be a day or two before I can arrange to come down again, but I'll let you know what's happening and will send you a full report as soon as I can.'

Peter Meredith showed him out and he walked back to his car, thinking that this all sounded a bit far-fetched, in that the QC was virtually suspecting his son-in-law of murder. But 'the usual fee and expenses' part sounded good, as well as getting his name known around the South Wales legal establishment.

SIX

'Why don't I drive you down there, Doc?' offered Jimmy Jenkins. 'It's a long 'ole journey and you want to be fresh to do your duty when you gets there, eh?'

It was Wednesday evening and Pryor had arranged to carry out the second post-mortem at noon the next day, having made all the arrangements through the coroner's officer in Gowerton, appropriately named PC Mort.

Richard wasn't all that keen on Jimmy's suggestion, but Angela thought it a good idea.

'You're paying him to do odds and ends about the place, but there's no hurry about the gardening, so he might as well make himself useful driving you,' she pointed out.

He gave in and at half past eight next morning, they left for the three-hour drive. Richard refused point-blank to sit in the back as if he was a grandee with a chauffeur and sat alongside Jimmy, where he could keep an eye on his driving.

He was soon aware that the man was an excellent driver, for he learned that Jimmy had spent much of the war behind the wheel of a three-ton Bedford, trundling across North Africa and then Italy.

'How are you getting on with the little widow woman, Doctor?' he asked. 'Nice little lady, she is! Do her good to get out and about a bit more, she's been keeping too much to herself since her husband died.'

He seemed to know everyone's business from top to bottom of the Wye Valley.

'She's doing fine,' said Richard sincerely. 'At least we're eating proper food now, not stuff out of tins! I understand her husband died in an accident.'

'Blown to bits, he was!' said Jimmy with ghoulish drama. 'Some chemical factory up near Lydney. Time she had a bit of cheerful company, after the bad time she's been through. Mind, that Sian will cheer her up, she's always on the go, ain't she?'

As Bridgend was left behind, Richard sat and studied the countryside, seeing things he missed when he was driving. It was more relaxed, he had to admit, though he resolved in future only to let Jimmy drive on long-distance trips. Talking of Moira Davison got him thinking about her – she seemed perfect for the job and he only hoped she stayed. He had known secretaries in the past to give up when they had to type post-mortem reports with descriptions of horrible injuries or decomposed corpses. Moira was very well organized, setting a routine on the first couple of days which first ensured that any office work was done, then the beds made and the lunch prepared, with some cleaning in the afternoon and more typing if it was there.

He sensed that both Angela and Sian were slightly wary of the new employee, though they were unfailingly friendly and pleasant to her. It never occurred to him that he might be the cause of this watchfulness, as they waited to see how his attitude to her developed.

Pryor had been married for nine years until his divorce in Singapore last year – it was one of the factors that persuaded him to take the 'golden handshake' and return to Britain. He had met Miriam, five years younger than himself, when he was serving in Ceylon. She was a civilian radiographer attached to the military hospital in Colombo. Later, he found that the old adage 'marry in haste, repent at leisure' was all too true and after a honeymoon year, things started to go downhill. She went with him to Singapore when hostilities finished and stayed for several years when he took the civilian post.

But after a series of 'affairs', she left him and went back to England, the final break coming with the divorce a year ago.

Though by no means celibate since the divorce, he had no burning desire to marry again. Ruefully, he thought that he now had no lack of feminine company, with three women under the same roof most of the time!

His reverie took them further towards Swansea and soon they were looking for the mortuary, which the coroner's officer had told him was in The Strand. This turned out to be a dismal street between the lower part of the town and

the river, which in former times had been a quayside. The
mortuary was housed in one arch of a disused railway viaduct,
each end being blocked off with brickwork, that on the street
side having large double doors. Jimmy parked outside and
declared that he was going off for an hour to find a pub.

Pryor knocked on the door and it creaked open to reveal
a small, dark-haired man who announced himself as the
coroner's officer. There were two other men present, who
PC Mort introduced as Dr O'Malley and Detective Inspector
Lewis. The other pathologist was about seventy, burly and
red in the face, dressed in an old-fashioned blue suit with
high lapels. He seemed an amiable enough man and had a
marked Irish accent when he told Richard, with tongue in
his cheek, that he still did a few coroner's cases to finance
his membership of his golf club. Pryor thought that it was
very likely that the coroner was also a member of the same
club.

The local detective was another small man, middle-aged
and with thick dark hair coming low on his forehead.

'The coroner had a word with my 'super' and he thought
it best if I came along, in case anything significant turned
up,' he explained.

The arch was divided into two halves, the outer part
containing an old cold cabinet like the one in Monmouth, only
larger. It was a 'walk-in' type without racks and looked as if
it had originally come from a butcher's shop. Beyond a door
in the central partition of the arch lay the post-mortem area,
merely a porcelain slab raised on two brick pillars, with a sink
and a table against the walls. A dusty fluorescent light hung
by chains from the distant roof. Standing by the table was a
tall, stooped man with a walrus moustache, already attired in
a long red rubber apron and thick rubber gloves that came
almost to his elbows.

'This is Mr Foster, from a local undertaker's,' explained
Patrick O'Malley. 'He's really an embalmer, but he comes
down to help here when required.'

Foster bobbed his head and muttered a greeting, then went
outside to pull a trolley from the fridge. He slid the sheeted
body on to the table whilst Richard opened his case on the
table and then put on an apron. There were several pairs of

grubby rubber boots under the sink and he chose a pair of
short, white ones which looked as if they were rejects from
a hospital operating theatre.

Foster removed the sheet from the body and to complete
the legal formalities of continuity of evidence, should it ever
be required, PC Mort confirmed it was the mortal remains
of Linda Prentice.

'I've no doubt it was a drowning,' volunteered the older
pathologist, as Pryor began to examine the body externally.
'There was no froth at the mouth and nostrils, but plenty
down in the air passages.'

He was slightly defensive, which was natural enough when
a colleague was being hired to pick any holes in his opinion
that could be found.

Richard nodded. 'As she wasn't found for a couple of
days, that's not surprising,' he agreed. 'Were all these marks
like this when you examined her?'

He pointed with a gloved finger at a number of scratches
and areas of peeled skin on the forehead, nose, arms and
legs. O'Malley came near, bending forwards to keep his suit
clear of the table. He peered at the superficial injuries, his
glasses on the end of his nose.

'They're much more obvious now, of course,' he observed.
'But that's to be expected after all this time. I did my examination a week ago.'

He was correct, thought Richard, as bruises could 'come out',
as his grandmother used to say, and appear more prominent
after a day or two.

Richard got Foster to turn the body on its side, holding
the upper arm so that the pathologist could look at the back,
where there were more irregular scratches, some in long
tracks.

'Where she was recovered was a very rocky place,' offered
O'Malley, still rather defensively. 'Deep gullies with the tide
surging up and down. The rocks are sharp there and those
limpets and barnacles make it even worse.'

'Some bruises as well,' Richard pointed out. He recalled
that O'Malley had not listed the injuries in any detail in his
brief report to the coroner, but that was not unusual in a non-
forensic autopsy in which there was no suspicion of foul play.

O'Malley peered again at some small areas of discoloration on the arms, neck and face, which varied from blue and purple through to pale green and yellow.

'Banging about on those damned rocks, no doubt!' he declared. 'I've seen it too often around this coast, it can be a very dangerous place.'

Richard made no reply, he was keeping all his options open. He produced a few instruments from his capacious bag and began reopening the neat stitching made by Foster at the first post-mortem. Carefully, he went through all the organs again, O'Malley being keen to point out the water-logging of the lungs which was still very apparent. Pryor took some small tissue samples from various organs into pots of formalin which he always carried in his bag, then turned his attention to the head. PC Mort and the CID man watched impassively as he felt all over the scalp with his fingers and parted the damp hair to look at the skin beneath.

'I didn't think it worth disturbing the poor lady more than necessary,' said O'Malley, as the other doctor took a scalpel and began shaving the auburn hair from several small patches near the back point of the head. Again, Pryor recognized that many pathologists – and other doctors who still did coroner's work – frequently omitted to open the skull and examine the brain in cases where another cause of death seemed glaringly obvious.

'Some more bruising here,' he commented, standing back so that O'Malley could lean in and look at a couple of bluish stains under the scalp, each about the size of a two-shilling piece.

The Irishman grunted. 'They're rough old places, those rock gullies. Perhaps you ought to have a trip out there to have a look at them.'

Richard remembered them well enough from his student trips to Gower – including one where he and a nurse from Cardiff Royal Infirmary spent a cosy afternoon lying in the grass above one of those gullies.

He stood back for a few minutes while Foster incised the scalp and removed the skullcap with a hand saw, though not making such a neat job of it as Solly Evans at Chepstow.

Richard spent a few minutes in making detailed notes on a

clipboard, recording the position and size of each mark on a printed outline of a body, back and front, using a celluloid ruler to measure the exact dimensions of the injuries. Then he looked carefully at the inside of the scalp, taking more tissue samples, and then at the skull itself, before removing the brain and examining that on the draining board of the sink.

Finally, he managed with some difficulty to get a clean blood sample from one of the leg veins and some urine from the bladder, which O'Malley had not opened.

'That for analysis, Doctor?' asked Lewis Lewis, the detective inspector, the first time he had spoken since they began.

Pryor nodded. 'I'd better fill in some exhibits labels and sign them, just in case,' he murmured and fished in his case for some buff luggage labels. 'I'll check for alcohol and anything else relevant,' he said. 'Though in drowning, the dilution of the blood by absorbed water spoils any accuracy. Still, the urine should be OK.'

O'Malley grasped at his words thankfully.

'So you agree with me that she drowned, Doctor Pryor?'

'I do indeed, no doubt about it,' he replied, thinking that this was safe ground, whatever else might materialize. After settling the tip with Foster – he reckoned the coroner's officer had already had his pound of flesh from O'Malley – he said goodbye to them all and went out to where Jimmy was sitting in the car, reading the *Daily Mirror*.

'All set, Doctor?' enquired his driver.

'I'm starving, did you see a café on your travels?' Dissecting bodies had never yet put him off his food and they walked around to Wind Street where Jimmy had noticed a 'Bracchi' establishment, the South Walian nickname for an Italian café. He had a ham omelette and treated his driver to bacon, beans and egg, all with chips, a plate of bread and butter and a pot of tea.

'Funny old town, this,' observed Jimmy. 'Can't decide whether it's ancient or modern!'

From what he'd seen of the place, Richard knew what he meant – the remains of a Norman castle and the oldest pub in Wales just up the street, but with ugly modern buildings springing up amongst the wide acres of bomb damage that had completely destroyed the town centre.

'It's called progress, Jimmy,' he sighed. 'And we may be seeing quite a bit more of Swansea and district before long.'

At a loose end, now that her current batch of analyses was finished, Sian wandered over to Angela's bench and stood watching what the biologist was doing.

'That's this diatom test, is it?' she asked, always eager to learn something new.

'Pull up a stool,' invited Angela. 'You'd better learn how to do this, in case I'm away when Richard needs one urgently.'

The technician watched as the older woman took a conical-bottomed test tube from a rack, containing a clear yellow liquid with a button of brown deposit in the tip. She sucked off most of the upper fluid with a teat-ended pipette, discarded it and then tapped the tube with a fingernail to mix the deposit into what was left.

'I don't really understand the principles of this test,' confessed Sian. 'How can it help diagnose drowning?'

Angela carefully sucked up a single drop of the fluid with another pipette and placed it in the centre of a glass microscope slide, covering it with a wafer-thin glass cover-slip.

'It's still not accepted by everyone, but I think it's reliable if done carefully,' she said. 'When someone drowns in water containing these microscopic algae called diatoms, it goes down their windpipe and into the lungs, taking the diatoms with it.'

'So if they're dead, there's no breathing, so the diatoms can't be found in the lungs!'

Angela laughed. 'I wish it was that easy! No, even if you throw a corpse into the river, the water still percolates down into the lungs. So finding diatoms in lungs doesn't mean anything.'

'So what's the point of looking?'demanded Sian, pointing to the tube, which had a label saying 'Lung'.

'To check that the water actually contains diatoms, though we always look at a water sample as well. If it doesn't, there's no point in looking further. Some waters don't, though even tap water often contains a few, especially if the pipe hasn't been used for a time.'

She pointed at the test-tube rack, where there were three other tubes. Sian looked at them and read the names written in grease-pencil . . . marrow, liver, kidney.

'Are these what you've been boiling up in the fume cupboard?' she asked.

'Yes, you have to dissolve little samples of internal organs taken at the post-mortem in nitric acid, which gets rid of all the organic material and leaves the diatoms.'

'Why don't they vanish as well, then?' demanded the knowledge-hungry technician.

'Because they've got a shell of silica, which resists the acid. Now, if the victim drowns, then these tiny things get into the lungs and some penetrate the lining, they're so small. The heart is still beating, so they get carried off in the blood stream and get filtered out in the bone marrow, liver, spleen, and kidneys.'

Light dawned in Sian's mind. 'Ah, I see! So you can tell if it was a live body or a dead body that went into the water. That's really clever!'

Angela smiled at her enthusiasm. 'Hang on a minute! It's not all that simple. You have to find a good number of diatoms in the target organs, not just the odd one or two, because we've all got some knocking around inside us. They are wafting around in the air, dust from all sorts of places. Filter material, toothpaste, chicken farm litter – it's everywhere.'

'You mean I'm breathing the damned things in even now?' demanded Sian.

'Probably . . . a researcher in a London hospital examined the air-conditioning filters on the roof and found plenty of diatoms in them. And because the sea is full of them as well, a chap from Norway found that eating shellfish produced plenty in the organs, as they can penetrate the wall of the gut!'

Sian looked dubiously at the slides that Angela was preparing from the other tubes.

'So is it worth doing?' she asked.

'Sure, if you can find a heavy penetration, especially in the bone marrow – and they match up with what's in the water – then it's good evidence of live entry.'

'What d'you mean, "match up"?'

'There are thousands of different types of diatom, which vary from place to place. If those in the organs have a similar mix to those in the lungs or the water sample, then it adds to the probability that they weren't just strays, especially if there are a lot of them.'

She began looking down the eyepieces of the microscope at the slide from the lungs. 'There we are! Plenty in the River Wye, have a look at those.'

She leaned aside to allow Sian to look and as she twiddled the fine focus knobs, the technician gave an exclamation.

'They're so pretty! Like little bananas or boats or pill-boxes, with lace patterns on them.'

'Now have a look at the kidney extract, see if there are any there. It might take some time.'

Sian used the stage controls to move the slide around and eventually gave a cry of triumph. 'Got 'em! Once you get your eye in, it's easy.'

Angela took her place and soon agreed that all the samples had diatoms which were a similar mix to that in the lung. 'So we can tell Richard that this chap undoubtedly drowned, though he probably knows that already. Still, it's nice to have a belt-and-braces confirmation.'

Sian went back to her own bench, happy that she had acquired a bit more forensic mystique.

That afternoon, Trevor Mitchell had again gone to see Molly Barnes in Ledbury. She was not pleased to see him and she later told her sister Emily, who lived further up the street, that if she had known who it was, she wouldn't have opened the door to him.

'Bloody cheek of the man – and that lawyer fellow who wrote to me!' she protested.

'What did he want this time?' asked Emily, who had a soft spot for her brother-in-law Albert. She privately wondered if he had just done a runner to get away from her difficult sister. He had once admitted to her that he had a lady friend in Hereford.

'Want? Only Albert's medical records,' said Molly, indig-nantly. 'At first I told him to get lost, but he said the coroner was in agreement and that because it had been an open verdict at the inquest, he could reopen it if he wasn't satisfied.'

Emily nodded sagely. 'You can't beat the system, Molly. It would look bad if you refused. They'd think you had something to hide.'

Emily was inclined to think that her sister did have something to hide, but she didn't know what. Since Albert had vanished, Molly had 'taken up' with a fellow from the other side of town and she wanted to get married, as soon as she could. The coroner had given her a paper to take to the Registrar for a death certificate, but now it looked as if someone had thrown a spanner in the works.

'So what did you do?' she persisted.

'I didn't have much choice, did I?' snapped her sister. 'I can't see what medical records from years ago have got to do with this. It was only a little accident at work.'

'Only a little accident?' squeaked Emily. 'He was knocked out and spent a night in the County Hospital.'

'I still don't see what they want them for,' she said sullenly. 'That private snooper said I should have told the inquest that he had been in hospital once.'

The private snooper in question drove away with a sheet of paper in his pocket, signed by Mrs Barnes, giving consent to an inspection of her late husband's medical notes. Trevor Mitchell had been told by John Christie that if it came to the crunch, the coroner could demand that the hospital produce the records, but it would be easier if the widow agreed.

As he had to pass through Hereford on his way home, he thought he might as well call into the County on the way. It was on the eastern side of the historic city and he parked and made his way to the Records Department, tucked away at the back.

The woman at the desk looked askance at the letter he produced and went off to talk to someone higher up the bureaucratic tree.

'I can't give you these, sir,' she said officiously, when she returned. 'It's quite out of order. How do I know who you are?'

'Do you know PC Christie, the coroner's officer? He must come in here now and then for records.'

She softened a little. 'Of course I know John Christie. What's he got to do with it?'

'If you can't give them to me, you'll have to give them to him on the coroner's order,' he said patiently. 'Then he'll give them to me.'

Long experience of people on the other side of her counter told her that this man was – or had been – a police officer.

'I'll have to ring him, sir,' she said half-heartedly.

'Yes, a good idea. I'll wait,' he replied politely.

She vanished for a few moments and then came back.

'It'll take some time, these are a few years old.'

Trevor Mitchell nodded. 'I'll go and get a cup of tea in the canteen. Half an hour be alright?'

When he came back, there was a thin brown paper folder waiting for him.

'The Records Officer says you can't remove it from the hospital, but you can look at it here,' she announced with a note of triumph in her voice. 'Only the coroner can have it taken away.'

Mitchell sighed, but pulled out his notepad and leaned on the counter to copy every word. It was not difficult, as the notes were only one and half pages long. He didn't understand some of the words, but transcribed them faithfully for Doctor Pryor to see.

Thanking the clerk with exaggerated courtesy, he left, wondering if the whole afternoon had been a waste of time. He drove his Wolseley back to Monmouth and then down the valley, deciding that instead of turning off near the bridge to go up to St Brievals, he might as well call at Garth House to show the doctor what he had found.

As he drove into the back yard, he saw that the Humber had also just arrived and Richard Pryor was hauling his black case into the house. Invited into the kitchen for a cup of tea, Trevor saw a new face, a neat woman with dark hair, who was just hanging up her pinafore.

'This is our new recruit,' said Richard heartily. 'Mrs Davison is our housekeeper, cook, secretary and general factotum! Moira, meet Trevor Mitchell, the Wye Valley's answer to Sherlock Holmes!'

Mitchell grinned as he shook hands. 'Is the doctor always like this?' he asked.

Moira gave him a lovely smile. 'It looks that way, but I've only been here a couple of days!' She turned to her employer. 'I've left the rest of the cottage pie in the fridge for your supper, Doctor. Just heat it up in the oven – and there's a new tin of Campbell's oxtail in the cupboard if you fancy soup to start.'

She took a light jacket from a hanger on the back of the door and slipped it on. 'Nice to have met you, Mr Mitchell. I'm sure we'll see you often.'

Trevor hoped so too, as she smiled again and went out into the yard.

'Nice woman, that,' he said appreciatively, then waved his notebook at Pryor. 'I've managed to copy Albert Barnes's hospital record, what there is of it.'

Richard wet the tea and set cups and saucers on the kitchen table. 'Angela's in the lab, I'll give her a call, she might want to hear this.'

A few minutes later the three heads were bent over the notebook, studying two pages of Trevor's neat handwriting.

'Not much help is it?' commented Angela, when they had read to the end.

Richard summarized what it said. 'He was admitted to Casualty after being struck in the railway siding by an empty truck that was rolling down an incline. Thrown to the ground, bruised chest and arm, two fractured ribs and a laceration of his scalp needing six stitches. Mild concussion, admitted overnight for observation. Discharged himself late next day, ribs strapped up, dressings on head wound, told to go to GP if any problems and to come back in ten days for the sutures to be removed.'

'What did you expect to find from hospital records that would help in identifying him?' asked the ever-critical Angela.

Richard shrugged, his lean face scowling at Mitchell's handwriting in the book. 'Well, say he'd had a fractured leg – that could have left a deformity on the bone that the patholo- gist might have noticed – some callus, for instance.'

'What's callus?' asked the detective.

'It's a lump of calcified stuff that forms around a break to join the two parts of the broken bone together. It gradually absorbs over months or years, but usually leaves some permanent sign, especially on X-ray.'

'Nothing here like that,' said Angela. 'Neither did the Hereford pathologist mention any old injuries.'

'So we're no further forward,' growled Mitchell, obviously disappointed that his efforts had been in vain.

'What's this you've written here, in the clinical examination?' asked Pryor, jabbing a finger at the notebook.

Trevor peered over Richard's shoulder. 'It says *'pec.rec'*, that's all. I don't know what it means, I just copied what was in the original notes.'

'*Pec.rec*?' asked Angela. 'What's that mean, for heaven's sake?'

The pathologist shrugged. 'Search me, it's no medical term I've ever heard of. The doctor who examined him, whoever he was, has just written it down at the end of his external examination, before he goes on to say that the heart and lungs seem normal.'

'Could it be of any use to us?' asked Mitchell.

'Until we know what it means, there's no way of telling. It might be worth asking the chap who wrote this, what he meant by it.'

Angela looked at the date on the notes. 'It's seven years ago. That doctor might have drained his brain to Canada or Australia by now.'

'Was his name on the original notes?' asked Richard.

Trevor shook his head. 'No, only the name of the consultant who he was admitted under that day.'

Pryor slapped his fingers on the edge of the table. 'That's good enough! The hospital staff records will show who worked for that consultant at that time. It would have been a house officer or a senior house officer admitting patients on surgical intake. We could track him down through the *Medical Directory*.'

'A lot of effort for two little words which may mean nothing useful,' said Angela dubiously.

Trevor drank his tea and got up to leave. 'Next time I'm near Hereford, I'll call in and make some enquiries. Nothing ventured, nothing gained,' he added, philosophically. 'When I was in the CID, we sometimes got a result from snippets just as unlikely as *pec.rec*!'

After their meal that evening, Richard and Angela brought a couple of chairs from the office and sat on the tiled area outside the front porch, between the two bay windows. It was a glorious evening, the setting sun lighting the opposite side of the valley, making the dense woods glow in different shades of green. He had unearthed a bottle of Gordon's gin from one of the boxes in his room and with some tonic water that Moira had thoughtfully added to the shopping list, they spent a peaceful hour relaxing.

The woman stretched out her legs luxuriously.

'Quite a change from my flat in New Cross, with the fog coming up from the river and the noise of the traffic outside.'

'I though you lived in posh Blackheath,' observed Richard, lazily.

'The estate agents always called it that, but really it was New Cross,' she admitted. 'But this is much nicer!'

The sat and sipped their gin for a time, watched the shadows change beyond the Wye as the sun slipped down.

'People would take us for an old married couple,' said Richard grinning at his partner.

Angela glared at him. 'Don't get any ideas, my lad!' she growled. 'We're just business partners, remember?'

Her feelings towards him were ambivalent, she realized. Richard was an attractive enough fellow, in a lean and wiry sort of way. He was clever, honest as far as she knew and generous, but was given to swings of mood that were so unlike her steady temperament that she doubted she could put up with him in anything other than an arm's length relationship. At the same time, she felt herself illogically irritated by the hero-worship attitude of Sian towards him – and even after only a few day's acquaintance, the respectful and admiring manner of Moira Davison.

'Right, tell me about today, we've not had a chance until now,' she commanded.

Pryor described the strange mortuary in Swansea and the people he had met there, then summarized what he had found.

'No doubt at all that she had drowned, it was just as obvious as that chap dragged out of the Wye at Chepstow,' he said. 'But I'm a bit concerned about some of the injuries on the body. I realize she was being bashed about on the rocks, but I need to know how old some of those bruises were. They certainly weren't all fresh.'

'Because of this story that the dead woman's friend told to her father?' asked Angela.

'Yes, she reckoned that the daughter claimed that her husband was being violent because she wouldn't agree to a divorce.'

Angela sipped her drink slowly as she pondered.

'What are you going to tell Massey?' she asked.

'I've got to be cautious, I don't want him rushing around yelling "murder" until I've had a chance to look at those injuries under the microscope.'

'The funeral has been postponed once already. Can they hang on to the body even longer?'

'That's up to the coroner. If it does turn out to be suspicious, then I don't see how he can allow it to be buried – certainly not cremated, as was the family's intention.'

'But there's been a second post-mortem. Won't that do as defence autopsy?'

'No, because I'm acting for the father, who's in the position of a complainant. If the husband was ever charged, then his defence lawyers would almost certainly want another opinion of their own, to counter mine.'

'We'd better get it right then, laddie!' said his partner, sagely. 'When are you going to tell the father what's going on?'

'I hope Sian can manage some decent histology, but that will take a few days. I'll have to say something to him before then, I'd better ring him tomorrow.'

They sat for a while longer, then Angela decided it was getting cooler as the sun went down. She stood up and collected the glasses, while Richard took the chairs back inside.

'I forgot to tell, you, the coroner's officer in Newport rang, he wanted to know if you could cover there from next week, as their chap is going on holiday. Sounds as if your pal Brian Meredith has been talking on the grapevine again.'

'Newport? Should be quite a few cases there. Perhaps we'll be able to afford another bottle of gin after all, partner!'

Next morning, Pryor had one routine post-mortem in Chepstow, but by mid-morning was back at Garth House, where Angela was busy with her paternity tests, checking blood groups of the mother and child against the putative father, who had denied that the child was his and therefore had no obligation to finance its upbringing. Sian was assembling her histology equipment, ready for Monday, when the tissues that Pryor had taken would be sufficiently fixed in formaldehyde for her to process them for examination under his new microscope. Unlike the big hospital laboratories, which were beginning to get the new automated processing machines, she would have to do it by hand, placing the tissues in jars of varying grades of alcohol and then xylene until they could be embedded in paraffin wax, ready for cutting into diaphanous slices, ready for staining.

Richard looked in briefly on this earnest labour, then backed out and went to the telephone, where he placed a trunk call to Leonard Massey's chambers in London. Fortunately, the barrister was available to talk to him, as he had cancelled many of his commitments, due to this family tragedy. Carefully, Pryor summarized his post-mortem findings at Linda's autopsy, emphasizing that these were provisional conclusions and would have to be further investigated over the next few days, possibly a week.

'But you feel that some of these injuries were made before death, not in the sea?' demanded Massey, well-used to interrogating witnesses.

'Yes, but I don't know yet how long before death – and I may never be at all accurate,' answered Richard, cautiously.

'This last letter that my daughter wrote to her friend Marjorie, was about ten days before she disappeared. Could they be that old?'

'It's possible. They would be unrelated to the events surrounding her death, so perhaps made during an assault. I can't be more specific at this stage – and as I say, dating injuries is notoriously inaccurate.'

There was a silence over the miles of phone line between them, but Richard could sense the wheels going round in Massey's head.

'So where does that leave us, Doctor?' he asked eventually. 'What am I to say to the coroner and the police?'

'I need at least a few days to check on these wounds. I'm afraid that these laboratory investigations inevitably take time. It's not my place to become involved in the legal aspects, but I doubt that the coroner would want to hold on to the body after two post-mortems, given the tenuous evidence we have so far.'

Massey seemed of the same opinion. 'Naturally, my wife and I are distressed enough as it is without having to again delay laying poor Linda to rest. Do you see any merit in postponing burial any longer?'

Richard shook his head at the telephone, even though the recipient was over a hundred miles away.

'I think I have every sample that is necessary, Mr Massey. I doubt the coroner would grant a cremation order in the circumstances, but I see no reason why you could not go ahead with a burial, if he agrees.'

This was because the slight possibility of an exhumation existed, should any future defence lawyer insist on a further opinion.

Massey switched to another aspect of the case.

'I'd like to know more about this alleged affair that Michael Prentice was having with some woman. I presume she was down in South Wales, so do you happen to know any reputable enquiry agent who could get some information?'

Richard was happy to be able to recommend Trevor Mitchell, telling him that the former detective superintendent was working with him on another case. He gave Mitchell's phone number to Massey and they left it at that for the moment, Richard promising to send a written preliminary report that day and keep him informed the following week about the results of the microscopic examination.

He sought out Moira in the kitchen, where she was preparing a couple of trout for lunch, new potatoes and peas already waiting in saucepans on the Aga cooker.

She always slipped home for an hour at lunchtime, as it was only five minutes away and she wanted to feed her cat.

'When you come back, can you type out a report on this Swansea case and get it in the post tonight?' he asked. 'I'll write it out in longhand now and leave it in the office.'

'I can take shorthand, if you ever need it,' she offered.

Richard grinned and made a show of sniffing the air like a Bisto Kid. 'I'd rather you finished making our lunch, thanks all the same!'

As she went back to flouring the glistening fish, she had another suggestion.

'A lot of offices now are using these small tape recorders, Doctor. I've seen a portable one in a little carrying case that you can take around with you and record straight into it when you do your work.'

Moira used the term delicately, still not quite used to his macabre occupation.

'A good idea, when we get some cash under our belt, we'll think about it. There's so much stuff we need, it's frightening.' As he went back to his room to start writing, he thought of the shopping list that Angela had for the laboratory, especially on the chemistry side. It would take a lot of mortuary work and paternity tests before they could even think of some of that equipment.

With a sigh, he sat down and pulled out his fountain pen.

An hour later, Moira was clattering away on her new Olivetti, copying Richard's draft report. He had good handwriting for a doctor, and she had no difficulty in transcribing it, even the unfamiliar medical terms.

After only a few days, she was enjoying her new job very much – it was a strange one, a little housework, some cooking and now this, describing the dissected remains of a young woman. After several years of mourning and apathy for her lost husband, she felt as if life could restart properly once again and she was grateful to the inhabitants of Garth House for giving her this unexpected opportunity. She realized that Doctor Bray was slightly wary of her, though she was friendly and communicative enough. Moira also knew that this might be due to an almost subliminal feeling of competition over

Richard Pryor – she had not yet worked out what the relationship was between the two partners, or what it might
develop into in the future.

As she was typing away and musing on the new turn her
life had taken, Richard was answering the telephone in the
hall. He had earlier brought a spare stool from the kitchen
to put alongside the small table that carried the heavy black
instrument, as he anticipated spending a lot of time there
until the GPO got around to putting in some extensions in
the other rooms.

It was the Gower coroner on the line, a local solicitor
called Donald Moses. He had just been contacted by Leonard
Massey about Richard's preliminary findings.

'This leaves me in a difficult position, Doctor,' he said,
sounding rather agitated. 'If I feel there is any substance in
these suspicions raised by Mr Massey, then I'm bound to
pass the matter to the police.'

Pryor repeated what he had told Massey, that he could not
be more specific until he had examined the sections of the
bruises under the microscope, which could not be until sometime the following week.

'There was a detective present at the post-mortem,' he
added. 'But he just verified the continuity of the samples I
took and I didn't discuss any findings with him, they are too
uncertain at present.'

Donald Moses sighed. 'Mr Massey is very persistent, I'm
afraid. But I don't want to start a wild goose chase and then
find it comes to nothing. To even approach the husband of
the dead woman at this stage would be most unfortunate if
nothing came of the matter.'

Richard saw a flaw in this argument.

'But he must already know that something is going on, as
the original funeral date was postponed for my examination?'

The coroner accepted this 'He never contacted me to ask
why, which is a little odd. I suspect that his father-in-law
had it out with him. He's a forceful personality, to say the
least!'

Pryor wanted to avoid getting too involved in aspects that
were none of his business.

'I'll be sending you a copy of my preliminary report today,

it's being typed as we speak. And as soon as I see the tissue sections, I'll get back to you.'

The coroner seemed relieved by this breathing space.

'I'll hang fire until then, Doctor. But if you find nothing definite, I'm going to allow a burial to go ahead whenever the family want it. Mr Massey told me that you said you had all the material that was necessary.'

After he put the phone down, Richard sat on his hard stool for a few moments to think about the situation. It seemed that a lot might hang on his examination of the bruises next week, as the coroner was right in saying that it would be both embarrassing and unjust to start a possible murder investigation, based only on the angry dislike of a father-in-law, fuelled by a letter alleging a domestic dispute.

Well, he thought, there was nothing more he could do until Sian came up with the microscopic sections in a few days' time, so he might as well enjoy the weekend.

He had seen in the newspaper that the new film *Richard the Third*, with Laurence Olivier, John Gielgud and Claire Bloom was playing in Cardiff and decided to go down on Saturday. He wondered if Angela would like to go with him – maybe they could hold hands in the back row, he thought facetiously!

SEVEN

As a Shakespearean performance was being played out in a Cardiff cinema, another drama was taking place in a Swansea hotel.

The Osborne was a small, but exclusive, hotel perched on the edge of a low cliff at Rotherslade. About six miles from the town centre, it was at the eastern end of the Gower peninsula, overlooking the popular Langland Bay.

In one of the best bedrooms, with a perfect sea view, a furious row was going on.

'You've got a bloody nerve, interfering in my affairs like this!' ranted Michael Prentice, his face suffused an angry red. He was a tall man, though not so heavily built as his father-in-law, who stood facing him in a colder type of fury.

'Your affairs! That's what's led to this, according to Linda's best friend,' he responded scathingly.

'Watch what you say, Leonard, or I'll have you for slander, barrister or not!' snarled the younger man, his handsome face contorted with hate. 'You accuse me of assaulting my wife and I'll break you!'

The two large men stood just inside the door, squaring up to each other like a pair of boxers before the fight.

'Do you deny pushing and punching Linda when she discovered you were having it off with some tart?' said Leonard, in intense but measured tones.

'Don't you call her a tart, damn you!' howled Michael, then stopped dead, as he realized he had been tricked by the experienced advocate.

The Queen's Counsel gave a cynical smile. 'No use denying it now, Michael? Who is she?'

'Mind your own damned business. If Linda and I did have a row, what's that to you?'

'As I'm her father, a great deal, blast you!' rasped Massey, losing his temper for a moment. 'She writes to her friend that you want a divorce and that you assaulted her, then within a couple of weeks, she ends up dead! Do you wonder that I feel that it's my business?'

Prentice glowered at the barrister. 'Are you accusing me of murder now, instead of assault? Good God, man, I could sue you for thousands for this!'

Massey looked around the room with exaggerated care.

'Indeed? Where are the witnesses? I think you'll be talking to people soon who have no fear of slander. I'm talking about the police, Michael.'

The younger man took a threatening step nearer Massey.

'You wouldn't dare, damn you! Your reputation would be ruined when the farce was exposed!'

The barrister did not flinch, but glared at his daughter's husband with utter contempt. 'It won't be my decision, it's up to the coroner. It's his duty to report any suspicious circumstances to the CID. You'll be getting a visit from them soon, I don't doubt.'

He turned away and went to a table, where he picked up a cheque and handed it to the other man.

'Meanwhile, we have to do the decent thing and see that my poor daughter is put to rest. The coroner will be calling you on Monday about a disposal order for burial, so this is for whatever funeral director you choose.'

Michael Prentice snatched the cheque and violently ripped it in half, dropping the pieces on the floor.

'I don't want your damned money, blast you! I can bury my own wife, thank you very much!'

He swung around, and went out, slamming the door behind him.

Massey stood for a moment looking down at the fragments of paper on the floor, then he took a diary from his breast pocket and looked up a telephone number. He went to the phone and asked for an outside line.

'Is that Trevor Mitchell? . . . this is Leonard Massey.'

On Sunday, Richard Pryor spent much of the afternoon in his large plot behind the house. He was increasingly keen on starting a vineyard, in spite of Jimmy's scathing remarks and with the help of a long tape measure, was pacing off a large patch about the size of two tennis courts.

In the house, Angela was standing in the window of one of the back bedrooms with a mug of coffee in her hand, watching him as he banged lengths of wood into the ground with a brick, making off the margins of his chosen area. She smiled, much as a mother would humour a child who wanted to build a spaceship in the garden.

'Enjoy yourself, Richard, but it'll never happen,' she murmured. Probably by this time next year, he would be full of keeping turkeys or pigs there instead, or some other impulsive and equally impracticable scheme.

As she stood sipping her Nescafé, she idly tried to analyse her feelings towards him. It was a strange situation, she thought, living alone in a house with a man in a totally platonic relationship. Or was it all that platonic, she wondered?

Richard Pryor was an attractive fellow, with that frequent wry grin or a ready smile. He seemed free of any vices, never angry or sarcastic or mean-spirited. Impulsive, yes, and sometimes swinging between exuberance and depression, but his moods were like quicksilver, never lasting long. He sometimes needed pulling back from going down some irrelevant diversion, but on the whole, he was a really nice guy.

But what did she want with another really nice guy? The last one had left her in the lurch after four years' apparent happiness, with an imminent walk up to the altar in view. No, she would try a bit of celibacy for a time, until something really special came along – and if it didn't, well, she wasn't going to risk another shaming debacle.

Looking out at Richard's antics in the plot, she wondered what had gone wrong with his own love life. They had met at a forensic congress in Edinburgh last year and had hit it off from the first moment. Both recently crossed in love – or in his case, a bitter divorce – and she disgruntled with her employers, they had hatched this plan to set up in business together.

Angela mused over what might have gone wrong with his marriage. He had leaked out bits of information over the months, as he was much less secretive than she. Her private life was always played close to her chest, but he had told her that his wife Miriam had been playing the field with the limitless supply of men available in Singapore – the army officers and expatriate businessmen who abounded in the Singapore Swimming Club, the Golf Club and the famous hotels like Raffles.

Angela wondered if the fault had all been on Miriam's side, but then decided that it was none of her business and that she should be glad that meeting him had led to her coming to live in this lovely valley in a job where she could be her own boss. Please God, let it succeed, she prayed to herself, as she finished her coffee and took one last look at a sweating Richard wielding his brick.

As she went downstairs to the kitchen with her empty mug, the phone started to ring again. Far from being irritated at a disturbed Sunday, she picked it up, knowing that it must be something to do with their business, as virtually no one else knew they were here.

It was Trevor Mitchell, another man she had taken to at first sight. A typical senior detective, he was impassive and dependable and though they had only met once, she liked him and trusted him, not like another senior detective who had let her down so badly.

'What can we do for you, Mr Mitchell? Do you want to speak to Richard?'

'Please call me Trevor, Doctor!' he said. 'And you're in this bones job as much as him, so shall I tell you what I've found so far?'

She liked him even more for that, for not assuming that the male half of the partnership was the chief honcho.

'Sure, Trevor, what's new?' she replied.

'Remember those cryptic words on Albert Barnes's medical notes? Well, I've tracked down the doctor that wrote them.'

'That's great!' she enthused. 'Who is he?

Mitchell explained that he had got John Christie to persuade the hospital to look up their staff records at the request of the coroner. The consultant mentioned in the notes had an SHO named Andrew Welton at the time of Barnes's admission. By searching the Medical Register, he had found that he was currently a Senior Registrar in neurosurgery at Frenchay Hospital near Bristol.

'Maybe Doctor Pryor could arrange to see him and take the notes, hoping that this chap would remember something about it?'

Angela promised to tell Richard and he would get back to him. 'Anything else happening?' she asked.

'Yes, big stuff!' replied Trevor enthusiastically. 'A barrister called Massey rang me last night and said that Doctor Pryor had recommended me as an enquiry agent in a case he's involved in. He's going back from Swansea to London tomorrow and he's breaking his journey at Newport to meet me and explain what it's all about. All I know is that it's an eternal triangle job.'

Angela gave a quick summary of the problem and their involvement, saying that Massey wanted to know more about this alleged 'other woman'.

'Well, it's all grist to the mill – thank the doctor for mentioning me, I can see we're going to be a good team!'

Angela told her partner about Trevor's call, when he came in from his vineyard planning. 'Would it be best if I went to see this chap in Frenchay or could I just ring him up?' he asked.

'I think you'll have to see him, you could be anyone on the phone,' she advised. 'Maybe you ought to get a note from the coroner, as it concerns a patient's confidential record, even if he is dead.'

'Especially if he isn't!' added Richard, cynically.

Monday took Pryor to the large Royal Gwent Hospital in Newport, about fifteen miles away, where he was pleased to have the coroner's work for the next fortnight while the resident pathologist was on holiday in Spain. It was a change to have a proper hospital mortuary to work in, rather than skulk in council yards or under boarded-up arches. There were three cases there that morning and after he had gone home and enjoyed another of Moira's lunches, he drove up to Monmouth to deal with a single autopsy rung in by PC Christie.

'Trevor Mitchell told you that we found the name of that surgeon at Hereford?' asked Christie, as he was sewing up the victim of a carbon monoxide suicide who had killed himself with car-exhaust gas in his garage. Pryor nodded as he picked up the two pound notes that the coroner's officer had left on the table.

'Thanks for your help. I rang Frenchay this morning and I'm driving over tomorrow to see him. My partner thinks I should have some kind of authorization from the coroner to show him, so I'll call on Dr Meredith after this and get some sort of billet-doux.'

Rather guiltily, he was glad that as it was mid-afternoon, he could avoid buying another expensive lunch for his portly friend. He found him in his surgery, just returned from house calls in time for his four o'clock clinic and explained the situation. As Meredith wrote out a quick authorization on a sheet of headed notepaper, the coroner asked about the likelihood of finding any more information.

'I've never heard of this *pec.rec* either, Richard. It seems a bit unlikely that it's relevant.'

'I agree, but without something new, we're not going to be able to twist your arm for consent to an exhumation,' he admitted.

Next morning, armed with his piece of paper, Pryor drove to Bristol after another three-body stint at Newport. Rather than drive an extra sixty miles around Gloucester, he decided to take the Beachley–Aust ferry across the Severn, just above Chepstow. A ferry had been there from ancient times, being given to the monks of Tintern Abbey in the twelfth century.

Richard queued up behind a dozen cars at Beachley, a small village on the riverbank and waited for the return of the flat-bottomed vessel from Aust on the other side. Thankfully, it was not the busiest time of day and soon he was gingerly driving the Humber down the ramp on to the open deck. As they glided across the water on the *Severn Queen*, he wondered if this bridge they were talking about would ever be built.

Half an hour after reaching the muddy shore at Aust, he was turning into Frenchay Hospital. Originally an old sanatorium, it had been expanded into a military hospital for American servicemen during the war and now was a large general hospital providing various surgical specialities.

The head porter's kiosk directed him to the neurosurgical

department and as he trudged down long corridors in the wartime blocks of single-storey brick buildings, he wondered if Welton was still 'Doctor' or had advanced to 'Mister' in the strange way that British surgeons do after gaining the Fellowship of their Royal College, a memory of the times when surgeons were barbers, not proper physicians. He decided that as it was seven years since Welton had written those notes in Hereford, he must surely by now have passed his final examinations to land a job as Senior Registrar in these competitive times. When he eventually found the cubbyhole that was his office, a cardboard label on the door confirmed that it was indeed 'Mr A Welton'.

The surgeon was a thin, rather haggard-looking man in his mid-thirties, with a cow-lick of fair hair hanging over his forehead. He had a strong Liverpool accent when he spoke. He greeted Pryor courteously and he spent a few moments reminiscing about Hereford and the Royal Army Medical Corps, in which Welton had done his two years' National Service in Catterick.

Then Richard produced his coroner's clearance and the copy of the County Hospital notes and they stood over a cluttered desk in the tiny room to look at them. The pathologist explained the problem and then pointed to the cryptic two words with his forefinger.

'I'm sure you don't recall Albert Barnes after all this time, but I wondered if you could explain this abbreviation – it's a new one on me!'

Welton's response was rather unusual. He opened his white coat, threw his tie over his shoulder and unbuttoned the middle three buttons of his shirt.

Pulling aside the material with both hands, he looked down at his bared chest.

'That's one – a *pec.rec*!' he said, almost proudly.

Richard stared at the surgeon's thorax and saw that his breastbone was pushed deeply inwards in its lower part.

'Well, I'm damned – a funnel-chest! That's what we used to call them, or a "salt-cellar sternum"!'

Andrew Welton grinned. 'I was always interested in the abnormality, as I have one myself. Doesn't matter tuppence, unless it's part of Marfan's syndrome.'

Richard dug around in his memory, but failed to find anything left on the matter from his long-ago student days. He looked enquiringly at the surgeon, who responded.

'Whenever I saw a patient with a depressed sternum, I could never resist mentioning it in the notes. *Pec.rec* is my shorthand for *pectus recurvatum*, the proper Latin name for it.'

'And this patient Barnes must have had one?'

Welton nodded. 'No doubt about it. I don't recall him now, but no way would I have written that unless he had one. Does it help at all?'

Pryor closed the folder with the notes and picked it up.

'It may well do, as the thorax was still present amongst the remains. It all depends now on whether the first pathologist has any recollection of it.'

After thanking Welton for his time and patience, Pryor found his way back to his car and began the journey home. Was this another useful step on the quest, he wondered? If the older pathologist in Hereford had no clear memory of whether the benign deformity was present in the bones or not, they were no further forward.

Feeling more like Sherlock Holmes than a doctor, he decided that there was only one way to find out. Instead of going back to the ferry, he drove up the A38 to Gloucester, then turned to Hereford through Ross-on-Wye. Near there, he stopped at a small roadside café with a National Benzole petrol pump alongside. After egg and chips and a pot of tea, he had the Humber filled with petrol, scowling at the recent price increase which had taken it up to four shillings and sixpence a gallon.

By mid-afternoon he was in Hereford, where he found the County Hospital and sought out the pathologist who a month earlier had examined the remains from the reservoir.

Dr Bogdan Marek was about sixty, a thickset man with cropped grey hair. He rose from behind his microscope when a technician brought Pryor in and as they shook hands, the visitor noticed a pile of cardboard slide-holders on the bench alongside the instrument.

'I'm sorry to disturb you, Doctor Marek, you look as if you're snowed under with biopsy reports. I know the feeling!'

This broke the ice nicely and soon the two pathologists were exchanging common ground. Marek, who still had a thick Polish accent, had escaped from his home country in 1939 and come across to join the Polish Forces as a medical officer. Already a pathologist before the war, he had stayed on in Britain in 1945 and was now an SHMO in the speciality.

'I make no claims to knowing much forensic medicine,' he admitted frankly. 'But someone has to do the coroner's work here. If there's anything suspicious, of course, the police get someone from Birmingham or Cardiff.'

He gave Richard a sudden beaming smile. 'Maybe in future, it should be you, I've heard a lot about you lately!'

Pryor said he would be only too happy to come up at any time, but that it was really up to coroners and the police to decide.

'They didn't think it was worth getting a Home Office fellow up here for this one,' said Marek, when Pryor told him the purpose of his visit. 'So has it turned suspicious now?'

'No, it's a bit of a dispute over identity. I've just turned up a piece of evidence that might possibly help.'

He showed the other pathologist the medical notes and pointed to the words *pec.rec.*

'I've just discovered what the clinician meant by that,' he explained.

Bogdan Marek looked at him in mild surprise.

'Surely that must refer to *pectus recurvatum*?' he said mildly.

Richard's mouth did not sag in astonishment, but he felt deflated at Marek's instant recognition.

'Good God, I've just been all the way to Bristol to find that out!'

'Maybe it is because I qualified some time before you, when we used much more Latin in my medical faculty in Krakow!' he answered with another broad smile.

Pryor swallowed his chagrin and came straight to the point.

'The man whose wife claims the remains are his, undoubtedly had this abnormality of the sternum. Now you are the only doctor who has seen those bones, as they've been buried

since then. Can you by any chance remember whether the
sternum you saw had this defect?'

He felt tense as he waited for the answer, hoping that
Marek would dig deeply enough into his recollections of the
case. But the wait was but a few seconds, as the Pole soon
shook his head.

'I can definitely say that it did not,' he said firmly. 'As I
said, I'm no forensic expert or a physical anthropologist, but
I would undoubtedly have noticed a *pectus recurvatum* and I
would have written it in my report to the coroner.'

Richard felt a surge of relief that his efforts had not been
wasted. 'And you'd be willing to confirm that to the
Monmouth coroner?'

Bogdan Marek turned up his hands in a typically conti-
nental gesture. 'Of course! Why not!'

Trevor Mitchell's Wolseley was travelling across Clyne
Common, a large area of rough heathland and bog, a few
miles to the west of Swansea. He was reminding himself to
keep a strict check on his mileage, as this job was likely to
generate a lot of travelling.

The former superintendent liked his 'Six-Eighty' model,
as it was a favourite with so many police forces and he
admitted to a bit of nostalgia after having spent so much of
his life in similar black cars.

On the seat alongside him was a road atlas opened at the
appropriate pages, as well as a folded Ordnance Survey map
at a one inch to the mile scale. He was making his way to
Pennard, just beyond Bishopston, with no clear idea in his
mind how he was going to proceed. The London barrister
who had hired him was not very specific about his needs;
he had said that he just wanted to confirm that his son-in-
law had been unfaithful to his wife and to discover the other
woman's identity and whether this alleged demand for a
divorce was true. As he could hardly knock on Michael
Prentice's door and ask him those questions, he would have
to use a more roundabout method.

A few miles farther on, he turned down to Pennard, a
small hamlet ending on the high cliff tops between Three
Cliffs Bay and Pwlldu Head. Passing a golf course, he drove

slowly through a quarter-mile ribbon settlement of houses and bungalows, with a post office, chemist and a general shop at the end, where the road petered out into stony tracks running right and left across the cliffs. He was hoping for a pub, which was often a useful place to pick up local gossip, but here in common with much of Gower, the place seemed to be teetotal.

At the far end of the road, some cars were parked on the grass, where there was a breathtaking view down a steep valley that intersected the limestone cliffs. He pulled in amongst them and went in search of information. Massey had given him the address of Michael Prentice, a house called *Bella Capri*, presumably from some romantic episode in a former owner's life. However, he wanted a more 'softly-softly' approach and went across to the small shop and ice-cream parlour that was the last building on the approach road. He went to the counter, got himself a cup of over-milked coffee and a jam doughnut, and went to one of the small tables in the outer half of the shop. There were a dozen other people sitting there, all trippers brought out by a dry day, though the hot weather had gone and it was cloudy for June.

Trevor soon decided he would get nothing from either the visitors nor the adenoidal girl serving in the shop, so he finished his snack and went outside. Here he found a middle-aged man in a brown warehouse coat, sweeping ice cream and sweet wrappers from the concrete patch in front of the shop.

'Not the best weather to attract the crowds, eh?' he said, to strike up a conversation. The man, who he guessed was the proprietor, leaned on his broom, ready for a chat.

'Bit early in the season, mind,' he said. 'Things should buck up soon and then we'll get the crowd when the schools go on holiday.'

Trevor brought the conversation round to the direction he wanted.

'I suppose most of the kids want sandy beaches, like Three Cliffs and Oxwich? It's a bit dangerous for nippers down there, isn't it?'

He pointed to the valley, where grey rocks could be seen

where the grass and bracken ended, several hundred feet below. The shopkeeper nodded and said the very thing that Mitchell had angled for.

'That's true enough. We had a nasty accident a bit further along the cliffs. It was only a week or so ago, when a swimmer got drowned.'

'Some tripper who didn't know the dangers, I suppose?' said Trevor, guilelessly.

'No, it was a local lady, as it happens. Strange, because she often went swimming along here, she lived in the village and knew the coast well enough.'

'Swimming alone, was she? Not very wise, if you get into trouble,' said Mitchell, probing.

The proprietor shrugged. 'She never came to any harm before and she's been swimming here regular for a year or more. I often saw her walking in her swimming costume, she used to wear a sort of terry-towel coat over it to get dry on the way back. She only lived along there.'

He pointed with the handle of his brush to the track that led eastwards from the parking area. It was set back quite a way from the gorse and bracken that covered the undulating cliff top. The roofs and chimneys of several houses could be seen in the distance.

The detective knew when to stop his questioning, knowing he would get little more of any use. He moved back to his car and after the man had gone back inside the shop, he started the engine and drove very slowly along the rough track, the car rolling and pitching slightly over the irregular stones.

He passed a house and a bungalow, spaced well apart behind wind-blown hedges, but neither was *Bella Capri*. There was a gap of a few hundred yards before the next dwelling, the track passing between thick gorse bushes on the cliff side and dense elder and blackthorn on the landward verge. A pair of wrought-iron gates came into view, set back a little from the track and on one of the masonry turn-ins was a metal nameplate bearing the name he was looking for. He did not stop, but drove on a little until he found a gap between the bushes sufficient to make a three-point turn. The track deteriorated beyond this point and there seemed to be no more houses further on.

Mitchell went back towards *Bella Capri* and stopped the Wolseley opposite the gates. Without getting out, he looked up the drive from his seat and saw a low house, with bay windows downstairs and two gabled windows in the slate roof. There was a long front garden, entirely grassed, through which the gravelled drive went up the centre, until it swung around the right-hand side of the house, where a separate garage was visible. The main door was in the centre between the bay windows and a few yards in front of it was a circular rockery with a small ornamental pond in the middle.

Trevor sat looking for a few moments, prepared to act the nosy voyeur of a tragic house if anyone came out to challenge him. But the place remained silent and deserted. The curtains were drawn and no dog barked at him. He pondered what to do next, with such a dearth of anyone to question. Presumably, Michael Prentice would be at his factory, which Massey had told him was in an industrial estate the other side of Swansea, near the docks.

As he sat there, his problem was unexpectedly solved when an elderly lady appeared from the gate of the next bungalow down and began walking up towards him, a large black retriever running ahead of her, sniffing the bushes and cocking up its leg at intervals. Trevor expected her to pass the car, but she came to his driver's side and rapped peremptorily on the glass.

'What are you doing here, may I ask?' she snapped, when he wound the window down. 'Are you a policeman?'

Mitchell, who looked every inch a copper and was sitting in what looked like a police car, was glad that he could honestly say that he was not. 'I'm a journalist, madam, writing an article on the dangers of solitary bathing on this coast. I've been looking at some of the more dangerous spots.'

It was a harmless lie and in fact, he had written a few articles for magazines on various aspects of policing in Britain, which almost made him a journalist. The rather hard-faced woman, her grey hair crushed under a scarf tied tightly under her chin, seemed mollified at his explanation.

'We have to be careful of loitering strangers,' she snapped. 'We've had several break-ins along here.'

'I understand that this was the house where that poor lady

Mrs Prentice lived?' he asked humbly, pulling out his notebook and pencil to validate his guise as a writer. 'She was
the reason I was asked to write this article, to point out the
risks before the summer season gets going. Did you know
her well? I presume she was an experienced swimmer.'

The neighbour fell for the ploy, unable to resist airing her
knowledge.

'Oh yes, she loved the sea. In good weather, she was in
almost every day. I think that's partly why they came to live
here. I'm not sure that Michael was all that keen on it, I got
the feeling he was more of a city man.'

Trevor also got the feeling that the old lady did not care
for the man of the house nearly as much as she did for Linda.

'Did you see her the day of the accident?' he ventured.
'No possibility of her being unwell and this contributing to
the tragedy?'

The grey-haired woman looked thoughtful. 'I didn't actually see her for a few days before that,' she admitted, rather
regretfully. 'In fact I thought she looked a little out of sorts
for a week or two. I do hope that wasn't anything to do with
her death – getting cramp or something like that.'

Mitchell felt he would be sailing too near the wind if he
probed much more, but he had one last try.

'I suppose there's no one else I could ask, to get more
background on this awful business?' he said solicitously.
'Have any local friends or family been here since it
happened?'

The neighbour thought for a moment, then shook her head.
'They kept very much to themselves, especially the husband.
I did see a blonde lady come in with Michael in his car on
Friday, but I don't know if she was family or not.'

Trevor knew when to bow out gracefully and with thanks
to the lady, he said goodbye and let her march away up the
track, snapping commands at her uncaring dog.

He went back into the village, which he saw from a sign
was called Southgate, and found a red telephone box.

With a fistful of change, he rang a Reading number that
Leonard Massey had given him, that of the dead woman's
schoolfriend, who had raised all this suspicion after receiving
Linda's letter. When he got an answer, he pressed Button A

and spoke to her for several minutes, having to push several more pennies into the slot, then came out with a few more words written in his notebook.

About twenty-five miles from Pennard, on the main A48 going towards home, Trevor turned the Wolseley off onto a secondary road and made his way towards the seaside town of Porthcawl. As he drove along the promenade and out towards Rest Bay, he could see Gower on the western horizon and even identify the cliffs of Pwlldu Head, on the further side of which *Bella Capri* lay.

Here in Porthcawl, Trevor found the coast was very different, low cliffs and beaches giving way to miles of sand dunes, under which lay buried the medieval town of Kenfig. He was not going that far, however, and guided by the sparse information that Marjorie Elphington had given him over the telephone, he found the road that was an extension of the Esplanade, going towards the burrows and golf clubs.

All Marjorie had been able to tell him on the telephone, was that Linda had learned that her husband's mistress was a blonde called Daphne and that she lived in a maisonette on the front in Porthcawl. Mitchell parked his car in a side street and began walking along the road which fronted the sea. The houses were built only on the landward side and included thirties modernistic houses with curved corners and flat roofs, mixed with some larger classical dwellings. Further on were smaller bungalows and he could see only one block of maisonettes. This two-storey building had four apartments, each with its own front door, two on the front, the others at each end. He walked slowly past, trying to get a glimpse of the bell pushes to see if there were any names on them, but they were too far away from the pavement for his eyesight.

Rather stumped as to his next move, he carried on up the road until he came to the next side turning, another suburban collection of houses and bungalows.

He could hardly walk up to the doors and push all the bells in turn, then ask each occupant whether they were the fancy woman of Michael Prentice! His brief from Leonard Massey was only to confirm the existence of the mystery woman and to obtain her name and address.

Turning round, he walked slowly back to the main road and
ambled towards the maisonettes, hoping for some inspiration.
The patron saint of private eyes must have been in good form
that day, for as he approached the block, the door of the further
apartment on the front opened and a woman stepped out
and began walking briskly ahead of him. She was young and
very blonde indeed, wearing a light sling-back coat and high
heels.

He could not see her face, but making a bet with himself
that a smart blonde living in those maisonettes might well
be the mysterious Daphne, he followed her at a discreet
distance. There were a few other people about and he had
little fear of being challenged as a stalker as she turned into
the road where he had left his car. Now he could see her
face in profile, and decided she was in her mid-twenties,
attractive but with rather sharp features. The blonde walked
past the Wolseley and headed for the centre of the small
town, but stopped after a few hundred yards and turned into
a newsagent's shop.

Seeing no reason why he should not do the same, as she
could not know him from Adam, he went in and saw her at
the counter at the back of the shop. He stopped just inside
and began looking at magazines on a rack, taking off a copy
of *Picture Post* and looking through the pages. He heard the
woman asking for twenty Gold Flake cigarettes and laughing
over something with the middle-aged shopkeeper, who she
called 'Tom'. Then she walked out of the shop past Trevor,
without glancing at him. He managed a good look at her and
confirmed that she was attractive, but perhaps wore too much
make-up.

As soon as she had left, he went to the counter to buy his
magazine and as he waited for his change, he spoke casually to the proprietor.

'That was Daphne from the maisonettes, wasn't it? I live
a few doors away, but I can never remember her surname,'
he lied.

'Daphne Squires? Yes, she's a good looking woman.'

The shopkeeper was obviously appreciative of young
blondes and assumed that Mitchell's interests lay in the same
direction.

'I heard that she was leaving soon, going to live in Gower,' said Trevor, with false innocence.

The man behind the counter shrugged. 'I wouldn't know. Pity though, she buys fags and magazines from me – and she's better looking that most of my other customers.'

Trevor knew when to stop probing and he left to go back to his car. Before he drove off, he was able to write another line in his notebook.

EIGHT

When Richard Pryor returned to the Wye Valley late on Wednesday morning, after having done his duty at Newport, he found Sian waiting for him with a tray of microscope slides.

'Here we are, Doctor, a set of 'H and E' and one of Perl's.'

'H and E' was probably the best-known acronym in pathology, standing for 'haematoxylin and esosin', which for a century or more had been the main method of staining tissues for microscopic examination.

She proudly set the cardboard tray alongside the small microscope that stood on a table in his room. Their big new microscope was in the laboratory for communal use, as it was so expensive that Richard and Angela had to use it between them until their finances improved. However, he had this smaller monocular in his own room, the same one he had had as a student. Sian hovered over him as he sat on his high stool.

'Are they OK?' she demanded, as soon as his eye was settled on the top of the instrument. He made no answer until he had studied and replaced several of the glass slides on the stage of the microscope, moving them around with the pair of control knobs. Then he looked up at the pert little technician, who was staring at him in tense anticipation, a cloud of blonde hair like a halo around her pretty face.

'Damned good, Sian, first class! Nice and thin, fully de-hydrated and beautifully stained!'

They were good, but he laid the praise on thickly as he knew it meant a lot to her, the first histology she had produced for him. Technicians were very proud of their expertise and took it personally when things went wrong.

She beamed and looked as if she had just won the foot-ball pools.

'Thank God for that,' she said fervently. 'I hadn't used a

Cambridge rocker for years, we had a sledge at the Royal Gwent.' Sian was referring to the devices used to cut slices a few thousandths of an inch thick, gadgets like mini bacon slicers, which passed the paraffin-wax blocks containing tissue against the edge of a blade like a cut-throat razor.

'They're great, Sian, now I can spend a happy hour looking at your handiwork!'

She took the hint and almost skipped out of his room in satisfaction. Pryor sat for a long while on his stool, eye glued to the eyepiece of the microscope, except when he changed slides and once when he got up to take a thick textbook from a shelf. Then he sat back and stared out of the window for a while, gazing unseeingly at the trees above Moira's house further down the valley. When he finally moved, he drew a lined pad towards him and began writing a supplementary report.

By that afternoon, two conferences with different coroners had been arranged, each requiring Pryor's presence. Phone calls between the solicitor in Lydney and Trevor Mitchell had resulted in the first appointment being made with Brian Meredith for the following morning.

'You'd better come with me, Angela. I may need some biology expertise, as well as your moral support!' said Richard as they were having their mid-afternoon tea.

She nodded and, with a grimace, stretched her legs out from the chair.

'It would be nice to get out for a change, after sitting doing all that blood grouping. You get all the fun, Richard, going to all those glamorous mortuaries.'

'Fun? Abattoirs have more glamour than those awful places I have to work in.'

Moira and Sian had taken to joining them in the staff lounge – in fact, it was Moira who now made all the tea and coffee. 'I'll have that extra report typed up for you to sign in an hour, then I can get it in the post tonight,' she promised.

Sian, itching to know whether her efforts with the tissue sections had proved useful, asked Richard to explain.

'I saw the report on Moira's desk,' she admitted. 'What's it actually mean?'

'The bruises were of different ages,' he replied. 'That was obvious to the naked eye from the colour, as fresh ones are blue or purple, but the haemoglobin decays after a time and then they turn green and yellow.'

'My grandmother could have told you that!' said Angela, softening the sarcasm with a grin.

'Sure, but she couldn't put a date on them,' he countered. 'Neither can I for that matter, except in very approximate terms, as different people react differently, as well as there being other factors.'

'So what use was my histology?' persisted Sian.

'In a fresh bruise only red blood cells have leaked out from the damaged blood vessels, but soon white blood cells start accumulating to start the clear-up and healing process and their type changes with time.'

'Why did you ask me to do a Perl's stain on them? That's to show iron, isn't it?'

Pryor nodded, he liked to teach others the mystique of his profession, which was why he was happy to have been given those medical student lectures in Bristol.

'The haemoglobin in the red cells gets broken down and the contained iron is set free, so that it shows up in a Perl's stain as blue specks. That doesn't happen for a day or two, usually longer. So if it's Perl's-positive, then the person must have lived for at least that length of time after the injury.'

Sian nodded her understanding.

'That means she couldn't have sustained the bruises knocking around against the rocks, because she was dead too soon afterwards?'

'That's it, my girl! Trouble is, I can't put a definite date on them, apart from some which are undoubtedly fresh. Whether they go back a week or so, to when she was supposed to have had this punch-up with her husband, is hard to tell.'

Moira listened to this with fascination. After years of humdrum life in a local solicitor's office, typing letters about house conveyancing, divorces and motor claims, this erudite talk of blood, bruises and suspected homicide brought home to her how a week or two had changed her outlook on life. Richard had taken her aside early on and tactfully empha-sized that everything she heard in Garth House must be kept strictly confidential, as some might be sub judice, though he softened the warning by saying that he was sure that she already appreciated that, after having worked in a lawyer's office.

He had given the same homily to Sian, soon after she started with them and he had every confidence that these two sensible women would keep their mouths shut outside working hours.

The other conference was set up after he had telephoned Massey to give him a cautious interpretation of his examination of the bruises, telling him much the same as he had explained to Sian. Within an hour, he had had a call back from the Gowerton coroner's officer, asking him to attend a conference with the coroner on Friday, to determine exactly what the significance of his findings were.

Richard realized that this coroner was treading very carefully in such a sensitive matter. Leonard Massey must have phoned him straight after speaking to Pryor about the bruises and Richard hoped that he had not painted too strong a picture.

Next morning, a bright but breezy Thursday, he drove up to Monmouth, with Angela sitting in the passenger seat, revelling in the sunlit appearance of the valley as they followed the winding river through meadows and woods. Richard thought she looked very elegant today. Around Garth House, she normally wore a blouse and slacks under her laboratory coat, but for this professional meeting she had on a light grey suit with a narrow waist and long slim skirt. Angela was keen on the fashions of the day, being an avid student of *Vogue*. He knew she went on shopping expeditions in London with her sister and suspected that her wardrobe was now subsidized by her parents, as their present earnings from the new practice were negligible.

Brian Meredith's partner was taking morning surgery for him, as the coroner had put aside the morning for a short inquest, followed by this meeting. They met in the empty magistrates' court where he had just held his inquest. It was housed in the historic Shire Hall, which bore a statue of locally born King Henry V on its front, but the court itself was a gloomy chamber lined with sombre wood panelling.

There were two pews for lawyers and benches at the back for the public, all set below a raised bench for the Justices of the Peace, dominated by a large plaster Royal Coat of Arms.

This morning, the participants sat in the well of the court, around a large oak table normally used by the clerk of the court and a shorthand writer.

The coroner claimed the clerk's chair in the centre, the others present being the pair from Garth House as well as Edward Lethbridge, Trevor Mitchell and rather to Richard's surprise, Dr Bogdan Marek, the pathologist from Hereford. Pryor was half-expecting to see the old battleaxe Mrs Oldfield there, but presumably her solicitor had managed to keep her out of the proceedings – neither was there any sign of Molly Barnes.

PC John Christie hovered in the background as Meredith cleared his throat and began by welcoming the gathered participants.

'This is an informal meeting, not an inquest. In fact I did not actually call this gathering. I am responding to a request by Mr Lethbridge here, so I think he should explain the position.'

The solicitor made a performance of changing his spectacles for a different pair, then produced some papers from his old briefcase and shuffled them about on the table before speaking.

'Thank you, Coroner. As you say, I have asked for this meeting with you, to put forward some new facts which I hope will persuade you to reopen your inquest on the human remains found on May the twelfth at Glasfryn Reservoir. I was not involved at that time, but it is a matter of record that you returned an open verdict and declared the remains to be that of Albert Barnes, aged forty-five, resident in Ledbury.'

Richard suppressed a sigh, as Lethbridge droned on, making a meal of facts about which everyone present were already well aware.

Dr Meredith nodded his chubby head. 'I did indeed, the identification was made by Mrs Molly Barnes, who declared that the remains were those of her husband.'

Apologetically, the solicitor hesitantly ventured to disagree with the coroner.

'In actual fact, sir, she did not identify the remains themselves, which she never saw. She claimed to have identified his watch and his wedding ring.'

Dr Meredith nodded in agreement.

'That is so, but in view of the strongly positive manner in which she said that those items of property belonged to Albert Barnes and in absence of any other evidence to the contrary, I felt it justified to accept what she claimed – and I still do, unless you can provide me with fresh information.'

Lethbridge almost fell over himself in his haste to dissociate himself from any criticism of the coroner's decision.

'Of course, sir, it was most understandable that this was considered the right course of action given the information available at that time,' he brayed. 'But some further investigations undertaken on behalf of a client, who claims that the remains were that of her relative, has since cast doubt on the identification as that of Albert Barnes.'

He peered over his glasses at Trevor Mitchell and suggested that he take up the tale. The detective described first how he had some doubts about the dating of the wedding ring and the Omega watch, especially as Mrs Barnes's claim that her husband had obtained the watch during his wartime service in Germany could not be true, as the watch had not been made until 1950 at the earliest.

Brian Meredith had some objections to these disclosures.

'I admit those facts are odd, but I can't accept them as sufficiently relevant,' he said mildly, but decisively. 'The ring might genuinely have been much older than the date of their wedding, if it was second-hand, as she claimed. And though the husband may not have obtained the watch in the way he said, there are many things that a man fails to tell his wife. He might have won it in a game of poker – or even stolen it!'

Mitchell was too old a campaigner in the witness box to be thrown by such legitimate criticisms.

'That's very true, sir, but they raised my threshold of suspicion. I then found from further enquiries that Mr Barnes had been in hospital for injuries sustained several years earlier, which his wife failed to disclose to you. We obtained a view of his medical notes – with Mrs Barnes's consent, I might add – and found that he had been X-rayed, which I understand might have been conclusive evidence of identity had they been available when the remains were examined.'

Meredith already knew the general thrust of the new argument, because he had given a note to Richard Pryor to authorize the doctor in Frenchay to clarify his notes, but he was not yet aware of the details of the result.

'Perhaps this is now more within Dr Pryor's field of expertise to explain,' cut in Edward Lethbridge.

Angela winked at him as her partner leaned forward to speak. This was not the Old Bailey, she thought, but let's see how he performs. Some of her forensic colleagues, experts though they might be, were hopeless witnesses, humming and hawing and mumbling technicalities without any attempt at making them understandable to judge or jury.

'Put simply, Coroner, the clinical examination of Albert Barnes in Hereford County Hospital seven years ago, recorded a harmless anatomical abnormality, which according to Dr Marek here, was not present in the bones he examined.'

Top marks, Richard, thought Angela. Short and sweet!

The coroner's fair eyebrows rose on his cherubic face.

'Indeed! What exactly was this abnormality?' he asked.

'The hospital notes recorded a *pectus recurvatum*, which you obviously know as a "salt-cellar sternum", Doctor Meredith.'

The coroner shifted his gaze to the Polish pathologist.

'What do you say to this, Doctor Marek? You are the only one who actually had the opportunity to examine these remains.'

The big man from Hereford shifted uneasily. He was not sure whether his professional skills were being called into question.

'It is unfortunate that these notes and especially any X-rays were not available when I did my examination,' he rumbled. 'But as far as the sternum is concerned, I am almost certain that there was no depression. I am familiar with *pectus recurvatum* and I am sure I would have noted it if it had been there.'

'How sure are you, Doctor?' asked Meredith. He suddenly had assumed a penetrating manner, at odds with his usual benign nature.

Bogdan Marek backtracked a little.

'I'm very sure, sir. Of course, there are different grades of depressed sternum, but if it had been marked enough for a junior doctor to have recorded it, I feel sure I would have recognized it.' His accent was more pronounced as he spoke with extra emphasis.

There was a heavy silence as they waited for the coroner to digest what had been said.

'So where does this leave us, Mr Lethbridge?' he asked at last. 'I suspect you are going to make an application to me?'

The lawyer cleared his throat. 'In order to at least clear the way for my client's pursuance of her own claim, I submit that the new evidence is sufficient for you to reopen your earlier inquest, the verdict of which was left open and to annul the stated identification of the remains as that of Albert Barnes.'

Brian Meredith shook his head sorrowfully. 'I don't think I can do that on the sole evidence of the recollection of Dr Marek, Mr Lethbridge. With the greatest respect to Dr Marek, the consequences of rescinding an already-certified death are profound, not least in the bureaucratic processes involved, as well as the distress caused to the putative relatives.'

Lethbridge nodded, not at all surprised at the rejection of his first attempt. He fiddled with the papers in front of him before offering a second course of action.

'If you feel unable to do that at this stage, sir, then I would respectfully request you to consider applying for the exhumation of the remains so that a definitive answer be obtained.'

The coroner took a deep breath and let it out slowly, his cheeks puffing out in a gesture midway between resignation and exasperation.

'I suspected it would come to this,' he said sorrowfully. 'The thought of doing battle with the grinding machinery of the Home Office frankly appals me! Are you sure that re-examining the bones will give us the final answer, Doctor Pryor?'

Richard nodded confidently. 'No doubt about it, sir. As

well as settling the issue of the sternum, the fact that we can get the X-rays from Hereford will clinch it.'

'What films did they take, then?' asked the medically qualified coroner.

'I understand that they are of the skull, pelvis and leg.'

'There was no head, so the skull films will not help,' growled Dr Marek, fighting a final rearguard action.

'We can X-ray the remains and compare the internal structure of the major limb bones in the two sets of films,' said Pryor decisively.

Angela Bray spoke for the first time. Justifying her attendance at the meeting. 'And I can determine the blood group. There are sure to be records of Barnes's group either from the hospital or from his Army records.'

The coroner resignedly closed the file in front of him.

'And you are absolutely sure that this will be a hundred per cent reliable?' he asked Richard Pryor.

The pathologist nodded confidently.

'I won't be able to tell you who he is, Coroner – but I'll certainly be able to tell you who he isn't!'

Moira was busy typing up some of Angela's paternity test reports when the two principals returned from Monmouth and she stopped to listen to their news. Sian hurried in from the laboratory just in time to catch Richard announcing that the coroner had agreed to an exhumation.

'Can you just walk into a churchyard with a shovel and dig someone up?' asked Sian rather indignantly. She had strong views on human rights and social justice, coming from a strong Labour-voting family.

'Good God, no!' responded Richard. 'It's a hell of a performance and is not always granted.'

'But if the coroner says it must be done, isn't that sufficient?' asked Angela, who was perched elegantly on the edge of the desk.

Pryor shrugged. 'I'm not sure. I have an idea that if the coroner still had jurisdiction, he could order an exhumation off his own bat, though even then, I seem to recall that he always plays safe and goes through the Home Office, which is the usual route in seeking consent.'

Moira Davison listened with interest to these discussions; she was finding every day more fascinating as bits of the forensic world were opened up to her.

'But how can he *not* have jurisdiction, as you call it?' she asked, her typing forgotten for the moment. 'Surely that's his job, to sort these things out.'

'As far as I can make out, a coroner has jurisdiction over a body lying within his area, up to the point where he arrives at a verdict at an inquest,' explained Richard. 'Once that verdict is given and the certificates issued, then he loses control over what happens to it.'

'So then he can't tell the chap with the shovel to go and dig it up?' concluded Sian, still harbouring her image of some arbitrary bodysnatching.

'I'm no lawyer,' said the pathologist. 'But I understand that an "open verdict", as was given in this case, really means "no verdict yet" and therefore the inquest can be reopened at any time in the future if new evidence is found. So the coroner still keeps his jurisdiction!'

'Where are these remains, as you call them?' asked Moira, with a slight shudder at her mental image of what they must look like by now.

'Buried in the public cemetery in Ledbury, according to John Christie. But knowing how slowly the Home Office wheels grind, it'll be some time before we get our hands on them.'

'If we prove that they are not those of Albert Barnes, what happens then?' demanded Moira, already using the 'we' as an indication of her immersion in the Garth House team.

'That'll be a totally different ball game,' said Angela. 'No doubt Mrs Oldfield will be back on the warpath, championing the cause of her nephew. But how she's going to get any further, I can't imagine.'

'Maybe she'll find a new set of bones to send Lethbridge chasing after,' suggested Sian, cynically.

'How could she claim that these remains were that of her nephew?' asked Moira. 'Did she also say that the ring and the watch were his?'

Richard Pryor shook his head. 'I asked Trevor Mitchell about this. It seems she never noticed his watch, she said all men's watches looked the same to her. But as for the ring, apparently he *had* been married. According to Mrs Oldfield, he was divorced fifteen years ago and still wore a ring.'

'But the hallmark would be as wrong for him as it was for Barnes,' objected Sian. 'He couldn't have been married as far back as 1931.'

Angela got up to go back to her workbench.

'The coroner wouldn't dismiss Molly Barnes's claim on either the ring or the watch,' she observed. 'So he'll have to apply the same logic to Agnes Oldfield.'

Richard also pushed himself to his feet.

'She'll have to do better than that, though! Brian Meredith will be much more cautious next time, if we rubbish his Barnes identity,' he said as he went to the door. 'He'll demand cast-iron proof before putting another name to the bones.'

'We can only do our best!' said Angela philosophically, as she went back to her racks of blood-grouping tubes.

With the next day's conference in Gowerton in mind, Richard spent another hour that afternoon looking at the microscopic sections of the bruises from Linda Massey.

Sian had stained some spare sections with other staining techniques that he had asked for, but he felt that they didn't add anything to more accurate dating of the injuries. He had heard of some new research from Finland, involving these new methods of 'histochemistry' where enzymes were used on fresh tissue, but he knew nothing of the details. He was discovering that 'going solo' had its disadvantages compared with working in a university or large teaching hospital, where library facilities and all the current medical journals were available. He subscribed to a couple of forensic journals, but it was too expensive to take a whole raft of publications.

'Must spend a day in the library in Bristol,' he muttered to himself, as he stared down the eyepiece of his microscope. 'And maybe I can wangle a ticket to the one in Cardiff medical school, as I'm one of their old students.'

After their tea break, he abandoned the sections to give his eyes a rest and wandered out into the plot behind, where Jimmy Jenkins was using a scythe on the patch marked out with stakes for Richard's vines.

The lush grass of early summer had grown up to knee height and with his rhythmic sweeps of the curved blade, Jimmy had already laid almost half the area low.

He stopped to sharpen the scythe with a short rod of carborundum as Pryor approached.

'You still set on planting this with them grapes?' he demanded, his tone suggesting that he thought his boss was mentally defective for wanting to do such a thing.

'Yes, of course. But I can't do this until the spring, so we've got time to get the ground into shape ready for them.'

His scanty knowledge of viniculture came from a slim booklet he had bought in Bristol recently. Jimmy grunted, pushing the peak of his cap further up from his forehead. With cooler weather, he had taken to wearing a plaid lumber-jack shirt, tucked into corduroy trousers, which were tied below the knees with lengths of binder-twine to keep them clear of the scythe.

'Far better to plant forty rows of strawberries!' he advised. 'Grows a treat here in the valley. You could sell 'em to passing tourists or up in the market in Monmouth. Make more money than with your doctoring, I wouldn't wonder!'

That wouldn't be difficult at the moment, thought Richard.

'Whichever it is, Jimmy, we'll have to get this plot turned over somehow.' He looked at the large area on the slope and wondered how many men with spades it would take to turn the grass in and make a decent tilth. Jimmy seemed to be reading his thoughts.

'Need machinery for that, Doctor! Near on half an acre, this is! Either a tractor with plough and disc-harrow – or maybe I could borrow one of them "walk-behind" rotavators.'

They talked on for a while about the problem, though Richard was often hazy about what Jimmy was telling him. He had never before shown any interest in horticulture, having been either in the army or living in servant-rich idleness of colonial comfort. But now he felt that this might be a pleasant release from the tensions of a stressful profession, a welcome change from corpses, courts and coroners. He listened to Jimmy extolling the virtue of the various types of strawberry, in his crusade to wean Richard off his determination to plant vines. In the contest between Royal Sovereign and Cambridge Favourite, the pathologist happily forgot his concern about the ratio of polymorphs to lymphocytes in those bruises back in the house.

But later that evening, the concerns crept back with the prospect of the conference next day and he pulled down his textbooks and pored over them yet again to get the salient facts clear in his mind before he went to Swansea next day.

NINE

Though the post-mortems on Linda Prentice had been carried out in the mortuary in Swansea, the coroner who covered Gower was not the same official whose jurisdiction was the borough itself. Neither was Pennard in the Swansea police area, but was part of the Glamorgan County Constabulary, the larger force that covered all the county except for the three major towns of Cardiff, Merthyr and Swansea.

So it was not in Swansea itself that the Friday meeting was convened, but in Gowerton, a small industrial town on the northern neck of the peninsula. It was not far from the edge of the Burry Inlet, a vast sandy estuary where the Penclawdd cockle beds lay – totally different from the southern coast of Gower, blessed with miles of cliffs and golden beaches.

Today, the coroner had not commandeered the local magistrates' courts for the meeting, but held it in his office nearby. Like most coroners outside London and some other big cities, where they tended to be medical doctors with an additional legal qualification, he was a local solicitor. These tended to pass the appointment down through their partners for generations – often the deputy coroner and assistant coroner were also part of the same firm.

Mr Donald Moses carried on his practice from all three floors of a terrace house in Mill Street. As senior partner, he had the best room, the first-floor front, and it was here that the meeting assembled at eleven o'clock. Richard Pryor had again been chauffeured by Jimmy Jenkins, who had gone off to find a cup of tea, promising to be back in an hour.

The coroner was a small man of about sixty, with thin black hair spread carefully over his rounded skull. He had a small toothbrush moustache that caused his junior staff to refer to him secretly as 'Adolf'. Pryor was intrigued to see that he wore a wing collar with his black jacket and striped trousers – almost a stage caricature of a lawyer. But it was soon apparent that though a small-town solicitor, he was a very sharp character with an ability to cut through any waffle.

He sat behind an old leather-topped desk in the bay window, with his coroner's officer, PC Mort, standing against a nearby wall. A motley collection of chairs faced him, as he conducted his inquests in this room, except for ones requiring a jury or where there was a need for lawyers and press to be present.

Already seated were Leonard Massey, Doctor O'Malley and two plain-clothes police officers. One was Detective Inspector Lewis Lewis, who Richard had met before at the mortuary, and Detective Superintendent Ben Evans who headed the local Divisional CID. He was a large, red-faced man with bristly fair hair, looking every inch a policeman.

No tea or coffee were on offer and Donald Moses, after naming all those present, cut straight to the chase.

'I opened my inquest on the lady Mrs Linda Prentice last week,' he began in a surprisingly deep voice for such a small man. 'That was for identification purposes only and I issued a burial certificate in the usual way.'

He straightened a buff folder in front of him and placed his fountain pen precisely in its centre.

'I intended resuming the full inquest into this tragic death in about two weeks' time, but following representations from the father of the deceased, Mr Leonard Massey, I had the funeral postponed so that a second post-mortem examination could be carried out.'

He made a small nod of recognition towards Richard.

'I did this with some reluctance, due to the inevitable distress that it would cause the relatives, but given the legal experience of Mr Massey here – and the letter he produced from his daughter's friend, I felt I had no option but to accede to his request.'

He produced a wire-framed pair of half-moon spectacles from his top pocket and laid them alongside his pen.

'Now Doctor Pryor has offered a report that takes this matter a stage further and in view of that, I decided to request the presence of the police here today, in case they feel the need to intervene.'

DS Evans cleared his throat at this point, which sounded like the first rumblings of a volcanic eruption.

'Mr Moses, I am afraid I come into this with very little background knowledge, except what my inspector here has told me about the post-mortem.'

The coroner nodded jerkily. 'Very well, perhaps Mr Massey would summarize what made him uneasy about the circumstances of this death.'

The Queen's Counsel opened a folder which was on his lap and took out some sheets of paper. He handed one each to the detectives.

'These are typed copies of the relevant parts of the letter that my daughter's close friend received from her, as well as a report which I commissioned by a private investigator, who is a former detective superintendent.'

He looked across at Donald Moses.

'You already have a copy, sir, as well as the original letter. In essence, that contains allegations that there was a serious marital dispute between my daughter and her husband, Michael Prentice, and that he had shown violence towards her during the weeks before her death. The cause was her discovery of his affair with another woman and her refusal to agree to divorce proceedings.'

There was a short delay while the two policemen read through the transcripts, Lewis Lewis getting the fainter carbon copy. At the same time, the coroner put on his glasses and opened the file before him, refreshing his memory from his own copy.

'The second part is the report of the investigator I employed,' continued Massey. 'You will see that he confirms the identity of the woman suggested by Linda's friend, as a Daphne Squires who lives in Porthcawl and who I have no doubt was the blonde woman seen by a neighbour in Michael Prentice's house some days after my daughter's death.'

Ben Evans looked up from his copy. 'So the only knowledge we have of the violence upon your daughter, sir, is this hearsay evidence from the friend?'

Massey nodded, rather impatiently. 'But you will see that at one point, she says that "I was afraid for my life, he was so violent." That is very significant, I submit. The friend told me – and as her father, I can vouch for it – that Linda was not given to dramatic exaggerations, in fact she usually played things down.'

The superintendent nodded, but did not look all that convinced. 'There were no other useful witnesses who could corroborate this, I presume? Friends or neighbours?'

Massey shook his leonine head. 'They live in a rather isolated house in Pennard. There are neighbours, but everyone drives in and out by car without much social contact. The only thing my investigator found was that the nearest neighbour said that Linda looked "out of sorts" for a while before she died.'

Lewis Lewis scribbled something in his notebook at this, but the coroner began to look a little fretful at being out of the loop for a while.

'I think we should hear from the medical men now,' he said. 'Dr O'Malley, you performed the first examination at my request. Was there anything that suggested that death was due to causes other than drowning?'

The retired pathologist shifted rather uneasily on his chair.

'Absolutely no reason to doubt that the poor lady drowned,' he declared in accents suggestive of County Cork. 'Of course, there were numerous marks on her body, as I mentioned in my report – scratches and bruises, but she had been washing around in the surf for at least a day, against a very rocky coastline.'

Donald Moses picked up O'Malley's very short report from his file. 'You say there were many abrasions and bruises on the legs, arms, back and face?'

'Indeed I did, sir. They were too numerous to describe individually.'

The coroner then picked up and perused the several pages of Pryor's report, in which every injury was described, but he made no comment.

'Did you do any special tests of any sort – using the microscope, for instance?' he asked at length.

O'Malley looked a little crestfallen at this.

'Unfortunately, since I retired from my hospital post three years ago, I have no access to any laboratory facilities. If any of your cases require that, the samples must be sent away, as you know. Or if there is any suspicion about the death, the Home Office chap is called.'

'And you felt there was no such necessity here?' asked Moses.

The pathologist shook his head. 'None at all, sir. I have dealt with dozens of drownings in my time, and this was typical of the condition.'

Moses now turned his head towards Richard.

'Doctor Pryor, do you agree that she drowned?'

'Like Doctor O'Malley, I have no doubt about that,' he said, keen not to embarrass the older doctor. 'Drowning can often be a difficult diagnosis, especially in sea water, as opposed to fresh – and made more difficult if there is a delay before the recovery and examination of the body. But here there was ample frothy fluid in the air passages and the lungs were waterlogged and showed the typical brownish patchy haemorrhages and alternating areas of emphysema and collapse.'

He spoke rather diffidently, trying not to be too graphic in the presence of the woman's father, but he seemed to show no emotion.

'But you recorded some other findings, Doctor,' persisted the coroner.

'Yes, as Doctor O'Malley has said, there were many relatively minor injuries scattered over the body, some consistent with being knocked by the waves against sharp rocks and barnacles. But there were other less explicable injuries in rather characteristic situations.'

This statement injected a new tension into the atmosphere, which until then had been a little soporific.

Ben Evans hauled his big body more upright in his chair.

'And what were they, Doctor?' he rumbled.

'The scratches were all very recent, and I have no reason to think that they were not caused when she was in the water. They had no "vital reaction" at all and some or even all of them could have been sustained after death.'

'What about the bruises?' asked Evans.

'Ah, that's a bit different. You can't bruise a dead body, as once the heart stops, there's no pressure to force blood out of damaged vessels into the surrounding tissues – which is what a bruise actually is.'

'So they were all ante-mortem?' ventured Lewis Lewis, who had picked up the term from other cases.

'Yes, but some could have been caused immediately before death or during the drowning process, as the heart needn't stop instantly, especially in sea water. If, say, she fell off a low cliff, she could hit herself on the way down and get scratches and bruises. Even in the water, before she drowned, she could still sustain some bruises from being battered against rocks by the waves. There were two quite large ones on the back of the head, but again they were very fresh and one could make a case for them knocking her out, so that she drowned. As I understand she was a good swimmer and might well have survived if she was in full possession of her senses.'

'So what's the problem, Doctor?' said the senior detective, almost belligerently.

'The problem is that some of the bruises were in places where you wouldn't expect them to be caused by falling or swilling around in a rock gully. But even more significant is that these were not sustained immediately before death. Some were certainly at least a few days' old.'

This caused a thoughtful silence. The coroner came back first. 'And you consider the position of these bruises suggestive of violence?' he asked.

'Some were on the upper arms, each side of the biceps muscle, a typical position for gripping during shaking – and possibly from a punch on an obvious part of the body. One of these was actually greenish-yellow, so it must have been inflicted a number of days previously. Also, there were two small older bruises on the neck, one on each side under the angles of the jaw.'

'From gripping the throat?' said the superintendent, who in his time had seen his fair share of attempted strangulations – and a few successful ones.

Pryor nodded, but O'Malley raised an objection.

'With a body being tossed about by big waves on that coast, surely bruises could have been inflicted anywhere on the body?'

Richard shrugged. 'Maybe, though it's a coincidence that some of them were in just the right place to indicate an assault. But the real proof is that they couldn't have been inflicted in the water, because some were days old!'

'Could they have been sustained during a previous swim, a couple of days earlier?' asked Lewis Lewis.

'That's not for me to say, it's not a medical matter,' answered Richard. 'But it wouldn't explain the position of the injuries, which are classically those of a struggle or assault of some sort.'

The coroner nodded and scribbled something on a notepad with his large pen. 'Can your microscope date these bruises with any accuracy, Doctor?'

Ruefully Richard had to admit that the science was very approximate in this area. 'This iron test can pick up injuries more than a day or so old – and then changes in the scavenger and inflammatory cells can suggest a number of days earlier still – but there's no accuracy in it, unfortunately, though researchers abroad are trying to develop new techniques.'

Donald Moses made a few more notes with his pen, then laid it down and looked at the two police officers.

'How does this appear to you, gentleman?' he asked courteously.

As a mere inspector, Lewis kept his mouth closed and his superintendent answered after a pause.

'If Doctor Pryor is correct – and I've no reason to doubt him – then the fact that some of these bruises must have been inflicted at least a day or more before death needs investigating, especially as they are the sort that can be suffered in some sort of domestic violence. Coupled with the allegations in that letter, it makes it all the more obvious that we need to interview a few people.'

Leonard Massey nodded his agreement. 'I'm glad to hear you say that, Superintendent. I've naturally taxed my son-in-law with the matter, but he denied it and became abusive.'

The two detectives murmured together for a moment and then Ben Evans spoke again.

'I must refer this back to my chief superintendent, at Headquarters in Bridgend, as it may become a sensitive issue, especially when the bloody Press get hold of it, if you'll pardon my language. Then if he agrees, we'll set about seeing the people concerned.'

A few moments later, after exchanging addresses and telephone numbers, the two policemen left, along with a rather subdued Dr O'Malley. The coroner had asked Richard to stay, as he discussed with the dead woman's father the logistics of a funeral.

'I can't allow cremation until all this is cleared up, one way or another,' he said. 'Dr Pryor, do you see any reason why the body should not be buried, in view of the perhaps remote possibility of another post-mortem being required by any future defence?'

Richard explained again that in view of the agreement about the actual cause of death, he could see nothing that would help a defence pathologist, given that he already had tissue samples preserved from the bruises and that he had taken samples for blood and urine analysis. At the same time, he pointed out that it was not for him to prejudge the issue and perhaps it might be as well to wait until the police decided whether or not they intended to pursue the matter. Donald Moses eventually decided to wait for another week until issuing Leonard Massey with a burial order and Richard left them to discuss the details, leaving to find Jimmy and the Humber.

Now that they were technically in Gower, he decided to go and look at the scene of the death and with Richard's memories from his motorcycling days, they set off for Pennard. In Bishopston they found a café that catered for passing tourists and he treated Jimmy and himself to cottage pie, chips and peas, followed by apple tart. They washed this down with a glass of beer at a nearby public house, Jimmy bemoaning the recent rise in price of a pint of bitter to nine pence.

'It'll soon be a shilling at this rate!' he complained. 'I blame this new Tory Government, battening on us working-class folk!'

Though Jimmy was a good enough worker when the mood took him, Richard grinned to himself at the thought of him being one of the downtrodden masses. The Conservatives had trounced Labour again at the recent General Election, with an increased majority of fifty-eight seats, but neither Jimmy nor Sian Lloyd had taken kindly to having Sir Anthony Eden as Prime Minister.

Their break over, they carried on to Pennard, retracing the route that Trevor Mitchell had taken. He had described the location of the house and Jimmy carefully took the Humber along the stony track past *Bella Capri*.

Richard had no idea what he hoped to gain just by looking at a house, but he always liked to visit crime scenes, if indeed this was one. They stopped outside the gate and looked up the windswept garden, taking in the general appearance of the oddly named house. Then Jimmy noticed a curtain being pulled aside in one of the front rooms and a woman's face stared out. He let in the clutch and moved on quickly.

'We've been rumbled, Doc,' he said cheerfully. 'Some blonde giving us the evil eye.'

'Just keep going,' ordered Richard. 'According to Trevor Mitchell, the place where the body was recovered was about half a mile further on.'

Mitchell had been given the location by Leonard Massey and had marked it on the one-inch Ordnance Survey map which Richard held, so they bumped along the track until they reached the nearest spot on the road.

'Park here and we'll go and have a look,' he commanded. Jimmy pulled off on to the rough grass and locked the car, then they walked a few hundred yards across to the edge of the spectacular limestone cliffs.

A jagged, almost sheer drop went down into the sea below, though there were some ravines here and there, where steep slopes of turf ran down to the rocks a few feet above the heavy swell.

'I suppose you can stumble down there, but it's not easy,' said Richard, looking at the greenish-blue swell that even on a fairly calm day such as this, threw up spray over the rocks.

'But she didn't go swimming here, surely?' asked Jimmy. 'Too bloody dangerous by half!'

He was a countryman and the Severn Bore was the only wave he was used to seeing.

Pryor consulted his map again. 'No, this is where the coast-guards hauled her body out. Must have been in that gully down there.' He pointed to a narrow channel cutting into the cliff slightly to their left. It was about twenty feet wide and forty long, lined with jagged grey rocks.

'So where did she go swimming?'

Richard put a finger on the map, at a spot further west, almost to where *Bella Capri* sat well back from the cliff top. 'She did her swimming nearer home, according to her father. This map shows a little patch of sand at low tide.'

They paused there to have a look on the way back, but this time driving past the house without stopping, because of the curtain-twitcher.

'Think that was the fancy woman?' asked Richard. 'If it is, she didn't waste much time moving in!'

His chauffeur shrugged.

'Takes all sorts, dunn'it!' he said.

TEN

The following week was a busy one for Garth House, as Richard's stint as a locum in Newport produced a steady stream of sudden deaths, a couple of suicides, a fatal road accident, a death under anaesthesia and a fall from a factory roof. Angela was also busy, as her reputation in the blood-grouping field for disputed paternity had spread rapidly and she had half-a-dozen new cases to deal with.

Sian also had her hands full with several blood and urine alcohol estimations, using the time-consuming Widmark method, as well as some more histology for Richard. One of the two suicides needed a carbon monoxide analysis, as the victim had her head in a gas oven – and the other one was more obscure, being a mixture of barbiturates and an unknown number of tablets from an unmarked bottle.

'We'd better ask the coroner if this can be sent to the Cardiff Forensic Laboratory,' said Richard, after Sian had explained that she had no facilities for doing a blind screening test on the blood and urine samples that he had brought back from the Newport mortuary. The Cardiff laboratory was one of the seven that the Home Office had set up across England and Wales and although it specialized in the forensic examination of documents, it also did the full range of investigations.

In addition to Pryor's work in Newport, there were a number of routine post-mortems in Monmouth and Chepstow, so there was little time to think about the more curious cases.

'I've heard nothing from Trevor Mitchell so far this week,' observed Richard, as he and Angela sat over the ham and salad supper that Moira had left for them on Wednesday evening.

'We can't expect any progress on the exhumation yet,' replied Angela, sampling a glass of sweet cider that Jimmy had brought in from a farm a few miles away.

'Knowing the speed the Home Office reacts, the application is probably still sitting in someone's 'In' tray in Whitehall.'

Her partner drank some beer, his preferred drink, this time a bottled one from Brain's Brewery in Cardiff.

'I wonder if the police have decided to lean on Michael Prentice?' he mused. 'I thought that Superintendent Evans was quite a capable chap, he reminded me of Trevor. If they don't make their minds up soon, the coroner is going to let them bury that poor woman.'

'Would it matter if they did?' asked Angela. 'You said there'd be nothing to be gained by a third post-mortem, given that you've got all the samples.'

Richard grunted. 'All the same, any decent defence counsel would complain that they were at a disadvantage if they couldn't get their own expert opinion. They could hardly get much joy out of O'Malley's report.'

The biologist speared the last piece of local ham with her fork.

'The coroner won't allow cremation, you said – so they could join our club and get an exhumation order.'

Richard grimaced. 'The value of what they could get out of that will get less by the week, once the body is buried,' he observed.

Perhaps the Glamorganshire Constabulary had the same concerns, as that evening, a maroon Vauxhall Velox saloon parked at the side of the track across the cliffs at Pennard and two police officers went across to the gate of *Bella Capri*.

Ben Evans led the way up the long gravel drive and his inspector followed, looking about him with a professional eye.

'He's in, as there's a car at the side of the house,' muttered the superintendent, nodding at a black Jaguar parked outside the garage at the rear of the house.

'He can't be short of a bob or two,' growled Lewis. 'That's a Mark Five, and brand new by the look of it.'

The senior officer went to the front door and banged on the brass knocker, discoloured by the constant salt spray that blew up from the sea. He heard some muffled voices, then a shape appeared beyond the coloured frosted glass of the top half of the door. When it was opened, a tall man in a

Fair Isle jumper stood there, but there was no sign of anyone behind him.

'Mr Michael Prentice?' queried Evans. 'Could we have a word with you, please?'

He identified himself and Lewis Lewis as police officers, but Prentice needed no introduction to know that this pair were detectives. He sighed and stood aside, opening the door fully.

'You'd better come in, I suppose. No doubt that bloody father-in-law of mine has set you on to me with his crazy notions.'

'In fact, sir, we are here at the behest of the coroner,' began Ben Evans, heavily. 'We thought it better to visit you at home, rather than at your place of work.'

Prentice led them into a room on the left of the hall, one of those with a bay window that overlooked the front garden. It was expensively furnished with a leather three-piece suite around a thick patterned carpet. A baby grand piano stood against a further wall and there were two glass-fronted cabinets filled with porcelain.

Prentice motioned them to sit on the settee, but remained standing in front of the stone Minster fireplace in which was fitted a coal-effect electric fire, now switched off.

Lewis produced a notebook and pencil, leaving his DS to do all the talking, but Michael Prentice beat him to it.

'I know you are only doing your duty, but this is really intolerable! My late wife's father has disliked me since the moment he set eyes on me, years ago! This is a great chance for him to embarrass me, but I must warn you that I intend taking legal action against him for defamation of character.'

Evans, who had heard similar threats so many times before, remained imperturbable.

'We just need to establish some facts about your wife's death, sir. I'm sorry I have to trouble you at a sad time like this, but there are some points which need clearing up.'

Prentice, somewhat deflated, gave up his 'master of the house' pose before the hearth and subsided into one of the buttoned armchairs.

'What is it you want to know?' he sighed. 'I've given all

this to the uniformed men who came at the time of my wife's death, as well as to the coroner's officer.'

'What is your occupation, sir?' asked Evans, thinking of the very expensive car outside.

'I'm a partner and technical director of a company that develops new equipment for the motor industry – electronic ignition systems, lubricating additives, disc brakes and the like,' he said with obvious pride. 'We have a research and production unit on Jersey Marine, just beyond Swansea docks.'

'And how long have you been married?'

'Just over five years. My wife was twenty-eight when she drowned and we married on her twenty-third birthday.'

Lewis scribbled away as the other detective carried on with his questions.

'I understand that your wife, Linda, was a keen swimmer. She went in almost every day, is that right?'

'In the summer, yes. We've been in this house for a year and she only stopped swimming from about last October until this April.'

'So where did you live before?' asked Ben Evans.

'In Slough, where our first small factory was based. We were offered a good deal on a new building and rate-relief in Swansea, so we moved here. Linda wanted to be near the sea, she loved the coast.'

Evans paused for a moment, while he leaned across to look at what Lewis had written.

'Is all this necessary, Officer?' said Prentice testily. 'I've said all this over and over before!'

'I'm afraid so, sir. Now, let's go to the day she vanished. What exactly happened?'

Michael Prentice hunched forward in his chair, his hands clasped between his knees.

'This is very painful for me, Superintendent. But if you must know yet again, I was at my office as usual, leaving after breakfast and working late, getting back here about eight in the evening. It's almost an hour's drive at rush hour. There was no sign of Linda, which was unusual.'

'No one else lives here?'

There was a momentary hesitation. 'Not then, no. Since the tragedy, a friend spends some time here to keep me company.'

Evans decided to leave this topic alone for the moment.

'Where did you think your wife had gone? Was she always here when you came home?'

'Almost invariably. She doesn't drive, so has no car. We're a bit cut off out here, just an infrequent bus service from the village.'

'What did you do next?

'I waited a bit, thinking she might have gone for a swim, though she always got back in time to make me a meal. After a couple of hours, I began to get worried and went out to look for her along the cliff track.'

'Did you take your car when you searched?'

Prentice looked up at Evans and twisted his hands in agitation. 'No, I left it at the side of the house all evening. I went over to the village to ask in the shop, but they hadn't seen her. Then I came back this way and walked along towards Pwlldu Head, but there was no sign of her.'

'Where did she usually go to swim?'

'It varied, according to her whims and the state of the tide,' he answered. 'To be honest, I didn't take much notice, as long as she was enjoying herself.'

'Did you never go with her, sir?' cut in Lewis, speaking for the first time. Prentice shook his head vehemently.

'Never, I can't even swim, for one thing. And I spend so much time at the unit now, I'm whacked when I get home.'

'But where was her favourite place to swim?' persisted Ben Evans.

'Just below the house, I suppose, what she called Broad Slade. The cliffs are less steep there, there's a sort of sloping valley going down to the rocks.'

'You looked there?' put in Lewis.

'Of course, it was the first place I thought of. I didn't go right down, but you can see from the top.'

He jumped up again and paced over to the window and back again to the fireplace. 'I walked back along the edge of the cliffs, rather than the track, so that I could look down at the edge of the sea wherever I could. In some places, the cliff bulges out, so you can't see the rocks below – and it was getting dusk by then.'

'What were you looking for?' asked Ben Evans.

Michael Prentice looked at the detective as if he was an idiot. 'Well, Linda herself, of course. She might have fallen and twisted her ankle or broken a leg. And if she'd gone into the sea, she would have left her robe on the edge, she always took a white terry-towel dressing gown sort of thing, as well as sandals and a bath towel.'

'And you saw nothing?'

Prentice shook his head. 'Not a thing. After she was found, the local police told me that her things were at the bottom of Broad Slade, but behind a gorse bush, so I couldn't have seen them from above. Not that it would have made any difference,' he added bitterly.

The superintendent waited until Lewis had finished writing in his notebook, then returned to his questions.

'You didn't report her missing until the next morning, sir. That seems rather a long time.'

Michael made an impatient gesture. 'Maybe it does with hindsight. But I had checked that she hadn't gone swimming, as far as I could tell, so I thought she had just gone off somewhere.'

'Gone off somewhere?' repeated Evans, sceptically. 'But you said she was always at home when you returned, having made you a meal?'

'Well, not always,' replied Prentice evasively. 'She did go out, you know, sometimes shopping in Swansea on the bus.'

'And not come back all night? Come on, sir, that's no answer.'

Michael flopped down into the armchair. 'All right, officer, I'll be honest with you, as I'm sure it's no secret after that nosy bitch in Reading has been telling tales. Linda and I had been through a rough patch lately. We had a bit of a tiff the night before and I thought she had got the hump and gone off to teach me a lesson.'

Evans and Lewis exchanged glances and the inspector began writing away busily again.

'A bit of a tiff, sir? Would this have been the previous evening or the same morning?'

'Well, it had been brewing for a week or so. She wasn't speaking to me the last day or two.'

'And did this "bit of a tiff" involve physical violence?' asked Lewis Lewis, who never believed in mincing his words.

'Good God, no!' snapped Prentice, his face flushing with indignation. 'You must already know, thanks to my damned father-in-law and that so-called friend of Linda's, that my wife suspected me of having an affair.'

'Suspected? Would that be with the lady who is in this house at the moment, Miss Daphne Squires?'

The other man stared in surprise. Did the whole bloody world know his business, he thought? Ben Evans, who had been informed by Leonard Massey of the result of Mitchell's visit to Porthcawl, registered Prentice's discomfiture with some satisfaction. Shake the tree and see what falls out, was one of his favourite maxims.

'I don't see what my private life has to do with you, officer,' blustered Michael.

'We have evidence that your wife suffered some injuries consistent with an assault, some time before she was found in the sea,' said Evans, bluntly. 'Have you any explanation for those?'

'Injuries? What injuries?' barked Prentice, shaken but still aggressive.

'Bruising of the arms and neck indicative of gripping by another person! Mr Prentice, did you assault your wife, in the days leading up to her disappearance and death?'

The man sitting opposite Ben Evans rose to his feet.

'That's enough, I refuse to answer any more of your insulting questions without my solicitor being present,' he grated. 'This is all the result of my father-in-law's slanderous motives. Just because he's a London QC, you police all sit up and beg!'

The superintendent got up and his colleague followed suit, still writing in his pocketbook.

'We are here because Her Majesty's coroner wishes us to follow up the results of the second post-mortem examination,' said Evans easily. 'I will have to report back to my senior officers and no doubt we will need to question you again, next time at a police station, where you are fully entitled to have your solicitor present.'

Prentice stood aside as they went to the front door, which he slammed behind them without another word.

The two CID men walked back to their car and sat in it to discuss the visit.

'No sign of the floozie,' observed Lewis. 'She's keeping her head down, but he didn't deny she was there.'

'We heard their voices, so he could hardly claim he was alone,' said Evans. 'But that's not our concern. Do you think he's lying about the assault?'

Lewis nodded. 'Through his teeth, boss!' he said. 'But it doesn't mean he killed her, does it? What about if she was so cut up about his affair with this blonde that she jumped into the sea to end it all?'

'It's a possibility, of course. A bit drastic, but stranger things have happened. He doesn't seem all that distressed, does he, but again that's not a crime.'

Lewis started the Vauxhall and they bumped along the track to reach the road into Southgate.

'Right, tomorrow we'll see these coastguard people and hear what they've got to say about it,' grunted his boss, as they headed back to their Divisional Headquarters at Gowerton.

That evening, Richard was in his office at the back of the house, writing a draft of a letter for Moira to type the next day. He sat at his desk, an old one his father had discarded from his surgery when he retired, slowly composing a notice for inclusion in the various medical journals that were devoted to forensic medicine. He was a committee member of the World Association for Medical Jurisprudence, an organization that had been going for many years. It held a congress every three years and the next one was to be hosted in Cardiff in November. Now being virtually a local, he was involved in organizing it and though most of the work was being handled by a commercial conference company, Richard had been saddled with some of the publicity, mainly keeping the medical profession aware of the congress, to get enough participants to make it viable. Pryor had become involved because the last meeting had been in Singapore and he had been drawn into the Association's activities then.

Angela wasn't involved, as the 'WAMJ', as it was known, was purely medical and was not primarily concerned with forensic pathology or science, but with all the other aspects of legal medicine, such as negligence, injury compensation, ethics, and professional misconduct – all the problems that besiege doctors worldwide. This was the stuff that he taught to medical students, rather than the details of forensic pathology, which the vast majority of doctors would never need.

As he laboriously composed his latest progress report to send to the editors of half a dozen journals, he sighed over the numerous crossings-out and rewrites he had made and hoped that Moira could make sense of it all.

It was almost a relief when he heard the telephone ring out in the hall. The GPO had promised to come this week to install the extensions, but so far there was no sign of them and he went out to answer it. Angela was upstairs in her own room, as they avoided living in each other's pockets, though they usually met in the evening for a drink or cup of coffee.

When he picked up the phone, he found it was Edward Lethbridge on the other end.

'Apologies for disturbing your evening, Doctor, but I thought you might like to know that I've heard from the coroner about this exhumation,' said the dry voice. 'He's had consent from the Home Office to go ahead.'

'That's damned quick!' said Richard, enthusiastically. 'We were all told that they usually drag their feet on this sort of thing.'

'It seems that the powers-that-be didn't really want to know, saying that as it was an open verdict, it was still within the coroner's jurisdiction. But they've rubber-stamped it as a formality. Dr Meredith says that he's arranged with the local council in Ledbury to open the grave early next Tuesday morning, if that suits you.'

Richard promised to liaise with the coroner's officer about details, such as which mortuary to use, then rang off and ran up to Angela's room to tell her the news.

She invited him in for a gin and tonic and they sat in the window to look out over the valley as the sun set.

'What do we need to do?' he asked. 'You need some tissue for blood grouping, though we'll have to search for Albert Barnes's group.'

'He was in the army, he should have it in his records,' she said. 'Trevor Mitchell should know how to go about getting it. Where will you look at the remains?'

Richard sipped his drink appreciatively. He was no drunkard, but he liked a glass of something every day.

'Ledbury is in Herefordshire, not Meredith's area, but he's got a permanent arrangement with his counterpart in Hereford to use the County Hospital. Hopefully, we'll need to have a bone or two X-rayed and then compare them with the Barnes's films that were taken when he had his accident.'

Business talk finished, they sat and talked for a while, mainly about their families. Angela had a much younger sister who lived at home in Berkshire, but she had taken up with a man of whom her parents disapproved.

'I'd better go up there next weekend and listen to all the angst,' she sighed. 'After the collapse of my romance, they're dead scared of another fiasco!'

Richard had never probed into her failed engagement to a detective superintendent in the 'Met' and she had never volunteered any details. Angela seemed to sense what he was thinking and smiled at him over the rim of her glass.

'This is an odd situation, isn't it?' she mused aloud. 'Here we are, two red-blooded people staying together in the same house with no chaperone. The village people must think we're living in sin!'

Richard's lean face creased in a grin. 'I always make sure my bedroom door's locked every night!'

His partner prodded him in the leg with her pointed court shoe.

'One of these nights I might break it down with an axe when I'm desperate!' she promised playfully, but they both knew that it was an empty threat. Theirs was the perfect platonic friendship – or so she told herself. As for Richard, he wasn't so sure. She was a very attractive woman, but he would never make the first move.

'Moira has got a real crush on you,' said Angela abruptly. 'You know that, Richard, don't you?'

He stared at her incredulously. 'Moira! Go on, she's only known me for a week or two!' he said scornfully.

Angela nodded wisely. 'I've seen her looking at you, with

eyes like a big soft spaniel! You could do worse, she's a very smart woman.'

'I don't want to "do" anything, thanks! I had enough problems with Miriam to last me for a bit. You'll be saying next that Sian fancies me!'

Angela nodded sagely. 'Of course she does! But you're a bit old for her, so I'm not sure if she wants you for a lover or a father figure!'

Pryor laughed and stood up. 'You've had too much of that gin, madam! I'm off before you get more fantasies – or start ravishing me! Don't forget, up early next Tuesday, you've got an exhumation to attend. That'll sober you up!'

He went back to his office in a thoughtful mood.

On Thursday morning, Ben Evans had arranged to speak to the men who had recovered Linda Prentice's body from the sea and the most convenient place to meet them was at the Signal Station at Bracelet Bay. This was perched on a rocky knoll just beyond Mumbles Head, a pair of small islands which carried the lighthouse that marked the western end of the huge sweep of Swansea Bay. The coastguard station was a low building with an observation deck above it, used to monitor all vessels passing up the north side of the Bristol Channel. The two detectives parked below and climbed the path to meet the pair of coastguards in a room below the operations level. It was half-filled with equipment, but had a table and a few chairs, along with an electric kettle. The two men were burly ex-seamen, dressed in thick blue jumpers and serge trousers. One was George, who made four mugs of tea before sitting at the table with his mate, Arthur, who did most of the talking.

'The local police called us about eight o'clock that morning,' he began. 'They'd been warned of a body in the sea by a chap going to do some early fishing.'

Ben Evans had already read the police report and knew that they had called the coastguard because it was impossible to get the body out of the water without proper equipment.

'Was it difficult to recover it?' he asked.

'We've had much worse places,' replied Arthur. 'But without

ropes and safety lines, it would have been bloody hard to get her up. She was obviously dead by the time the police responded to the chap's call, so there was no question of resuscitation.'

'Where exactly was she?' asked Lewis Lewis.

'At the foot of the last bit of cliff west of Pwlldu. There was a steep valley going down over the grass and scrub to the rocks, but then there was a ten-foot drop down to the water – a lot more at low tide.'

'Why would a fisherman want to go down such a hairy place?' asked Evans.

Arthur shrugged. 'You can get some good bass in those deep gullies.'

'Was she being knocked about much when you got there?' asked the inspector.

'It was near high tide and there was a fair swell running. She was close in to the rocks, being washed back and forth, rubbing against them sometimes,' explained George.

'The gully went in a long way, so she wouldn't have gone out to sea until the tide ebbed and pulled her back out,' said his mate.

Lewis wrote away in his notebook, while Ben drank some tea and thought of his next question.

'How long d'you think she'd been in the water?'

Arthur rubbed his bristly beard. 'Not all that long, but no way of saying exactly. She was still fresh, no signs of decay. The skin on her hands and feet was wrinkled badly, but that can happen in a couple of hours.'

'If she had gone swimming the previous day, could you guess where she went in, given where you found the body?' queried the detective superintendent.

Arthur grimaced. 'These chaps who claim to tell you that exactly are talking a lot of bullshit!' he declared.

'There's so many factors like tide, wind and coastal streams. With the usual westerly wind and the tidal drift along there, she would have gone eastwards, but I can't say how far.'

As the police had later found Linda's robe and towel at the bottom of Broad Slade, Ben knew the point was academic.

'No doubt in your mind that she drowned?' he asked.

'None at all – when we hauled her out on to grass, the movement brought up some froth from her nose and mouth. That goes with her not being in all that long, as when bodies reach a bad state, it's too late for that.'

'Do you get many drownings like this along that bit of coast?' asked Lewis.

The coastguard shook his head. 'Very few, thank God, only one or two a year. We get more damn fools who fall down the cliffs or get caught by the tide.'

'She was said to be a strong swimmer – and she went in along there very often. So why d'you think she might have drowned?' asked Evans.

Again, Arthur gave a shrug. 'Hard to say! She might have got cramp. The water's still cold even though it's June. Or she might have taken a knock on the head against the rocks if the swell caught her at the wrong moment.'

There was very little else they could extract from the men, helpful though they were and after some more chat and a refill of tea, the two detectives left, wondering what decision their senior officers in police headquarters in Bridgend were going to make about Michael Prentice.

ELEVEN

On Friday, Richard Pryor drove down to Newport and caught the train to London, where he had a meeting in St Mary's Hospital of the organizing committee for the conference in Cardiff in November. It was pouring with rain, but at least he had only a few yards to walk from Paddington Station to the hospital medical school in Praed Street. He got back to Garth House in time for supper, which he ate alone, as Angela had already left for her parents home to help sort out their problems with her sister over the weekend.

On Saturday, he went fishing further up the Wye, at a riverside farm where Jimmy Jenkins had got him permission to put a rod in the river. He had not used his kit for many years, though when he was a junior pathologist in Cardiff before the war, he had been quite keen on both river and sea angling. He had brought his rods from Merthyr, where they had languished since 1940, but he must have lost the knack, as he caught nothing during his six-hour vigil on the river-bank up beyond Llandogo. Still, he consoled himself, it had stopped raining and he enjoyed the solitude, with a Thermos of tea, a box of sandwiches and a couple of bottles of beer.

Once again Sunday seemed empty without any of the three women in his life – he especially missed the quiet company of Angela. If she had not been so damned good-looking and elegant, he thought, he would have liked her for a big sister! Richard Pryor liked women, not necessarily in the lustful sense, for he enjoyed their looks, their femininity and their company. In Singapore, since his wife left him prior to their divorce, he had had a few flings amongst the expatriate community, but after coming back six months ago, he had led a rather monkish life, being too absorbed in setting up his new forensic venture.

When things settled down more, he told himself, he would get himself a social life, join a golf or tennis club and maybe look around for a new wife. Angela's suggestion that Moira was keen on him seemed ridiculous. Attractive though she was, she was just their housekeeper-cum-secretary and he hardly knew her.

He mooched about all day on Sunday, feeling a little lonely, but occupied himself with cleaning his car and listening to the radio. Television was becoming more popular, now that the new BBC transmitter was broadcasting from near Cardiff, but he had not discussed with Angela whether they could afford to get one, even if they could get a decent signal in the confines of the deep Wye Valley. That evening, Leonard Massey phoned to say that the police had finally decided to investigate the death of his daughter.

'They have interviewed him and intend following it up,' said the barrister. 'Is there anything more you can do on the pathology side?'

'Not really, those older bruises are the main evidence for some previous form of assault,' replied Pryor. 'The cause of death is not in dispute, but I wonder about that rather nasty impact on the back of the head. Are the police going to examine the house?'

Massey followed his reasoning straight away. 'You mean there could be some physical evidence of what caused the blow?'

'Not necessarily a blow, a fall would be equally likely. The fact that it was a recent injury, not long before death, means it could have occurred in the sea, but it could have happened hours earlier and caused unconsciousness.'

'I'm sure that the CID will have a good look at the house and the surroundings,' replied Massey. 'They are having him in at their station to make a statement tomorrow. I think they are also going to talk to the friend who wrote the letter to Linda – and to this woman he's been carrying on with.'

Pryor had no more to contribute and after the lawyer had rung off, he sat wondering if the police had enough to proceed much further with Massey's claim that his son-in-law had murdered his wife. He also wondered if the father had not been an eminent Queen's Counsel, but a bus driver or a steel worker, whether the police would have pursued the matter on what was so far, rather scanty evidence. Richard decided that was probably an unfair thought, but still wondered if there was anything more than grounds for a domestic dispute, leaving a few bruises.

Still, more immediate matters took his attention and he went to the kitchen to attack the cold chicken and warm up the cooked vegetables which Moira had left in the refrigerator, amongst the other sustenance for the weekend.

On Monday morning, Michael Prentice grudgingly arrived at Gowerton Police Station to make a statement.

He parked his black Jaguar in the yard of the Victorian-vintage building and was directed to a gloomy interview room on the ground floor, where Ben Evans was waiting for him at the door. The detective had half-expected Prentice to come armed with a solicitor, but he was alone. The businessman looked with distaste at the room, which contained only a plain table and three chairs, on one of which a uniformed police constable was sitting, a notebook at the ready.

'Where's your other chap?' he asked coldly.

'Inspector Lewis? He's otherwise engaged,' replied the superintendent. In fact, Lewis was already in a small industrial estate in the shadow of Kilvey Hill, near Swansea Docks.

Ben Evans waved Prentice to one of the hard chairs and sat down opposite.'We need a statement from you about the circumstances of your wife's death, sir.' He pushed a few sheets of lined paper with a statutory heading across the table.

'I've already given all this to the coroner's officer for the inquest,' said Prentice testily.

'I'm not the coroner's officer, sir,' said Evans placidly. 'And then we were not aware of the old bruises on your wife's body.'

'Those were nothing to do with me,' snapped Michael.

'Our doctor says they were typical of an assault within a few days before her death. So have you any knowledge of anyone else injuring your wife during that time?' asked the detective.

'She said nothing about it,' said the other man defensively, then realized how silly it sounded. 'No, of course not, there must be some mistake.'

'Do you deny that you have been unfaithful to your wife recently? Specifically with Daphne Squires from Porthcawl, who I believe was in your house when we called on you?'

'As I said before, it's none of your damned business what went on in my private life,' snarled Prentice, rising from his chair. 'This is nineteen fifty-five, not Victorian times!'

Evans motioned him down with a wave of his hand.

'Just write down all the events, as I asked please, sir. Then we'll take it from there.'

Glowering, Prentice subsided and pulled out a fountain pen from his inside pocket. He grabbed a sheet of the statement paper and began to write with jerky, angry movements.

While he was doing this, a dozen miles away Lewis Lewis had parked inside a yard with a high fence, alongside a long steel-framed building with an asbestos roof. At one end, there was a two-storied brick annexe which was obviously the office block. From inside the larger building came the sound of machine tools and angle grinders. A collection of vehicles stood outside a pair of large closed corrugated doors which bore the name 'Dragon Motor Innovations Ltd'.

He went through a small door in the annexe with 'Reception' written on it and entered an office with several young men and two girls working at desks.

One of these came across and he showed his warrant card.

'Have you come about the van that was stolen?' she asked.

Thinking that a little discretion might be advisable, Lewis nodded. 'I'd like to see whoever's in charge, please.'

'Mr Prentice won't be in until later, but Mr Laskey is here. He's the other director,' she added helpfully.

Upstairs, he found Laskey to be a small, cheerful man with rimless glasses on a large nose. As soon as the girl had left the room, the inspector came clean and admitted that he was not here about any stolen van, but was making enquiries about the death of Mr Prentice's wife.

Laskey was taken aback and looked embarrassed. 'I don't know that I should be saying anything about that, Inspector. It's Michael's private business.'

'There are certain matters which need to be cleared up, sir. I don't want to open this up to other employees unless it's absolutely necessary,' said Lewis.

The director blinked at him owl-like through his glasses.

'But what on earth can I tell you?' he said plaintively.

'Did your partner mention anything about his domestic affairs in recent weeks?' began the inspector. 'Did you know that he was involved with another lady from Porthcawl?

Laskey's sallow face flushed. 'That's a very sensitive subject, Officer. And it's none of my business.'

'But I'm afraid it's mine, sir. From your answer, you did know he was having some marriage problems?'

'Well, Michael did mention it to me. He was thinking of a divorce and Mrs Prentice was dead against it.' A look of understanding crept over his face. 'Oh dear, do you mean she might have done away with herself because of it?'

Lewis had not meant anything of the sort, but he let it lie.

'Was his manner and behaviour any different recently, since this problem?'

Laskey thought for a moment. 'He was looking worried, I suppose, but that was presumably because of his troubles at home. Otherwise, nothing different as far as the business was concerned.'

'Did he come into the factory as usual on the days leading up to the death of his wife?'

'Yes, of course. After it happened, he was naturally away for a day or two, but he seemed to take the tragedy very well.'

After a few more questions, Lewis saw that there was nothing useful to be got from Laskey. On the way out, he casually asked what they did in the factory and full of enthusiasm – and relief at a change of subject – the other man offered to show him around. They went down to the large building, which was divided into bays, where a dozen men were working at benches and at machine tools. One part was filled with electrical equipment, including an oscilloscope. Lewis had a genuine interest in motor vehicles and asked some intelligent questions about the various operations. Laskey seemed happy to answer, keeping up the fiction to the employees that the inspector was here about the stolen van.

'That's where we're working on a better ignition system

than the usual induction coil,' he explained, as they passed the electrical section. He showed Lewis a new disc-brake device and then took him into a bay where a white-coated man was using a micrometer to measure the main bearings and big-end journals of a crankshaft. The place smelt strongly of engine oil and there was some chemical apparatus on a side bench.

'This is where we are developing a new oil additive that will reduce frictional wear on moving parts, like cylinder walls and bearings. It will make engines last longer and use less fuel.'

Lewis, who had been a motorized traffic officer before going into the CID, was intrigued. 'How can you do that – or is it a trade secret?'

Laskey grinned. 'The principle's been known about for years. There are several competitors working on the same problem of getting the correct concentration of molybdenum sulphide to stay suspended in the lubricating oil.'

They passed on to a couple of other experimental ventures, then Lewis took his leave, much to the relief of Laskey, who had been very unhappy at being questioned about his partner.

Back in Gowerton, the said partner had finished writing his statement and signed it with a defiant flourish.

'There you are, Superintendent! If there are any more questions, I'll only answer them in the presence of my solicitor, because I've had enough of this pointless harassment. I trust that coroner will now let my poor wife be buried with dignity.'

'That's up to him, sir,' said Ben Evans. 'The next thing we need is to examine your house. You are entitled to be present, as is your solicitor, if you so wish.'

Michael Prentice goggled at the detective, the veins on his forehead standing out like cords.

'Examine my house? Why in God's name would you want to do that?' he exploded. 'My wife drowned in the sea! What the hell's my house got to do with it?'

'Until we get an explanation of how those injuries were sustained, sir, we need to carry out all necessary investigations.'

'Well, I'm not having it, d'you hear! What right have you to intrude on my property?'

Imperturbable as ever, as he'd heard all these protests before, Ben Evans offered him a choice.

'We would like to do this with your consent, that's the easy way. Otherwise, we'll have to obtain a magistrate's warrant. It's up to you.'

'Do what the hell you like!' snarled Prentice, going to the door of the interview room. 'I'm going straight to Swansea to see my solicitor.'

Ben Evans followed him as he stalked out of the building and jumped into his car. After the Jaguar had scorched out of the yard, the detective superintendent shrugged and turned back into the building.

Richard Pryor and Angela Bray were up early on Tuesday morning, with breakfast at six o'clock. They were on the road well before seven and in Ledbury before eight.

'I don't know why it has always been traditional to have exhumations so blessed early,' complained Richard, as he drove the Humber through the gates of the cemetery. 'It used to be at dawn, for God's sake!'

'If it was December, it would be dawn now,' said Angela brightly, as unlike her partner, she was a morning person. 'I suppose it was to avoid the press and the public, though that's a faint hope these days.'

However, there was no sign of curious crowds as they drove into the deserted cemetery. All they met was a local police constable, who directed them to a parking space near a hut where the staff kept their shovels and made their tea.

'The others are up at the top end, Doctor,' he said helpfully, as Richard clambered out with his black bag.

They walked the length of the tree-lined path, Angela noticing that the headstones of the graves became more modern as they went. Soon they saw a police car and a plain black van parked opposite a canvas screen. It was stretched on poles around a few recent graves, which were still mounds of turf with wooden crosses instead of headstones. Inside, one of these had been excavated and a heap of red soil was piled to one side. A pair of undertaker's men lounged against their van, smoking until they were needed.

Also inside the screens was John Christie, the Monmouth coroner's officer, attired as usual in his tweeds and trilby.

With him was a council official from the Parks and Cemeteries Department, clutching a plan of the burial sites and two gravediggers, who had been removing all the earth that they had laboriously filled in a few weeks earlier.

'I've had the soil removed down to the top of the coffin, Doctor,' said the official importantly. 'Once the coffin plate is checked, my men can get it up for you.'

He stepped to the edge of the hole and waved his papers.

'I can confirm that this is Plot 275 E, occupied by Albert John Barnes.'

'Mebbe, mebbe not!' muttered Christie, under his breath, as one of the gravediggers went down the short ladder into the hole and, with a trowel, began excavating two tunnels under the coffin for ropes to be passed through. The soil was fairly dry and not hard-packed, as it had so recently been disturbed. Within a few minutes, the veneer-covered chipboard had been hauled out and laid on two timbers set across the top of the grave. One of the workers rubbed at the brass plate to remove the earth. The council official peered at it and nodded.

'Albert John Barnes, it says. Would one of you gentlemen please confirm that?'

John Christie bent to look at the nameplate and nodded.

'That's the one! We'll have it away to Hereford now.'

As the two undertaker's men carted it off to their van, Richard wondered what would happen to the empty grave if the remains proved not to be Barnes – but that was not his problem.

Angela was very quiet on the journey to Hereford.

'I've never been to an exhumation before,' she said suddenly.

'If you want the truth, neither have I!' confessed Richard. 'The need never arose in the Army, nor in Singapore. They are pretty uncommon events.'

Angela shuddered. 'I've led a sheltered life in a laboratory, I suppose. Seeing where you end up at the bottom of a deep hole is a powerful reminder of your mortality.'

Hereford was not many miles away and the road from

Ledbury came in past the County Hospital, so within a short time the cortège arrived at the mortuary. In the small office, a police photographer was waiting, organized by John Christie, as well as Dr Bogdan Marek, whose territory this was. In addition, Edward Lethbridge was there. He had had no desire to attend the exhumation nor view the disputed remains, but he felt that he should represent his client, on whose behalf he had set all this performance in motion.

The undertakers wheeled the coffin in on a trolley to the outer room where the body store was situated and proceeded to unscrew the lid. Richard Pryor put on a rubber apron and offered one to Angela.

'It'll keep the earth off your clothes, if nothing else,' he said cheerfully.

They stood at the side of the coffin as the lid was taken off and propped against the wall. As the contents were virtually skeletal and very incomplete, there was no satin lining, but a sheet of rubberized fabric covered the bottom and was folded over the remains, which were laid out in an approximately correct pattern.

'Better push the whole lot into the post-mortem room,' said Pryor to the mortuary attendant and they followed the trolley into the stark chamber next door. Angela had seen plenty of dead bodies when called out to London scenes of crime, some in all stages of decay and mutilation, so she had no qualms about being in such close proximity to what was left of a corpse, though after lying about in the open air for several years, it was not particularly offensive, being mainly bones.

Pushing the coffin close to the porcelain table, Richard took charge and folded back the flaps of fabric to expose what was left of the body. After he had had a good look, he asked the hovering photographer to take pictures in situ and, for a few moments, the room was dazzled by flashes of home-made lightning.

Then the pathologist began taking the bones out one by one and reassembling them in proper anatomical order on the white table, when Dr Marek began peering intently at them.

'There's quite a lot missing,' observed Richard. 'Some of

the ribs and quite a few vertebrae, as well as the skull. A lot of the smaller hand and foot bones have gone, too. There are small teeth marks on some of them, foxes and rats, probably.'

He waited until he had all the skeleton laid out before addressing the vital point.

'Thank God we've still got the sternum!' he muttered and though he had already handled it, he picked it from between the ribs and held it between the fingers and thumbs of each hand. The breastbone was blade-shaped, about six inches long and an inch and a half wide, tapering to a point. Richard studied it, turned it over, then held it out to the others, who were clustered around.

'Flat as a pancake!' he announced. 'Doctor Marek was quite right, no sign of a *pec rec* there!'

The Polish pathologist looked pleased at being proved right, though he had had no doubts about his memory of it. While the photographer took some close-ups of the bone, the coroner's officer wanted some firm assurance to take back to Brian Meredith.

'So we can definitely say that this is not Albert Barnes, Doc?'

Richard was more cautious. 'We mustn't jump to conclusions, there's a lot more we can do yet. Certainly there's nothing unusual about his sternum, but of course we're relying on Dr Welton's clinical examination for the truth of that. Mind you, I can't see any possible reason for him being wrong about Barnes having a depressed sternum, but after all the fuss we've caused, we've got to be a hundred per cent sure.'

Angela volunteered to write a list of all the bones for Richard, being a good enough biologist not to need advice about any but a couple of small wrist and ankle bones. While she was doing this, Pryor examined every bone minutely, looking for any signs of old injury, but he found nothing.

'There are still a few tendon tags here and there,' he said. 'As well as some joint cartilage, so death must have been within about the last five years.'

'But it could have been less, I suppose?' asked Marek.

'Yes, it depends on the appetite of all those predators out there. They haven't left much.'

When he had finished looking at the remains, Richard measured the surviving long bones of the legs and arms. He used an osteometry board which he had made himself in Singapore, a two-foot plank with a long ruler screwed to one edge. At one end was a ledge and a slider moved along a groove in the middle. He put a bone against the ledge, then slid the moving part until it touched the other end of the bone, reading off the length on the scale.

Angela wrote down all the measurements and after some hurried calculations on a sheet of paper, he turned again to the others.

'I'll do it properly when I get home, but I reckon that he was about five feet ten inches, with an error of up to two inches either way.'

John Christie nodded wisely. 'That's against it being Barnes, too. He was supposed to be only about five-seven.'

The photographer left, after being assured that there were no more pictures needed and Dr Marek went off to more pressing duties in his laboratory.

'What else can we do, Doc?' asked the coroner's officer, anxious to come to a final decision.

'We need some X-rays, certainly. Can you fix that? Tell the hospital that the coroner will pay!' Richard turned to Angela, who was finishing off her notes.

'What do you need for blood grouping? There's hardly any soft tissue left.'

'Any chance of some marrow? A vertebra or a small section out of a long bone would be enough.'

'His clinical X-rays would be from a leg, so I can't take any from a femur or tibia. A piece of ulna should do.'

Under the statutory Coroner's Rules, a pathologist was not only allowed, but was obliged, to retain any material which might assist the coroner in his enquiries. Richard used a small saw to cut a sliver from an arm bone that exposed the marrow inside, which was ideal for determining the blood group. Then he collected his instruments, washed his hands and went out to see the solicitor in the office.

He told him what had transpired so far and that it looked very much as if the remains could not be those of Albert Barnes. 'When I see the X-rays, I'll be in a position to give a definite answer,' he said. 'Perhaps I can phone you later today.'

The elderly lawyer remained impassive, but as he left, he gave a sigh. 'This means that Mrs Oldfield will be convinced that the remains are those of her nephew! I'll get no peace now, mark my words!'

While they waited for the radiographers to arrive, which was forecast as being at least an hour, Richard drove down to the town centre and found a parking place.

'A celebratory coffee is called for, partner,' he declared and taking Angela's arm they walked past the old jail and police station into the shopping streets. Finding a café of the 'Olde Tea Shoppe' style, they each ordered coffee and a cream cake, exhumation having done nothing to impair their appetite.

'It's nice to have things in the shops again,' said Angela. 'Ten years since the war finished and at last things are now virtually back to normal.'

They talked about their memories of pre-war days for a while. Both were from well-off families, Angela more so that the doctor's son Richard, who remembered the South Wales valleys in the depression of the early thirties. He had more sympathy with Sian Lloyd's pink politics than Angela, a 'true blue' who had been brought up in an affluent Home Counties' environment.

The hour went quickly and he realized again how much he enjoyed talking to his partner, who was highly intelligent, well educated and sensitive to other people's feelings. He began to wonder if their partnership would eventually take on another meaning.

When they got back to the hospital, a middle-aged woman was pushing a portable X-ray machine into the outer room of the mortuary. The device was like a washing machine with a thick chrome pole sticking out of the top, carrying a cabled tube on a side arm.

'Sorry about this,' apologized Richard, helping her push the machine into the post-mortem room 'Must be a bit different to your usual patients – but these don't smell or anything.'

The woman smiled and shook her head. 'Saw a lot worse than this in the war! What exactly do you want done?'

John Christie was there with the X-rays from Barnes's admission four years previously and he handed them to Pryor. There was an X-ray viewing box screwed to the wall and he held the four large films in front of the light.

'A right femur and tibia, AP and lateral. Is that OK?' he asked the radiographer.

She nodded and busily set about connecting up her set to a power socket, while he separated the appropriate bones from the collection on the slab. The mortuary attendant brought a small wooden table over, on which the lady put a large metal cassette containing the first blank film, with a clean towel over the top.

Pryor laid the first bone on it in the position he wanted and the radiographer swivelled the X-ray tube directly above it.

'Right, everybody out!' she commanded and the room was cleared to avoid stray radiation. She retreated to the doorway with a long wire in her hand and pressed a button. There was a whirring sound and she walked back to retrieve the cassette. Richard repeated this for another three exposures and when they were finished, the radiographer went off to develop the films, promising to return them in about half an hour. The mortuary man promised to trundle her machine back to the X-ray department and Richard, Angela and Christie had to sit in the cramped office, swapping stories of past cases to fill the time.

Eventually, the woman came back, carrying the developed films on metal hangers.

'They're still wet, but I thought you might like a quick look,' she offered. 'One of the radiologists will see them later and send you a report.'

Richard took one of the hangers and held it in front of the illuminated viewing box, then put up the corresponding film from Barnes's records. He did this for each of the four views before saying anything.

'That clinches it! Those bones are quite different.'

'Show me why you can say that,' demanded Angela and with Christie looking over her shoulder, Pryor shifted one of the old films across under the clips on the box, so that he could hold the corresponding damp one to the side of it.

'Look, a different length to the thigh bone, to start with. But the internal structure is different, especially up here towards the hip joint.'

'You mean that lacy-looking stuff, radiating up to the femoral head?' asked Angela, her biology expertise extending to quite a bit of anatomy.

'That's it, they're mechanical struts responding to weight bearing. I know they can change with age and injury, but in a man in his forties, there's no way they could alter this much in a few years.'

He showed similar differences to them in the other views and then told John Christie that he could confirm to the coroner that the remains were not those of Albert Barnes.

'I'll send him a written report as soon as we can get the blood groups done. Any joy with finding what Barnes's blood group was?'

For reply, Christie opened the folder he was carrying and produced a sheet of paper. 'I copied this from the pathology lab records. For some reason, the report form wasn't stuck into his ward notes.'

Richard took the sheet and looked at it, then handed it to Angela.

'"Albert John Barnes – Group A, Rhesus Positive",' she quoted. 'Well, that's the second most common in Britain. Thank heaven the bones were more unique.'

By later that day, Angela had determined that the remains were Group O Rhesus Positive, the first most common. Though Richard had had little doubt that the bones were not those of Albert, it was nice to have further cast-iron confirmation to give the coroner and Edward Lethbridge.

He phoned Brian Meredith at the end of the afternoon and told him of the findings. The coroner was not very enthusiastic about the news, but accepted the truth stoically.

'Now I've got to tell the wife and reopen the inquest. She'll make a bloody fuss, no doubt, but I'll get John Christie to have a word in her ear about giving misleading evidence, as she must have known that the ring and the watch didn't belong to her husband.'

'What about Albert's death certificate?' asked Pryor, out of curiosity. 'For all we know, he might be living in Birmingham with a fancy woman. He may not know that he's supposed to be dead!'

He could hear Meredith's sigh over the phone. 'It'll be a bureaucratic nightmare, getting that annulled. I had a clerical error once before that gave the wrong name and it took weeks for the Registrar and Somerset House in London to sort it out!'

With the coroner's permission, he next rang the solicitor in Lydney to tell him of the result and again he was not as overjoyed as Richard might have expected.

'Mrs Oldfield will get straight on the warpath now!' he forecast. 'She'll strain every nerve to prove that those remains are of her precious nephew. I expect she'll want me to carry on retaining you and Mr Mitchell to pitch in with the investigation.'

Even the prospect of a further fee was not all that attractive to Richard, if it meant running around at the behest of that autocratic old woman.

'I can't see where we could even begin, given that we don't have any physical details of this Anthony Oldfield,' he protested. 'If anyone can chase it up, it must be Trevor Mitchell. Perhaps he can somehow trace the chap's movements after he left home.'

'I'll see what he has to say, but if she really wants you for some medical advice, can I say you'll do it, Doctor?'

Rather reluctantly, Richard agreed, though he could see no reason for the offer to be taken up. He went to bring Angela up to date and then went to write a report on the 'man who never was', as Albert Barnes came to be known in Garth House!

TWELVE

When Michael Prentice arrived home from his office that evening, he had to squeeze his Jaguar past Daphne's blue Morris Minor which was parked near the top of the drive. It was normally hidden in the garage, so as not to attract too much attention from nosy neighbours so soon after his wife's death, so he wondered where his mistress had been. Inside the front door, he found the answer in the shape of two large suitcases left in the hall – Daphne had not *been* anywhere, she was *going*!

He marched into the lounge and saw her standing in the window, dressed in a cream shirt-dress with a wide flared skirt, a perky hat on her bottle-blonde hair.

'Where the hell are you going?' he demanded, the fuse already lit on his short temper.

'I'm going back to Porthcawl for the time being,' she snapped. 'I don't want to get mixed up in anything.'

'Mixed up in what?' he demanded, angrily stepping towards her. She backed away a little and pointed to the telephone on a side table.

'Those police again! They rang this afternoon to say that they are coming at nine tomorrow morning to make a forensic examination of the house. What's going on, Michael?'

He marched over to a drinks cabinet and poured himself a double measure of whiskey.

'Nothing's going on! It's that bloody man Massey, stirring up trouble for me. You know how he hates me, I would never have married his damned daughter if I knew he would be like this.'

He tossed back half the drink, without offering one to the woman.

'You haven't done anything silly, have you, Mike?' she asked accusingly. 'I'm not hanging about here if your troubles are going to involve me.'

He glared at her angrily. 'Anything silly? What the hell do you mean? Of course I haven't, you stupid bitch.'

Her face tightened and she stalked to the door, pushing him aside as he moved towards her.

'If that's what you think of me, I'm going. Probably for good!'

He stood aside sullenly and watched her go into the hall and open the front door.

'Are you going to carry my cases out or do I have to do it myself?' she demanded.

'There's no need for you to go at all,' he said, but he was making a statement, not pleading. 'Though if those coppers are coming to nose about, it might be just as well if you're not here at the time. I'll give you a ring when things have settled down.'

'I just hope they do, Michael, for both our sakes,' she said flatly and went to sit in her car while he put the cases on the back seat. A moment later, she had driven off without a backward glance, leaving him to close the gates that he had left open when he had arrived.

He stalked back to the house and slammed the front door. Going back into the lounge, he poured himself another stiff drink and flopped into an armchair to morosely ponder his situation and wallow in some self-pity.

In spite of his threat, Michael Prentice did not contact his solicitor to ask him to be present at the search of his house, as he was confident that there was nothing to be found. When the police arrived on Wednesday morning, he assumed an air of bored indifference.

'You won't want me hanging around while you waste your time, Officer,' he said nonchalantly, as he opened the door to Ben Evans. He had a bag of golf clubs on his shoulder and as he came out, he handed the officer a bunch of keys.

'I'm off to the club until you've finished. Here's the keys to the garage and the garden shed. Pull the front door to when you leave, there's a good chap.'

He walked off to his car and drove away, past the CID Vauxhall, a Standard Eight and a small Austin Ten police van that were parked on the track.

'Cheeky sod!' muttered Lewis Lewis as he watched him go. 'I'd like to find something here, just to pull him down a peg or two!'

'Now, now, Inspector, we are upholders of justice!' grinned Evans. 'Everyone's innocent until proved guilty.'

Lewis glared after the retreating Jaguar for a moment, then turned to the three officers unloading the van. One was a photographer from Bridgend HQ, the other two detective constables from Gowerton, one to act as Exhibits Officer if they found anything. The local uniformed man from the Southgate police station had just arrived on his bicycle and the whole team went into the house. Though it was June, it was overcast and the Home Service on the wireless was forecasting rain by the afternoon.

The superintendent had no idea what they looking for, but after a phone call to his chief superintendent, who was head of CID at Headquarters, they agreed that they should go through the whole routine. Then, if it turned out to be nasty, they would not be left with egg on their faces for not covering all possibilities.

'You've got a woman dead and an accusation that she was being ill-treated by her husband,' the chief had said. 'Now this pathologist says she has bruises indicative of gripping on her arms and neck – and not least, a London QC is her father and is raising hell. That's enough for me to give it the full Monty!'

Evans watched as the photographer took some establishing shots of the house, both from outside and indoors, while the inspector and two DCs made a methodical search of each room.

'Are we looking for anything in particular, guv'nor?' asked the older detective constable, an experienced man who had been involved in many searches.

Ben Evans shrugged. 'Flying blind, I'm afraid. She had an injury on the back of her head, so look for anything that might have blood and hair on it. Could be a corner of furniture or the fireplace – or it could be the good old blunt instrument.'

However, every effort to find evidence of a fall or a struggle came to nothing. They searched everywhere, including the garden, the garage and the shed. They even put a head up into the loft, which from the layer of dust, appeared never to have been entered.

'Are we interested in papers and stuff like that?' asked Lewis, as he pulled open a desk drawer in the right hand front room, which appeared to have been used as an office, as it had a portable typewriter on top and a small filing cabinet alongside.

Evans came across and began looking through some of the papers, but they seemed to be either household bills or documents relating to the factory in Swansea.

'No sign of a diary she might have kept?' he asked the searchers, but was answered by shaken heads.

He shrugged off his disappointment. 'I thought she might have left some record of him knocking her about, as she had written to her friend,' he said. 'Maybe he's clean after all.'

They gave up after about two hours, having covered every inch of the house, even pulling back carpets and moving beds. The superintendent was last out and slammed the door shut, leaving the keys inside on the hall table. They had a final conference in the front garden, Ben Evans perching his large backside on the low wall of the circular rockery. He looked morosely into the murky water of the small pond that lay in the middle, where two sad-looking goldfish swam around.

'We've got nothing, lads, and I'm not sure where we go from here. Any suggestions?'

Lewis Lewis scratched his head, then pulled out a packet of Players Navy Cut and offered them around. 'We've never actually seen where she went into the sea and where the body was found, have we?'

Two of his colleagues took a cigarette, Evans and the photographer declining. When they had lit up, the senior detective constable queried what could be gained.

'It's almost a couple of weeks now, and we've had some rain and plenty of wind. What's going to be left?'

Ben Evans thought for a moment, then whistled and beckoned to the uniformed man, who had been standing guard at the gate into the road. When he came up the path, Evans asked him if he was the one who had answered the call of the fisherman who had found the body.

'Yes, sir – and I was there when the coastguards hauled her ashore.'

'What about the place where she went swimming? Have you been down there since?'

The PC, a middle-aged man nearing retirement, nodded.

'I was the one who found her dressing-gown thing, behind a gorse bush above the rocks.'

'Can you show us both those places, Constable? We may as well have a look now we're here.'

They trooped off behind the officer, who went a few yards along the track to the right, then turned down between stunted bushes and across to the top of the cliff.

Here a wide, shallow amphitheatre sloped steeply down to the rocks below, lined with coarse grass and patches of gorse. There was a narrow, ankle-twisting path going down to the sea, marked by muddy earth and outcropping stones.

The PC set off, followed more cautiously by the others and eventually they reached a band of flatter grass immediately above the rocky gullies, in which grey water surged and sucked with the swell.

'Do people swim in that?' said Evans, pointing down to the water, ten feet below.

'Yes, plenty of them, especially at the weekends and in better weather than this.' The constable pointed up at the low clouds from which an intermittent drizzle came down.

'And this is where Mrs Prentice must have gone in?' asked Lewis.

The uniformed man pointed to a nearby gorse bush, where a few bright yellow flowers resisted the wind and salt. 'That's where I found her clothing, sir. One of these thick white towelling jobs, with a tie-belt, like you get in Turkish baths on the films. There was a blue bath-towel as well.'

'What about shoes?' asked the photographer. 'She'd hardly have come down that flaming path we just used in her bare feet?'

The constable shook his head. 'No shoes, nothing but that dressing gown and towel.'

Ben Evans looked at Lewis.

'That's a bit odd, unless she was one of these "back to nature" folks and despised shoes.'

'She may have some sort of sandals or rubber shoes and kept them on until she got down on the rocks,' explained the PC. 'I've seen a lot of people with those, it saves the feet until they're right at the water's edge.'

He pointed down at the grey rocks that formed the walls of the gullies. 'They get right down there, then jump or clamber down into the water. They say it's more fun than just walking in off a sandy beach, though at low tide, there's a little stretch of sand exposed here.'

'So where are the shoes now?' demanded one of the search team.

'Well they weren't there when I came down to find the clothes,' retaliated the constable. 'But that was a day later, they could have been washed off by a big wave or blown off by the wind.'

The superintendent had a few photos taken of the site, then they clambered back up to the top of the cliffs. Once on the track to the houses, Ben Evans decided to cover all his bases and look at the place where the body was recovered.

'It's about a quarter of a mile, sir. Do you want to walk or drive?' asked their guide. Opting to do it the hard way, the posse set off eastwards and passed the last of the houses, when the stony road became even more uneven.

'Really need a Land Rover along here,' observed Lewis, as they came to another dip in the high cliffs which went down to the rocks a couple of hundred feet below.

'That's Pwlldu Head further on,' said the local man, pointing to a blunt promontory beyond the dip.

He led them cautiously down another even more difficult path to a similar ledge above the waves and pointed out the place where the body had been seen in the water.

'Up against the back end of that narrow crack, it was,' he told them.

Ben Evans nodded. 'You reckon it could have washed along from where we were just now?'

The constable had no doubts about it. 'Twelve years I've been here, sir, I've seen many accidents in that time. They can end up anywhere from anywhere – as far as Porthcawl or even right up-channel. Sometimes, we never find them, they get pulled back out to sea.'

There was nothing else to look at, so they grunted and puffed their way back to the top. Once on the track again the group stood for a breather and a smoke, the photographer and the two DCs hoping that the search was over and that they could make for home.

The superintendent stood, deep in thought.

With absolutely nothing found, he failed to see that this case was going anywhere. Though he instinctively disliked Michael Prentice for an arrogant womanizer, that was no reason to accuse him of murder – and there was very poor evidence to even consider charging him with assaulting his late wife. He stood rubbing the bristles on his chin and staring at the ground, then realized that his eyes were actually focused on something.

Ben nudged his inspector and pointed to the ground near his feet. 'Reckon this is recent, Lewis?'

He squatted down and peered more closely at a dark stain on the grey limestone on the edge of the track. Just where the uneven surface gave way to thin grass was a smear of jet black, about six inches long and half as wide. In the middle, a jagged spike of stone poked up through it, the top clean and almost white.

Lewis Lewis crouched down and delicately touched the black stain.

'It's obviously engine oil. Somebody's stopped here and some has dripped from their sump.'

'Looks as if they've run the sump over the top of that rock. That's a fairly fresh scrape on it.'

Evans motioned to the photographer to unpack his kit again and get a couple of close-ups of the oil patch. Then he told the detective constable who was acting as Exhibits Officer to take a sample from it. The DC took a small screw-top glass pot from his case, the type used in hospital laboratories. With a clean wooden spatula, he carefully scraped off as much of the black smear as possible and put it inside, labelling it and attaching a brown cardboard exhibits ticket, which he signed after the place, date and time.

'Could be anyone, guv,' cautioned Lewis.

'Any port in a storm, lad,' replied Evans. 'We've got bee-all else. But let's go back to the house, before our golfer gets home.'

They retraced their steps to *Bella Capri* and Evans led them to the side of the house, in front of the garage.

'We left the keys inside,' pointed out Lewis.

Evans shook his bull-like head. 'Doesn't matter, he was leaving his car out here, while his floozie's was in the garage.'

He looked at the concrete hardstanding outside the garage and saw with satisfaction that a much longer black stain disfigured the ground.

'We'll have a bit of that, too,' he told the exhibits man and the DC repeated his operation, harvesting another sample in a different bottle.

Somewhat mystified, the party broke up, the others going off in the van and Evans driving away with Lewis in the Vauxhall. As they crossed Fairwood Common on the way back to Gowerton, the superintendent gave some instructions to Lewis.

'I want you to go back to that factory of his while Prentice is not there and speak again to that chap you saw. He seems to know all about the technology that's going on.'

He gave his inspector some more detailed instructions and when they reached the police station, he turned the car over to Lewis to make the journey into Swansea.

THIRTEEN

As Edward Lethbridge had gloomily anticipated, Agnes Oldfield was cock-a-hoop, as soon as she had the news that Molly Barnes's claim had been demolished by the exhumation. She insisted on a meeting with both her solicitor and Trevor Mitchell, so the lawyer thought it wise to invite Richard Pryor along as well, partly in order to deflect the inevitable demands concerning her own claim.

They arranged to meet at his office in Lydney on that Wednesday afternoon and the three men were already there when she arrived. As they rose, she swept in through the door opened by a secretary and imperiously took her seat alongside the desk. Richard, a keen cinema-goer, was reminded of Dame Edith Evans's portrayal of Lady Bracknell in Oscar Wilde's *The Importance of being Earnest*, as she wore a long black coat and an ornate hat. As it was raining outside, she also had a thin umbrella, upon which she rested a gloved hand, as she sat ramrod straight on her chair.

'Well, I told you it was Anthony!' she began without any preamble. 'I knew from the start that the Barnes woman was an impostor.'

As she had never laid eyes on the woman, Richard wondered how she knew that, but he kept his peace.

It was Lethbridge's task to try to put the brakes on Agnes Oldfield's certitude.

'Madam, we have only managed to prove that the remains were not those of Albert Barnes,' he said rather nervously. 'It does not advance us one inch in establishing that they are those of your nephew.'

She glared at the solicitor. 'Of course it must be Anthony. Now we must prove it!'

'That's what we've been trying to do for over a year, Mrs Oldfield,' said Lethbridge, in gentle exasperation. 'We have spent a lot of time – and I may add, you have spent a lot of money – in trying to trace your nephew, with no success whatsoever.'

'But now it's different,' she said triumphantly. 'You have had the actual remains to examine by a specialist.'

She gave Pryor a regal wave and a fleeting smile.

Richard felt he should make some contribution to help out poor old Edward.

'Yes, Mrs Oldfield, but unless we can discover some unique characteristic in your relative that can be matched to the bones, we are no further forward.'

'Such as what?' she demanded.

'Did he have any old injuries, for example? Had he been in hospital for anything?'

As he said it, he knew he was being false, because there was no sign of any old injuries or disease in the remains that could be matched to anything. In fact, if the missing Anthony had had any such features, it would exclude him from being the body at the reservoir.

The old lady pondered for a moment. 'I just don't know, Professor! You see, until the last year or so, my nephew was often abroad. For all I know, he might have broken a leg in the Alps or caught beriberi in Africa!'

She looked across at Trevor Mitchell, who was trying to keep as quiet as possible.

'Mr Mitchell should be able to help. He can find out from various hospitals and perhaps embassies overseas, if Anthony was ever treated there.'

The ex-detective groaned inwardly, trying to imagine himself touring the clinics of Europe and the consulates of far-flung countries.

'I'm not sure that's really feasible, madam,' he pleaded.

Agnes turned her attention back to Richard Pryor.

'I was told that one of the ways in which you destroyed that woman's claim was by means of blood groups? Surely that would give you the answer?'

Richard took a deep breath. 'I'm afraid it's a slim hope. The blood group of the remains was the second most common in Britain. Out of interest, do you happen to know your nephew's blood group?'

Mrs Oldfield looked severely at the pathologist.

'Indeed I do not concern myself with such matters! But there must be some way of discovering it.'

'Was he in the Forces?' asked Richard. 'They might have it in his records.'

She shook her head. 'No, he was exempt during the war. He had such an important job in his father's aircraft factory, you see.'

Trevor took a turn in the discussion. 'Was he ever a blood donor? There might be a card amongst his possessions.'

Again his aunt had no knowledge of this, but promised to search amongst the belongings he had left at her house. It then transpired that he had lived with her in Newnham only for a short time, having previously lived in a flat in Cheltenham. He was supposed to be seeking another place of his own and some of his furniture and other possessions were in store until then.

Having delivered her orders that proof must be found, she departed, leaving the three men to gratefully have the tea that Lethbridge's secretary brought in on a tray.

'She's a real old battleaxe, isn't she?' said Richard. 'I reckon her nephew is well out of it, dead or alive.'

'They didn't get on that well, apparently,' said Trevor. 'When I was snooping around at the start of this job, I talked to neighbours and friends of the family and they said they had heard the old girl and Anthony going at each other hammer-and-tongs sometimes. He used to push off on holidays and trips a lot, just to get away from her.'

'Didn't he have a job of any sort?' asked Richard.

'No, he was rolling in it. I don't know why he didn't get himself his own place again in the first week.'

'That's why she's so keen to have him declared dead, so that she can get probate, as there's a lot of money involved,' commented Lethbridge.

'Well, he *has* been gone for over three years,' said Trevor.

'Why is she so convinced that this chap at the reservoir is Anthony?' asked Pryor.

'This is the third time she's been convinced that a body was his,' said the solicitor. 'But this time, there was no head and no means of saying it wasn't him, which was what eventually happened with the others.'

'What about this ring and the watch, then?' persisted
Richard. 'Does she claim to have recognized those?'

Mitchell shrugged. 'She's deliberately vague about it.
He had been married many years ago, his wife died and
the old lady says he did wear a wedding ring. As for the
watch, she never noticed whether it was an Omega, just
says that being Anthony, it must have been an expensive
one!'

Their tea finished, Richard and Trevor rose to leave.

'So what more can we do now?' asked Lethbridge.

'If we could find Anthony's blood group, it might get her
off our backs, if it's not Group A-positive,' said Richard.

'I'll have a scout around and see what I can find in various
records,' offered Mitchell. 'But let's hope it's not A-positive,
or she'll be absolutely convinced it's him!'

Inspector Lewis was once again talking confidentially to
Michael Prentice's technical director at the industrial estate
on Jersey Marine. They were in his small office upstairs,
Lewis having checked that the black Jaguar was not in the
compound outside.

'I can't tell you why I need to know this, and I can't
legally tell you to keep it from your partner,' he said to Eric
Laskey. 'It's about that additive you told me about when I
was here last?'

The engineer looked puzzled, but went along with the
inspector's request.

'As I told you, it's only in the testing stage at present. We
add this compound to the engine oil, which reduces friction.
Several firms are working on it, success depends on who
gets it perfected and commercially available first.'

'Does it work?' asked Lewis. This query was not part of
the enquiry, he was just curious.

'Sure, there's no doubt of that! The problem is getting the
right concentration in the oil and making it stay there.'

'So what's the "it"? You did tell me and I've forgotten.'

'Molybdenum sulphide – physically, it's a lot like
graphite, the molecules are flat and slide over each other,
reducing friction and wear.' Laskey became enthusiastic
and insisted on getting into detail. 'The molybdenum atoms

are sandwiched between two layers of sulphur, which bonds to the metal of bearings, so the stuff slips sideways.'

Lewis, who years ago did General Science for his School Certificate, had a vague idea what Laskey was talking about, but returned to the purpose of his visit.

'Now then, have you started using it in engines yet?'

'God, yes, for the last three years! We have special fixed engines on test beds, which we run for a long time, then take to bits to see how they are wearing. Lately, we've been testing it on vehicles actually on the road.'

'That's just what I want to know, sir. Which vehicles in particular?'

Laskey looked a little furtive. 'Why on earth do you want to know that? Look, Inspector, there's a lot of competition in this field, until we get patents arranged on our final products, we wouldn't want any information to be bandied about outside this building.'

Lewis hastened to reassure him.

'This is purely a police matter, Mr Laskey. All I want to know is how many vehicles in the Swansea area would have molybdenum in their sumps?'

Still mystified, the other man began ticking off on his fingers. 'There are the two vans we use for running around – though one of them is God knows where, as it's been stolen. Then we have a Bedford truck for heavier stuff. Two of our floor engineers are trying it out – and then of course myself and Michael Prentice have joined in the testing.'

This was what Lewis wanted to know. 'That would be in his Jaguar, I presume?' he asked.

'That's right, he's been using it for almost a year, the same as I've had it in my Lanchester. These are very peculiar questions, Inspector. Can't you tell me why you want to know?'

The detective shook his head. 'Sorry, sir, not at the moment. What I would like is a small sample of this molybdenum that's in Mr Prentice's crankcase.'

Laskey was very reluctant to hand over any of their secret substance, but after Lewis had assured him that he was not involved in any industrial espionage and hinted that he could get a magistrate's order if it wasn't handed over, he caved in. Taking him down to the workshop floor, he took a small bottle of oil labelled with a serial number from a locked cupboard and handed it to the policeman. 'That's the one we're testing now, the code on the label refers to the strength of molybdenum in that particular batch.'

Laskey was very uneasy as he watched the inspector drive away, then went back to his office and picked up the telephone.

There was a hiatus in both cases for the next few days.

Agnes Oldfield went back to her gloomy house in Newnham and started searching through her nephew's belongings in the hope of finding something that would help in her crusade to prove that the reservoir remains were his. When he left his flat in Cheltenham, he had come to stay with her and had his own large room upstairs, for which he paid her rent, as well as a weekly contribution for food and household expenses. Their relationship was not always cordial and he spent a lot of time away, either staying with friends in various parts of England or going abroad on undisclosed trips. When he was there, he often went fishing or attending the races, both the Chepstow and Cheltenham courses being a favourite haunt for him to meet his friends.

The circumstances of his final departure had been gone over with her repeatedly by Edward Lethbridge and Tony Mitchell, but threw little light on where he might have gone.

'I went for a long weekend to stay with an old school-friend in Hove,' she had told them. 'When I returned on the Monday, he was gone. I thought little of that, as Anthony was always taking it into his head to disappear on an impulse without telling me, but this time he never came back.'

Pressed to explain why she thought he might have turned up at the reservoir, she had no real answer, except that he had often gone for walking trips in that area and was very fond of the Golden Valley and the borders of Wales and Herefordshire.

'He would sometimes spend a week there, staying in inns and small hotels,' she declared. 'So that place where the body was found was right where he might be expected to be.'

Now, with almost a hundred thousand pounds at stake, Agnes was more than keen to find evidence that would prove

him dead, but all her efforts to find something proved fruitless. She had vague ideas about discovering a receipt or a
guarantee for an Omega wristwatch or a Blood Transfusion
Service Donor's Card, but there was nothing in the few papers
he had left in a desk in his room. She wondered if he had
left anything with his bank or in a safe-deposit box somewhere, but had no idea how to follow that up – she must ask
Lethbridge about it, she decided.

While Mrs Oldfield was rooting around at her home, eighty
miles to the west Michael Prentice was pacing around his
living room at *Bella Capri* in a much greater state of concern.

He was trying to make sense of Eric Laskey's phone call,
to tell him of the detective's visit to the factory. What earthly
connection could their research into lubricant additives have
to the matter in hand? And why did the inspector insist on
taking some of the new product away with him? Like his
business partner, Prentice was unhappy that a sample of their
closely guarded innovation had left the premises, but even
he could not believe that a police officer had any commercial motives.

He poured himself a strong whisky and added a spot of
water, then marched out into the garden with the glass in his
hand. Walking around the corner of the house, he went to
where his car was parked in front of the garage and stared
at it, as if seeking inspiration. He circled the Jaguar, but saw
nothing that triggered any explanation.

Opening the boot, he looked inside and felt around the
carpeted floor, again without result. Mystified he slammed
it shut and stood back to sip his drink. As he stood there
contemplatively looking at the ground, his eyes focused
between his feet and became aware of scattered black stains
on the concrete.

'Bloody useless mechanics!' he hissed. After the first two
thousand miles his car had travelled since the molybdenum
had been added to the engine oil, the condition of the main
bearings and big ends had recently been checked. It seemed
obvious now that when the sump pan had been replaced,
either the ring of bolts had not been tightened sufficiently
or the gasket had not been renewed, leading to a slight oil
leak.

He hurried back into the house, then came out again with a raincoat and went to the garage, where he found a wire brush on the workbench, which he pushed into his pocket. With rapid strides, he set off eastwards along the track, scanning the uneven stones as he went.

FOURTEEN

Richard Pryor could stay up working or reading late into the night without protest, but once in bed, he detested having to get up again. That was the one thing about forensic medicine that he disliked, the frequency of being called out in the early hours.

It was fortunate then, that just before midnight on Sunday, he was still reading in his room when the phone went and his presence was requested in a wood about twenty miles away. The call came from a Detective Superintendent Tom Spurrel in Cheltenham.

'Sorry to disturb you so late, Doctor, but we're in a bit of a spot. We've got a shooting and no pathologist to attend the scene.'

He went on to explain that their regular Home Office pathologist from Oxford was already out on a double murder that would keep him occupied until late next day.

'My old friend Trevor Mitchell had told me about you and suggested that if we ever needed a backup, you might be able to help us out,' he added.

Richard was only too happy to oblige, as he was keen to get a foothold in the Home Office work. He asked the Gloucestershire officer for more details.

'We've got a chap shot dead in a car in a forestry area between Ross-on-Wye and Gloucester. It looks like a suicide, but the DI that was called is not happy about it, mainly because the deceased is a known villain from London. We can fill you in more when you get here.'

He gave some directions to Richard, suggesting that the best route was up to Ross via Monmouth, then down on the A40 towards Gloucester.

'I'll have a police car waiting for you on that road a couple of miles before you get to Huntley village. He'll lead you to the scene, as it's hidden away up some country lanes.'

With a promise to be there within an hour, Richard ran upstairs and tapped on Angela's door.

'Are you in bed or decent?' he called.

She was not in bed, but was in a dressing gown when she opened the door.

'What's this, Richard? Are you desperate enough to come knocking on a lady's door in the middle of the night?' she quipped.

He quickly told her about the phone call. 'Do you want to come?' he asked. 'Be like old times for you.'

She agreed readily. 'Give me time to get some clothes on. I'll see you downstairs in five minutes.'

The Humber's headlights were soon carving a passage through the slight mist that filled the valley as they drove. There were few other cars on the road and at Ross, they turned east towards Gloucester. Some miles down the A40, Angela spotted the illuminated roof sign of a police car parked in a field gateway. They slowed to a crawl until the big Wolseley flashed its headlights at them and Richard pulled up alongside.

'We'll go on a short way, Doctor and then turn left,' called the driver from his open window. They followed him for a couple of miles through a sleeping village called Dursley Cross and then along narrow roads with woods on either side.

Angela was looking at a folded road map by the light of a small torch. 'There's a huge area of woodland here, must once have been part of the Forest of Dean.'

After another half mile the brake lights of the police car came on and he slowed to turn left into a bumpy track which went deep into the trees, seen dimly in the reflected light of their headlamps. A few hundred yards more brought them into a clearing, where two other police cars, two unmarked cars and a plain van were parked.

The other driver came across to them as they were retrieving their bags from the back seat.

'We'll have to walk a little bit now, sir,' said the officer. 'The way we came in isn't the direct way to the scene, but we didn't want to drive over any tyre marks.'

Another uniformed bobby was standing guard over the cars and took their names down on a clipboard.

'I'll take you through, I've got a decent torch here,' said the police car driver, leading the way.

Walking through the forest was an eerie experience, as soon a glow appeared ahead where portable lights had been set up. A dense mist was hanging at head height between the trees and the dim light revealed only the straight black trunks of the larches on every side. The macabre effect was heightened when they overtook two men in black carrying a coffin through the ghostly scene, presumably the duty undertakers coming from the van parked in the clearing.

When they reached the lights, propped on tripods over car batteries, they saw a dark-coloured car at the end of a barely visible firebreak running through the wood.

Around it were half a dozen men, two of them in uniform. One of the others came to meet them as they approached.

'Good of you to come, Doctor! And you, miss' he added to Angela, assuming she was his secretary.

'She's a doctor too,' explained Richard with a grin. 'Doctor Bray, formerly of the Metropolitan Police Laboratory, until I stole her away!'

The superintendent introduced himself as Tom Spurrel, another large man, as most of Gloucester police seemed to be. Another officer approached them and Spurrel explained that he was Brian Lane, the DI who first attended.

'The situation is this, Doctors,' the superintendent began. 'There's a dead man in that car, shot through the neck. The gun's on the floor and it looks like a suicide – but maybe that's what it's supposed to look like.'

'You already know who he is, you said?' asked Pryor.

'Well, we know who the car belongs to and from the description we had over the phone from the Met, there seems little doubt that the chap is Harry Haines, a toerag from South London.'

'Harry Haines? I've heard of him,' exclaimed Angela. 'Wasn't he a villain from New Cross way, who got off on a murder charge a few years back? Some fight between rival gangs, that ended in a shooting. We had material from it in the Met Lab.'

Spurrel nodded in the gloom. 'That's him, his mob ran protection rackets and a bit of prostitution and drugs.'

'So what the hell's he doing in a Gloucestershire forest?' asked Richard.

The detective inspector, Brian Lane, answered. He was as tall as Spurrel, but leaner with a saturnine face.

'We've heard that his mob have been trying get in on the nightclub and dog racing scene here, to extend their protection scams. Same as what's happening in Tyneside and Manchester, the London boys are wanting to muscle in on the local action.'

'That's why we're cautious about accepting it as a suicide,' broke in Tom Spurrel. 'Why would he come all the way down here to top himself?'

Both the detectives wore belted raincoats and wide-brimmed felt hats, more reminiscent of the forties – or American B-movies, thought film buff Richard.

'Want to have a look now?' offered Spurrel. 'The forensic lab in Bristol is sending someone over, they should be here soon. We called them a couple of hours ago.'

'And there are officers coming down from the Met, to definitely identify this chap,' added the DI, as they walked to the car, sitting silently in the ring of lights. It was an almost new Rover P4/90.

Going round to the driver's side, Richard and Angela saw that the front door was wide open and a man sat there, his head lolling backwards against the top of the seat.

'Is it alright to go nearer?' asked Pryor, looking down at the ground. It was covered with a spongy mat of pine needles and there seemed no chance of footprints being left.

'Go ahead, Doc, we've got all the pictures. Just keep your fingers off anything but the body.'

Richard gingerly moved nearer and stood right against the door pillar, holding a large torch that Spurrel had handed to him. The man inside was dressed in a fawn check suit over a white shirt with no tie. He was thin and wiry, looking about forty years old, his brown hair cut short.

His mouth was open and blood ran from both corners, as it did from a wound in the front of his neck, just under the chin. There were runnels of dried blood on each side of the bristly skin of his neck. His hands lay on his lap and on the floor between his feet, there was a pistol.

Richard looked carefully at the corpse, his eyes running over every inch, from the crown of his head to the toes of his expensive brown shoes. Then he stepped back a pace and turned to the waiting onlookers.

'You're right, it's no suicide!' he said. 'And he wasn't shot here, either.'

The two senior detectives and three other officers who had gravitated to the group, looked at Pryor as if he was some Old Testament prophet.

'That's quick work, Doc!' said Spurrel. 'How d'you know?'

Richard grinned and winked at Angela. 'I'm sure Doctor Bray here will tell you!'

She rose to the occasion easily, blood stains and sprays being one of her specialities.

'Those dribbles of blood on the face and neck are going the wrong way for a chap sitting upright,' she explained, waving her own torch at the body. 'Look, that blood coming from the corner of the mouth goes straight across towards the ear, the same as the one coming from the gunshot wound. He must have been lying on his back when those were leaking.'

Richard added his own bit of expertise. 'And that post-mortem lividity, the blue staining of the skin on the back of his neck, could only have happened if he spent a few hours face-up after death, not sitting in a car seat.'

Richard knew that police always liked experts who would give them a dogmatic answer off the cuff, though it was a habit fraught with danger if it turned out to be wrong. Tom Spurrel rubbed his hands together and looked at his DI.

'Right, Brian, pull out all the stops on this one!'

As they started snapping instructions to the inspector and two detective constables, Richard saw torches bobbing towards them from the parking area and a moment later, two other men arrived, one carrying a large case.

As soon as this new arrival saw them in the gloom, he called a greeting.

'God God, Angie, what are you doing here? I needn't have come if I'd known the big chief from the Met was here already!'

The speaker was a moon-faced middle-aged man with wire-framed spectacles, short and rather plump. He dropped his bag well away from the car and advanced on Angela, giving her big bear hug.

'I thought I'd better come and show you how to do the job properly,' she chaffed and introduced him to Richard as Archie Gorman, her biologist counterpart from the Bristol Forensic Science Laboratory. The man with him, a younger, slim version of Trevor Mitchell, introduced himself as Detective Inspector Morrison, the liaison officer from the Bristol laboratory. These were detectives seconded for a period from one of the local forces, to act as links between the investigating officers and the scientists.

When everyone knew who was who, they turned their attention back to the job in hand. After Gorman had looked at the body and agreed with Angela and Richard, Tom Spurrel asked the pathologist what he wanted to do next.

'Very hard to do much with him stuck in that seat,' answered Richard. 'Do you want to get him out soon?'

'We've got all the photographs, so just tapings and whatever the lab wants,' answered the superintendent.

'Then we'll haul him out for you.'

The two from the laboratory opened their case and began dabbing lengths of Sellotape across the clothing of the corpse, picking up stray hairs and particles. They stuck these on to sheets of clear celluloid for later examination under the microscope. Then a detective constable who was acting as exhibits officer, carefully retrieved the gun from the floor, pushing the safety catch on with the end of a pencil. Wearing rubber gloves and holding only the edges of the trigger guard to avoid spoiling any fingerprints, he slid it into a brown paper bag, filling in the exhibits label before putting it safely into his own large box.

Now it was Pryor's turn and he tested the stiffness of both arms to look for rigor mortis.

'When was the body found?' he asked.

'About nine o'clock,' said Brian Lane. 'As usual, by a local chap walking his dog. It wasn't here at four this afternoon, as we've found two women who were riding horses up this firebreak then.'

Richard looked at his wristwatch. 'Just half past one now. He's in full rigor, not that that helps a great deal, except to suggest he died more than a couple of hours ago and less than a couple of days.'

With a torch, he looked closely at the wound just above the Adam's apple. 'No soot or powder burns, so it wasn't a contact or very close discharge. A lot depends on the weapon and the ammunition, of course. That's the lab's problem.'

He felt carefully at the back of the head, pushing against the stiffness of the neck. 'No exit wound, though there'd be blood soiling on the upholstery if there had been.'

He felt the face and forehead with the back of his hand.

'Doesn't feel warm, but I need to use the thermometer when we get him out. What's the air temperature, Angela?'

His partner had anticipated what he wanted and had taken a long chemical thermometer from his bag several minutes earlier, allowing time for the mercury to settle.

'It's just fifty degrees here. Better check it inside the car as well, though the door's been open for a time.'

Richard held the thermometer near the body for a minute or two. 'Just the same, fifty degrees,' he said, using the Fahrenheit scale.

The detective inspector and one of the DCs brought a large red rubber sheet and laid it out a few feet away from the car, then carefully hoisted the body out of the driving seat and laid it on the sheet. Due to the stiffness, the head remained bent back and the knees and hips stayed flexed.

Richard rolled the body over on to its side so that the two people from the laboratory could dab their sticky tape over its back and legs, then they carried on examining and taping the driving seat.

Pryor looked all down the back of the corpse and again noted the purple-red discoloration of the back of the neck from settling of the blood after death. He looked up at Spurrel, who was the officer in charge of the investigation.

'I'd like to take a rectal temperature before he cools down any more,' he said. 'Is it alright if I pull his trousers down for a moment?'

The superintendent nodded. 'OK by me, if the lab's happy about it. We've no reason to think there was any sexual involvement.'

Archie interrupted his work inside the car to agree with the detective but as Richard and the liaison officer wrestled with the dead man's belt and trousers, Angela held a swab ready, a test tube with cotton wool wound round the end of a stick stuck in the cork.

'Better use this first, just in case,' she murmured, as the corpse's buttocks were exposed. She did not want to appear as if she was interfering, as officially she was not there as a forensic scientist, except as the pathologist's assistant. Richard took the hint and as Angela held the glass tube, he pulled out the cork and prodded the swab into the victim's fundament. Replacing the swab in the tube, he put the thermometer in its place, two inches deep and waited until the mercury stabilized again.

'Eighty-four degrees,' he announced. 'There's still a bit of warmth to be felt on the backside.'

They hauled up the underpants and trousers and laid the corpse on its back again.

'I can't do any more here, superintendent,' he said. 'Are we taking it straight for a post-mortem?'

Tom Spurrel nodded. 'I'd like to, Doctor, if you can. The mortuary in Gloucester is laid on.'

As the photographer moved in to take more shots of the inside of the car and the body on the ground, the senior detective asked the inevitable question.

'How long do you reckon he's been dead, Doc?'

Richard hated answering this particular query, as where the time of death eventually became known from circumstantial evidence, the pathologist's estimate was almost always wrong, unless he gave a wide range of possibilities.

'It's fairly cool out here now, but we don't know where he was before he was brought here,' he began. 'It's the end of June and it was quite warm earlier today. The car door has been open, presumably since soon after nine.'

He did some mental arithmetic. 'His temperature has dropped about fifteen degrees. The old wisdom was a drop of a degree-and-a-half every hour, but that's always wrong. The problem is that there's often a variable time lag in the fall in temperature soon after death, which makes it impossible to be accurate.'

'So what are you going to tell us?' demanded DI Lane.

'You can't get within a bracket of less than four hours with a cat's chance in hell of being right, so I'm going to say he died between a maximum of twelve hours ago and a minimum of eight – and I wouldn't be surprised if I'm still wrong.'

The detectives did their own rapid calculations.

'It's getting on for two o'clock, so that means between about two yesterday afternoon and six in the evening,' said Spurrel.

'Gives them plenty of time to dump him, before he's found at nine,' commented Lane.

Morrison, the liaison officer, pulled his head out of the car. 'Got anyone in the frame for it, sir?'

Tom Spurrel frowned. 'There's a couple of local villains I fancy for it,' he replied. 'They run the Gloucester and Cheltenham protection rackets and one of our snouts has been telling us that some outsiders have been trying to get in on their act.'

He turned to the pathologist. 'I've spoken to the coroner, he's quite happy for you to do the post-mortem.'

Contrary to what most people thought, though the police could call a doctor to examine a scene of death, they had no power at all to order an autopsy, which was entirely the coroner's prerogative.

'If you want to get along to the hospital mortuary in Gloucester, Doctor, we'll get the body shifted as soon as we can. The undertakers are already here.'

Pryor was happy with this, for he knew that most mortuaries could rustle up a mug of tea at any time of the day or night.

'I'll just see the client into the shell and then we'll be off,' he agreed.

It was the pathologist's responsibility to see that the corpse was removed from the scene without damage or contamination of trace evidence – or if there was any, to check what it was, so that no artefact was misinterpreted at the post-mortem examination.

The two ghostly figures that Angela and he had seen on the way in, had all this while been patiently sitting on their

coffin fifty yards away, smoking and chatting in low voices.
Now they brought over their 'shell', a lightweight box of
five-ply that was used over and over again for collections.
Richard watched as the exhibits officer and the other constable
folded the rubber sheet over the body and secured it with
string, to ensure that no trace evidence fell out in transit.
Then the two undertakers expertly lifted it into the box and
fitted the lid. With a heave, they hoisted it up by its rope
handles and vanished into the dusk, preceded by a police
officer with a torch. When the macabre procession had
vanished into the trees, Richard and Angela followed them
back to their car and soon they were driving through the
silent countryside towards Gloucester, about ten miles down
the A40.

'Being a second string to this area would be an advantage
in getting us established elsewhere,' said Richard. 'If I could
get my name on the Home Office list, it would confirm our
respectability, so to speak.'

Angela laughed. 'I think you're respectable enough now,
Richard – but I know what you mean. Perhaps this superin-
tendent will mention you to his senior officers – and I thought
Brian Meredith also claimed to have some pull.'

The description 'Home Office Pathologist' was a title
beloved of the Press, though it had no great significance.
The Home Office, the ministry responsible for law en-
forcement, kept a list of pathologists in England and Wales
who were willing to assist the police when required. It was
more a matter of geographical convenience than any acco-
lade of expertise and, in some areas, no one wished to be
saddled with the job. It meant being called out at unsocial
hours, spending time in unsavoury conditions, such as
muddy ditches and scruffy mortuaries – and wasting days
in coroner's, magistrates' and assize courts, where they were
harassed by sometimes aggressive barristers. The financial
rewards were derisory, so the glory of having your name
in the newspapers occasionally was the only reason for
doing the job, a fact which tended to attract rather odd
characters. The exceptions were those who had academic
posts in the few university medical schools which still had
a forensic medicine department. This meant that London,

which had a number of such units, did not have 'Home Office Pathologists', as there was no lack of people to compete for the work.

The two partners talked about the situation as they drove along.

'Any regrets yet about taking the plunge, Angela?' asked Pryor, always slightly guilty at encouraging her to give up her safe job in London.

'No, I love driving around the countryside at three in the morning, when I could be tucked up in bed!' she replied flippantly. 'Seriously, it's a challenge. I was getting stale in the Met, every day filled with blood grouping and examining ladies' knickers for stains.'

She looked ahead at the lights of Gloucester appearing ahead of them.

'As long as we can keep our heads financially above water until we get really well established, I'm quite happy. It's a lovely place to live. I was thinking I ought to look for a place of my own, but Garth House is so pleasant, that I'm in no hurry to move out.'

Reassured once again, Pryor concentrated on finding the Royal Hospital and after stopping to ask directions from a policeman flashing his torch into shop doorways, arrived at the mortuary at the back of the large compound.

The attendant, called in on overtime at the coroner's expense, was expecting them and he lived up to Richard's hopes by having a kettle boiling on a gas ring ready to make tea. Soon, Angela and he were sitting in his pokey little office, with mugs of strong tea and even being offered biscuits from a battered tin marked 'Jacobs Cream Crackers'.

By this time, the body had arrived and was lying in its rubber sheet on the post-mortem table. The next arrivals were the photographer and Exhibits Officer, closely followed by the two from the Bristol laboratory. Then the detective inspector came alone, explaining that the superintendent had gone back to Headquarters to get the investigation moving. After more tea had been dispensed, the first mugs being rinsed and reused, everyone adjourned to the post-mortem room and set about their tasks.

The lab people unfolded the sheet and kept it bagged for

later inspection in case anything useful had fallen off during the journey. Then photographs were taken, while Richard set out his instruments and put on a rubber apron and rubber gloves. He directed the photographer, who had a big MPP camera on a tripod, as to the shots he wanted, including front and back of the body and close-ups of the wound in the neck.

The scientist, Archie Gorman, took swabs of the skin around the wound for propellant residues, though Richard again confirmed that there was no burning or tattooing around the very small entrance hole, the diameter of which he measured with a small ruler. The rim of the hole was discoloured, due to the friction of the hot bullet and contamination with oil and metal residues.

'Can't have been either contact or a short range discharge,' he announced to the group who were clustered around. DI Lane, still in his wide hat and raincoat, peered closely at the neck, as Pryor demonstrated the direction of the dried blood which had run from both the wound and the mouth.

'Any idea what the range of the shot would have been, Doc?' he asked.

Richard shrugged at this. 'All depends on the weapon and the charge in the cartridge,' he said. 'I'm afraid that's up to the lab to discover from test firing.'

Archie nodded. 'Probably have to send it off to Birmingham for that, they're the experts on shooters.'

The post-mortem proceeded, everyone knowing their role in the task. The exhibits officer was busy packing and labelling everything that might be needed for evidence, down to samples of blood and urine when Pryor had collected them.

He cut a circle of skin from around the bullet hole and kept it for possible analysis, as the soiling on the edge of the hole might contain substances that could identify a particular batch of ammunition.

Inside the head, the bullet had smashed its way into the thick bone at the base of the skull and had to be recovered. It was essential to retrieve it as intact as possible, so that it could be matched to a given weapon by the marks made on it by the spiral rifling inside the gun barrel.

'It's pretty much flattened, but there's a bit of jacket that is still in fair condition,' said Pryor, as he carefully fished out the missile with a pair of forceps with rubber tubing pushed over the tips, to avoid making false scratches.

The liaison officer packed it in cotton wool to stop it knocking against the glass of the small container in which it would be sent to Birmingham.

'Looks like a "two-two", which would suit the gun from the car,' he commented. Though it seemed almost inevitable that this was the weapon used, nothing could be taken for granted.

'No chance of tightening the time of death, Doctor?' asked Detective Inspector Lane, hopefully.

Richard had taken another rectal temperature before starting to examine the body. 'It's dropped another degree since we were in the woods,' he said, 'but that doesn't really help much. There are so many variables that anyone who claims to be more accurate is just guessing.'

The rest of the hour-long examination revealed little of significance. The stomach contents gave off a strong smell of beer, but there was no food present.

Richard was just about to finish and let the mortuary attendant begin to restore the body, when the door opened and two other men walked in. Once again, their large size and confident bearing marked them out as plain-clothes policemen. Richard happened to be looking at Angela at that moment and saw her face change expression. Her jaw tightened and her cheeks reddened as the first man identified himself.

'Sorry we're late, I'm Detective Superintendent Paul Vickers from the Met – and this is DI Waverley.' The other man nodded, but it was the senior officer who did all the talking. 'Hell of a drive down, pouring with rain until Cheltenham. We've come to see if your chap really is Harry Haines.'

Brian Lane went forward to welcome the superintendent from London and started to introduce the others in the room, but Vickers suddenly saw Angela and seemed to freeze on the spot.

'Good God, Angela!' he said. 'What the devil are you doing here?'

The local DI looked from one to the other. 'You know Dr Bray, then? She came to help Doctor Pryor.'

Angela nodded stonily at the newcomer.

'Hello, Paul,' she said icily. 'How are you?'

He mumbled something and turned his attention quickly to the body on the table. 'This is the chap, then?' he asked unnecessarily.

Pryor, wondering what was going on, stood back so that Paul Vickers could get a good look at the face of the corpse. It took him only a few seconds to confirm the man's identity.

'That's Harry Haines alright,' he said grimly. 'I can't say that he'll be any great loss to London.'

He fell into discussion with the Gloucester detectives about the case and Angela took the opportunity to move to Richard's side.

'Can you give me the keys to the car, please?' she murmured urgently.

'They're in my jacket pocket, hanging out in the office,' he replied. 'Anything you need from it?'

She shook her head. 'I'll wait for you there, this place has suddenly become overcrowded,' she said cryptically and quietly went out of the room.

It was only later, when they were driving out of the hospital grounds that he fully learned the reason for her strange behaviour, though he had begun to guess what had happened.

'Sorry about that, Richard, it wasn't very professional, but I wasn't really doing much in there, anyway.'

He looked sideways at her profile and saw in the dim first light of dawn, that she was staring fixedly ahead.

'Are you alright, Angela?' he asked solicitously. 'Anything I can do to help?'

She shook her head, angry at herself.

'You're a good chap, Richard, but no thanks. It's just me being silly.'

'That was him, wasn't it?' he said gently. 'What a coincidence! Perhaps I shouldn't have dragged you out tonight.'

She laughed more easily, rapidly returning to her normal poise.

'You weren't to know, were you! Yes, that was him, the

unfaithful bastard! Another reason why I'm happy to be out of London.'

She laid a hand briefly on his sleeve, in a rare gesture of affection.

FIFTEEN

Later that morning, Lewis Lewis drove one of the CID cars from Gowerton up to Cardiff, a large brown evidence bag on the passenger seat beside him. His face was set in a frown of concentration, as he tried to work out the possible ramifications of 'the Prentice case', as it had become known in the station. Lewis was a very conscientious officer, having risen through the ranks from the constable who had joined the Force in 1945, directly from his Army service. He had the deep-set eyes, black eyebrows and lean features of many South Walian descendants of the Iberian Celts, who came millennia ago before the bigger, red-headed Brythons. His father, three uncles and both grandfathers had been colliers in the Swansea Valley – he and his schoolteacher brother were the first generation to escape the pits.

Lewis knew the route to the Home Office laboratory well, as he had brought 'exhibits' there many times before. It was situated in a large enclosed estate in Llanishen, a northern suburb of the city. A high metal fence surrounded several acres of land adjacent to the 'ROF', an acronym for the Royal Ordnance Factory where local rumour had it that uranium was processed to make armour-piercing shells.

He turned into an entrance to what was euphemistically called 'The Government Offices', most of which was occupied by the Inland Revenue, who dealt with the tax affairs of all government employees worldwide. When Lewis was in the Second Battalion of the Welsh Regiment in Burma during the war, he always felt it rather comforting that the minute amount of tax deducted from his pay, was calculated back in South Wales!

He showed his warrant card to the gatekeeper and drove up one of the internal roads, past ranks of ugly single-storey brick buildings with flat roofs, looking like bomb-shelters with windows.

Two of them housed the Forensic Science Laboratory and in the small reception area in the nearest, he signed in and then recorded his delivery of his samples on forms given to him by the middle-aged lady behind the desk. He knew her from previous visits and they had the usual chat about the weather and where she was going on holiday next week.

'I'd better have a word with Larry McLoughlin,' he said. 'These are a bit out of the ordinary.' He pointed at the envelope on the counter.

She went to a door behind and a moment later, the liaison officer came out, a DI seconded from the Carmarthenshire Constabulary. They greeted each other, being old acquaintances, then Lewis explained the problem.

'I'll bet you've never had this request before, Larry,' he claimed. 'The super wants two samples of engine oil compared.' He explained the problem and after listening, McLoughlin raised the flap in the counter.

'Better come through and we'll have a word with the eggheads.'

After a quick cup of Nescafé in Larry's office, they went through into the second building, half of which was the toxicology laboratory, filled with benches of glassware, bottles and exotic electrical instruments.

From previous submissions of alcohol and drug samples, Lewis had a nodding acquaintance with Dr Archer, the man who ran this section. He again explained Ben Evans's request to examine the exhibits from Gower.

'This chap's car has got a slight oil leak and he wants to know if he had parked in a particular spot where he shouldn't have been.'

Archer, a tall, stooped man with a small pointed beard, made a sucking noise through his teeth to express doubt.

'I don't know if we can tell one brand of oil from another, Inspector. It might have to go away to some specialist place, like the Shell laboratories.'

Lewis hastened to elaborate on his story and told Archer about the testing of the additive in Prentice's Jaguar.

'Molybdenum sulphide? Bloody hell, that's a new one on me!' exclaimed the chemist, pushing his half-moon spectacles up his long nose. He turned to a bookshelf above a nearby desk and took down a volume from the middle shelf.

'Let's try good old Sherwood Taylor, he usually covers most things.' After running his finger down the index, Archer turned to a page in the middle and began muttering under his breath, Lewis catching words like 'ammonium phosphomolybdate'. Then, closing the book, he turned back to the police officers.

'I think we can make a stab at it,' he said confidently. 'It's not as if we need to measure the concentration at this stage, but just to be able to identify the stuff, eh?'

Lewis agreed, glad that the scientist had not kicked the possibility of helping into touch.

'There's hardly likely to be anyone else in South Wales with molybdenum sulphide in their sumps,' he said. 'Except for the other people in that company and one of their stolen vans. That's something we would have to sort out.'

Leaving the brown envelope with the chemist, he left with the promise that they would try to get a result back to Gowerton within the next week.

After being up all night, Angela Bray took to her bed on returning to Garth House and stayed there until noon, but Richard had to go to Newport to carry out the day's post-mortems. He made some breakfast for himself at about half past six, then wrote out a report on the night's activities to send to the Gloucester coroner and police, when Moira had typed them up. Afterwards he took the opportunity to catch up on some medical journal articles until eight, when he washed, shaved and departed.

Soon afterwards, both Moira and Sian arrived and were intrigued to find a note from Richard telling them that Angela was in bed and that he had gone to Newport.

'Why has she gone to bed?' asked the technician, wondering if her boss was unwell, but Moira soon found the handwritten report on her desk.

'They've been up all night, that's why,' she exclaimed, after scanning the papers. 'They've had a murder!'

This called for an early cup of tea and the two women sat

down in the kitchen to discuss their first definite homicide
with almost an air of pride.

'If we get in with the police, there should be more work
like this,' said Sian eagerly, again identifying strongly with
the partnership.

'Richard will surely have to go to the Assizes with this
one,' said Moira. 'I hope he's got a nice dark British suit for
that, not those funny tropical ones he's so fond of wearing.'

She was very conventional when it came to clothes, either
her own or other people's. Though she dressed nicely, her
tastes were always subdued compared with either Angela,
who was a fashion plate – or Sian, who favoured the young
and trendy. Richard's safari suits, with button-down pockets
and half-belts at the back, made Moira think of big-game
hunters or coffee planters.

Sian immediately came to Pryor's defence.

'I quite like the way he dresses,' she declared. 'Makes him
look younger and more romantic!'

Moira thought that was because Sian wanted to narrow
the age gap between her and her employer. Though the two
women had become good friends, whenever Richard Pryor
was the subject of the conversation, each became a little
possessive, even if they didn't realize it.

The crunch of heavy boots outside the back door heralded
the arrival of Jimmy Jenkins, who seemed to have a sixth
sense for detecting a pot of tea, as he did for a pint of beer.

'Came to have a go at all those weeds in the front,' he
explained. 'Proper disgrace they are, the old lady would have
a fit if she saw them.'

However, he seemed in no hurry to attack the offending
vegetation and sat down for his tea. He even had his own
large mug in the cupboard, obscurely inscribed 'A Present
from Bognor Regis'. The drive down from the house to the
main road was quite steep and ran at the side of a long stretch
of coarse grass, which could hardly be called a lawn. At the
edge adjacent to the gravel drive, there had been a narrow
flower bed, still sporting a few straggling rose bushes, but
since Richard's aunt had died, it was filled with a luxuriant
growth of weeds.

'It would be nice to see it looking tidy again,' said Moira, having known the house when it was kept in excellent condition.

'The doctor would rather have me mess about getting his vineyard ready,' grumbled Jimmy. 'I told him no good will come of that, but he's got his mind set on it.'

Moira rose and washed out her cup at the sink.

'Well, have a go at the front while he's not here,' she advised. 'But keep it quiet, as Doctor Bray is asleep, poor woman. She's been up all night, gallivanting around mortuaries!'

Angela was wide awake by the afternoon, having joined Richard for lunch, for which Moira had prepared a cottage pie, with local potatoes, carrots and peas, followed by strawberries from higher up the valley.

'These are what Jimmy's always telling me to plant instead of vines,' said Richard, liberally pouring cream over his fruit. 'I suppose I'll have to humour him next year, but there's plenty of room for both.'

Sian sometimes felt that she was living in a slightly schizoid world, where murder, suicide, skeletons and blood were discussed alternately with weeding gardens and growing grapes and strawberries. But she enjoyed every minute of it and was determined to get this additional qualification in biochemistry. Then she could help make the laboratory more versatile and hopefully get some more sophisticated equipment to expand their capabilities.

They talked about the midnight escapade into the Gloucestershire forest and Richard explained the reasons for declaring it a murder, not a suicide.

'The blood and the lividity showed that the chap must have been lying down after the shooting, but before he was propped up in the driving seat,' he said. 'But apart from that, the pistol must have been fired from well over a foot away, possibly a yard or more, so unless he had abnormally long arms, he couldn't have shot himself!'

'How could you tell that?' demanded Sian, who always wanted to have cast-iron reasons.

'When a gun is fired, all sorts of gunk comes out of the muzzle, apart from the bullet,' said Pryor. 'Flame, soot and unburned propellant. I admit there's a huge difference in how far these things travel, depending on the type of gun and the type of ammunition, but suicides are usually contact or near-contact wounds, as the person tends to press the muzzle against the skin. Here there was nothing except a clean hole.'

Moira wanted to know what was the background to the killing, but Richard had not much to tell her.

'We pathologists often don't get to know all the details, as we may never hear any more about the case for a year, until it comes to trial,' he complained. 'And then, if there's a guilty plea or the evidence is uncontested, we may never even be called to court and never hear a damn thing more.'

Angela remained very quiet and Pryor guessed that she was thinking of the unexpected visitor in the mortuary that morning. Later that evening, they sat in her room having a gin and tonic, which was now becoming a routine to unwind after the day's work. The rain had cleared off and through the bay window, the valley could be seen in its green beauty once again.

They both knew that each of them was thinking of the same thing, but Richard wisely held his tongue until she brought up the subject.

'I'm sorry I was so tiresome in Gloucester this morning, Richard,' she said quietly. 'But it was a bit of shock to see him just appear like that.'

'I could see that you were upset,' he said lamely. 'Is there no chance that you might get back together?'

She shook her head vigorously. 'Not the slightest! He did the dirty on me for months and was too cowardly to tell me. He just walked away one day, as if I'd never existed.'

'Has he married her – or is he going to?'

'I don't know – and I don't damned well care,' she said fiercely. 'As far as I'm concerned, he can go to hell.'

Richard felt it was time to change the subject and he turned the conversation to the two other cases in which they were involved.

'It looks as if Mrs Oldfield's crusade has run into the sand,' he observed. 'Unless she finds another set of bones for us to look at.'

'I don't see what else can be done,' replied Angela, glad

that the previous topic had been suppressed. 'If her nephew's blood group could be found, and was different to the bones, then at least she would have to give up.'

He sipped his gin reflectively. 'A pity there isn't some characteristic in tissues that's absolutely unique to every single person. I expect it'll come one day.'

'But not in our time, Richard,' she sighed. 'Is there nothing else in those bones that would help?

'Not a hope! Even if we had the head for dental identity or frontal sinus pattern, without the corresponding data on dear Anthony, we'd be no further forward.'

Their talk shifted to the Gower drowning.

'I wonder what's happening down there, they've gone very quiet,' said Angela.

Richard repeated what he had said to Moira. 'That's the trouble, once the pathologist has shot his bolt, that's often the last we ever hear of it, unless we read about in the *Western Mail.*'

He finished his drink and stood up. 'I remember in Singapore, giving evidence in court, then never even knowing whether the accused was convicted or not, unless I happened to see it in the *Straits Times.*'

Angela nodded. 'I know what you mean, it used to happen to us in the Met Lab. But I'd still like to know what those Swansea bobbies are up to.'

SIXTEEN

Those Swansea bobbies had plenty of other work to occupy them for the next few days, while they waited for a response from the Forensic Laboratory. They decided to hang fire on most aspects of the case, though Lewis Lewis did go across to Porthcawl and interview Daphne Squires, whose address he had obtained from Trevor Mitchell.

It was a fruitless exercise, as the blonde hotly denied any knowledge of anything, apart from being a 'friend' of Michael Prentice, which she stridently proclaimed as being the right of any British citizen. No, she had never met or even seen Michael's wife, as she had never been to the house until after her death. No, she knew nothing of any strife between them, though she did admit to knowing that he was seeking a divorce.

She certainly knew nothing about any physical violence taking place and she managed to distance herself so well from the man that it sounded as if she hardly knew him.

Lewis gave up the struggle before long and drove home in disgust at a wasted journey. Ben Evans had considered sending Lewis on up to Reading to interview Marjorie Elphington, the friend to whom the dead woman had written the letter that had started all this – but he decided that unless and until the case was a 'runner', it would be a waste of the inspector's time.

The ball was now in the court of Dr Archer, the chemist, and knowing of the case overload from which all the forensic laboratories suffered, Ben Evans and Lewis Lewis settled down for a long wait, as many police requests took weeks to come back.

However, the unusual nature of their problem played in their favour, as Archer was intrigued by an analysis that he was certain none of his colleagues in the other six Home Office labs had ever come across. The scientist even thought he might give a talk about it sometime at one of their regular scientific meetings. He read up more about molybdenum and decided that a 'spot test' was a fairly straightforward procedure, just to determine if any of the substance was present.

Archer even gave up his Saturday morning to come in and start playing about with the methods described in the manuals and on Monday, he finished off the analysis.

By the afternoon, he was able to ask the liaison officer to phone Gowerton with the result. Lewis took the call and moments later, came into Ben Evans's cramped office next to the CID room.

'Here's what you want, boss! The lab have broken all records this time.'

He put a page from a message pad in front of the superintendent. Evans picked it up and read Lewis's neat handwriting aloud.

'All three samples contain molybdenum sulphide. Two control samples of similar commercial motor oil are free from that substance. Written confirmation to follow.'

Ben laid the note back on the table and looked up at his inspector. 'The bastard! Let's see how he explains this one away!'

Lewis Lewis was not so enthusiastic about the significance of the discovery.

'So now we know his Jaguar was parked on the cliff above where his wife's body was found. But he can wriggle out of that, surely?'

Evans hoisted himself out of his chair and reached for his hat on top of a filing cabinet.

'Well, let's go and see what fairy tales he'll spin us this time.'

As it was still too early to expect Michael Prentice to have returned from his office, the two detectives drove past his house in Pennard and carried on until they reached the spot where the oil leak had been found.

Lewis parked the Vauxhall a little further on and they walked back, the long slope running way down to the rocks on their left. The sky had scudding clouds and there was a stiff breeze, but it was still a pleasant day to be by the sea.

Ben Evans scanned the ground at the edge of the stony track and his broad brow furrowed as he failed to find the black smudge which had been sampled the previous week.

'Where the hell's it gone?' he muttered to himself. Realizing that he had overshot the spot, he turned around and bent almost double, retraced his steps.

Suddenly he stopped and beckoned to Lewis, who was watching his boss imitating a bloodhound.

'Come and look at this! The silly fool, hasn't he learned that when you're in a hole, you stop digging!'

The inspector came across and stooped to see what the senior officer was pointing at.

'That was the rock, you can see that rubbed-off white tip where the sump dragged across it. But most of the black stuff has gone!'

Lewis saw that a six-inch strip of limestone looked cleaner than the surrounding rock, but there were still hair-like streaks of black visible.

Ben Evans straightened up, his hands on his hips.

'He's used a wire brush on it, the idiot! If he'd left it alone, he might have got away with some excuse.'

'We'll have to get this photographed again,' said the inspector. 'Then the "before and after" difference can be proved.'

They walked back to their car and drove back to Southgate village. As the car they had taken from the transport pool had no radio, Lewis telephoned Divisional Headquarters and arranged for a scene photographer to come out, for they did not want someone to drive over the rock and obliterate the evidence. As he came out of the phone box, he saw a black Mk IV Jaguar drive past and in a leisurely fashion, they followed it back to *Bella Capri*.

Prentice was just closing the garage when they arrived, after having put the car inside. As Evans walked up towards him, he noticed that the hardstanding outside the garage also appeared to have been cleaned, though a faint discoloration from dropped oil was still visible.

'My God, you lot again!' snarled Michael. 'What d'you want this time?'

The superintendent jabbed a finger towards the concrete.

'Your car leaks oil, by the looks of it.'

Prentice scowled. 'Yes, it did, a little. I had my fitters tighten the sump bolts today, as it happens.'

'A bit too late, I'm afraid, sir,' said Evans easily.

'What do you mean by that?' demanded the other man, though he had a dreadful feeling that he knew where this was leading.

'When we questioned you the other day, you said you walked almost to Pwlldu, when you were looking for your wife on the evening she disappeared.'

'What about it?'

'You said *walked*, not drove.'

'Did I? I don't really remember which it was. I was worried and confused,' said Prentice, desperately trying to fudge the issue.

Ben Evans waited a moment before delivering his knockout blow.

'If you don't remember, why have you been down there since and used a wire brush to try to remove the oil stain you left?'

'I don't know what you're talking about!' blustered Michael. 'Scores of cars use this track, there are oil drips everywhere.'

'Not ones with molybdenum sulphide in them, sir.'

Prentice looked like a stag at bay, but he made one final attempt. 'That van that was stolen – it could have been that.'

'You mean the thief was trying to return it to you at your home?' suggested Lewis, sarcastically.

Prentice stared at him desperately. 'It could have been one of my staff, they all have to test the stuff. Yes, that'll be it, one of my engineers came out to see me not long ago, it must have been him.'

'In that case, we'll interview them all, and see if any went and parked half a mile away,' replied Lewis remorselessly.

'If it was your engineer, why do you think he came all the way back here with a wire brush to clean up the drip?' asked Ben Evans. 'Come on, sir, don't play silly buggers with us, we all know you drove over to that cove where your wife's body was found. What were you doing there?'

Ben had bet his inspector a packet of Gold Flake that Prentice would yell for his solicitor at this point, but he lost the wager. The new widower's face became ashen and he seemed to crumple. A tall man, he suddenly became bowed, as he buried his face in his hands.

Then he recovered and groped in his pocket for his keys.

'You'd better come inside, there's something I must show you.'

Mystified by the turn of events, but still suspicious of the man, Ben Evans and his assistant followed him into the room on the left of the hallway. No one sat down and they watched him carefully as he went to a small table and pulled open a drawer.

'You'd better read this,' he said dully, handing the super-intendent a folded sheet of paper. Lewis moved closer so that he could also see it. It was typed and quite short.

> *Michael, I cannot go on like this. You have betrayed*
> *me with that woman, as you have done so often before.*
> *You have been cruel and violent and now I know you*
> *have never loved me. Life is no longer worth living, so*
> *I shall end it in the place I have found so much pleasure.*
> *Linda*

Evans placed the letter on the table, carefully avoiding touching it other than by the edge he had been gripping. If he had known what it was, he would not have handled it, to avoid adding to any more fingerprints.

'Are you now trying to tell us that your wife committed suicide?' he demanded, with incredulity in his voice.

Prentice nodded, standing head bowed and with his hands behind his back, like an errant schoolboy before the headmaster.

'I found that in the typewriter when I came home that evening,' he said in a low voice.

'It's all typed, there's no signature!' rasped Lewis. 'You could easily have written it yourself.'

Michael looked up, then slowly shook his head.

'But I didn't, believe me. It was waiting for me when I came home.'

Lewis hauled out a notebook and a pen, as the senior officer began his questioning.

'Start at the beginning, please. Tell us exactly what happened. You'll have to make a full statement later, but that will be at the police station.'

Prentice gave a great sigh and rubbed his eyes with a handkerchief before answering.

'I came home late, about ten o'clock and called out as usual, but had no reply. I looked in here and in the kitchen and called up the stairs without any response. Then I walked into the other room across the hall and saw that the cover was off the typewriter. This sheet of paper was still wound on to the roller.'

He spoke in a dull monotone, unlike his usual confident and often hectoring style.

'Then what?' prompted the senior officer.

'I couldn't take it in at first. I poured myself a drink and sat down in a daze. Then I thought it was some cruel hoax she was playing on me, to get even.'

'Get even for what? The note says you physically abused her, which is confirmed by the pathologist.'

Prentice rubbed a hand fiercely across his mouth.

'That was no big deal! I admit I grabbed her once and shook her, when she was ranting on to me about Daphne. She repeatedly refused to even consider a divorce and I lost my rag a bit, but I wasn't beating her up, for God's sake! It was just temper.'

Evans had his own ideas about that, but he carried on with his questions. 'What did you do then?'

Michael sank down onto the nearest chair and sat on the very edge.

'She said "the place that's given me most pleasure" so I knew she meant the little beach below the house. I rushed out and though it was starting to get dusk by then, I went down the path opposite, to the edge of the sea. The tide was out and that little bit of sand was showing in the gully.'

He stopped and dropped his face back into his hands.

'So what did you find?' persisted Evans, whose heart was not softened by the man's apparent distress.

'She was lying there, rolling in the surf just at the water's edge.'

'Dressed in her bathing costume, was she?' interposed Lewis.

Prentice nodded. 'The blue one, she had several. Her hair was streaming back and forth, as the small waves pushed at her. I knew she was dead.'

'So did you try to revive her?' grated Ben Evans.

The widower lifted his head. 'Of course I did!' he said hoarsely, with a hint of anger in his voice. 'I waded in and picked her up, but I could tell she was gone, as she was so limp. I carried her out and put her face down on the beach and started squeezing her back, though I knew it was pointless.'

'Did you know how to give artificial respiration?' asked Lewis. Prentice shook his head. 'Not really, I've never been taught. But it was just a gesture anyway, she was long dead.'

'Then what happened?' demanded Evans, in a tone that suggested that he didn't believe a word of it.

'I gave up pumping her back, all I was doing was forcing up froth from her mouth and nose. I decided to carry her back up here to the house.'

'Didn't you think it better to run for help – send for an ambulance or a doctor?' snapped Lewis.

Prentice raised his face to look up at the detective inspector. 'What would be the point? I knew she was dead. I just wanted to get her home.'

'Was there anyone about who could have seen you?' asked Evans.

'No, it was getting late and almost dark. I had a job stumbling back up the path, especially carrying her in my arms.'

'It takes a big stretch of the imagination to accept that you could get back up that rough slope lugging your wife's body,' grunted Lewis.

'I'm a big chap, officer – and Linda was very short and slim . . . and desperation lends strength.'

'Yes, I'm sure you were desperate enough,' said Ben Evans, cynically. 'So tell us the next part of this unlikely story.'

'It's not unlikely at all!' cried Michael, with another flash of anger. 'I brought her into the house and laid her on that settee.' He pointed dramatically at a velvet-covered sofa against the opposite wall. 'I fact, you can still see the dried stain where she leaked sea water from her mouth over the cushion.'

Neither officer took him up on his invitation to examine it, though Lewis made a note in his book.

'I sat shivering and confused, then had a stiff drink and thought about what I should do.'

'What you should have done was to run to the phone and call a doctor, ambulance and the police,' said Evans, sardonically.

'So how did the poor woman get back into the sea?' added Lewis Lewis.

Prentice took a deep breath and then sighed. 'I took her there in the car, of course. I must have sat thinking for a couple of hours, too afraid to call anyone.'

'And why was that?' demanded the superintendent.

'She had left a note saying it was all my fault and then gone and killed herself. How would I look when all that came out? She would be just as dead if it was thought to be an accident.'

'So it was your callous need to protect your good name?' snapped Evans.

'And *her* reputation and the feelings of her family. It avoided the stigma of suicide, and having that note read out at an inquest. It might just as well be called an accident, a swim which went tragically wrong.'

'From what I've heard, the feelings of her family, especially her father, weren't very high in your list of priorities!' retorted the detective.

'It seemed the best solution at the time,' muttered Prentice, sullenly.

'So what was the next act in this remarkable drama?' demanded Ben Evans.

'It must have been gone midnight before I made up my mind what to do,' muttered Prentice. 'I wrapped her in a blanket and put her in the boot of the Jaguar. There was no one about, so I drove down towards Pwlldu and stopped where that bloody oil must have leaked out.'

'Then you just carted your dead wife down the path and chucked her into the sea,' said Evans harshly.

'Why go to all that trouble?' asked Lewis. 'She was already in the water back nearer the house. One bit of sea is much the same as another, if you want to drown.'

Michael swung his head from side to side, as if he was a bull being baited by dogs.

'I don't know, I just don't know!' he groaned. 'I had brought her up to the house on impulse, it seemed the right thing to bring her home, not leave her almost naked on that lonely beach. Then when I decided to put her back in the water, I thought that deeper water near the headland might take her out to sea.'

'Oh, charming! You wanted to save yourself the cost of a funeral, did you?' snapped the superintendent.

'What difference would it make, if you were fabricating an accident?' contributed Lewis.

Michael Prentice grabbed at his hair with both hands.

'I don't know, I tell you!' he shouted. 'I can hardly remember that awful night, I came back here and drank half a bottle of whisky!'

'So what about your wife's dressing gown – the one found under a bush?' asked Evans, remorselessly.

'I don't even remember seeing it that evening,' grated the husband. 'It was found where it should have been, I suppose. I don't know where she usually left it while she was in the water.'

Evans looked at his inspector, who closed his notebook.

Then he turned back to Michael, who was still sitting on the edge of the chair, staring at the carpet.

'Mr Prentice, we're going to take you back to the police station in Gowerton now, where for a start, you'll be formally charged with obstructing Her Majesty's coroner in the pursuance of his duties. Other charges may follow in due course.'

Michael Prentice rose slowly to his feet, his face drained of all colour. 'I want to telephone my solicitor,' he said dully.

'You'd better do that from here, and ask him to arrange representation for you at Gowerton as soon as possible. You won't be going home tonight, I can assure you, so you'd better collect a few things in a bag now.'

He nodded at Lewis to accompany the man to his bedroom,

in case he either tried to make a run for it or even cut his wrists.

As the inspector passed his boss on the way out of the room, he murmured 'You still owe me twenty Gold Flake.'

SEVENTEEN

A couple of days later, Trevor Mitchell called at Garth House, perhaps not altogether accidentally at the time of their afternoon tea break. He sat with the team in the staff room and brought several items of news.

'The first thing will probably make you groan,' he said, as he accepted a McVities Digestive from the biscuit tin.

'I've tracked down Anthony Oldfield's blood group at last.'

'Don't tell me,' said Angela, with a sigh. 'He was A-Positive?'

The private detective nodded. 'Murphy's Law, I suppose, though it is very common.'

'How did you find out?' asked Moira.

'The obvious way, I suppose. Mrs Oldfield couldn't find a donor card in the stuff her nephew left behind in the house, but that didn't necessarily mean that he had never given blood.'

'So you went to the BTS records,' suggested Angela. 'Would they give you confidential medical information?'

'I got a letter from Edward Lethbridge explaining the problem and one from Mrs Oldfield giving her consent as next of kin. As some people have it engraved on a bracelet or tattooed on their arm, it's not all that confidential, anyway. The problem was that there are quite a number of Blood Transfusion Service centres and each keeps it own records, unless the groups are very rare and needed for making antisera.'

'And you struck lucky – or unlucky, depending on how you look at it!' said Richard.

'Yes, after a few false starts, I tried the Bristol centre, who turned up a record of Anthony Cyril Oldfield who was a single-time donor back in 1947.'

There was a thoughtful silence as they digested the implications.

'There's nothing more we can do about it,' said Angela

eventually. 'The coroner isn't going to get very excited about a marker that exists in about thirty-five per cent of the British population.'

Trevor's broad face creased into a grin. 'And who's going to convince Agnes Oldfield of that?' he asked.

'But while you're worrying about that, I've got a bit more news. Have you seen this morning's *Western Mail*?'

Moira lifted a folded copy from the chair beside her.

'I've only looked at the headlines so far – why?'

Trevor leaned back on his chair, his bulk making it creak.

'Inside, you'll see a short report of a hearing yesterday at Gowerton Magistrates' Court. "*Swansea Industrialist remanded on charges of obstructing the coroner*", but there are no details worth talking about.'

Richard leaned forward, intensely interested.

'What's it all about, Trevor? They haven't charged him with murder, have they?'

The former police officer shook his head. 'I rang Ben Evans, I've known him for years. He gave me the bare bones of it, there'll be a lot more to come.'

Mitchell passed on what the Gowerton superintendent had told him, that Prentice had claimed that his wife had killed herself and that he had suppressed the suicide note to make it look like an accident.

'Then he dropped her back in the sea at a different place! Ben doesn't believe a word he said, but the lawyers are going to have a field day with this.'

Moira and Sian were agog with excitement at this first major case they had become involved with and their house-keeper hurried to open her newspaper and find the report. The headline on the second page was prominent, but the actual content was notable only for its brevity.

'It says he was released on bail until the next appearance in two weeks' time,' announced Moira in a somewhat disappointed voice. 'I thought he would have been locked up until the trial.'

'So did Ben Evans,' agreed Trevor. 'Prentice must have a pretty persuasive solicitor. The father-in-law will be spitting tacks at the fact that Prentice wasn't held on remand.'

'I suppose obstructing the coroner isn't exactly a capital

offence,' observed Angela. 'Richard, you'll be called as a witness for the prosecution in this case, as it was you who confirmed the bruises. They are bound to go into that aspect.'

Trevor nodded his agreement. 'No doubt about it. I expect Ben Evans will be in touch with you soon, the prosecution will probably have a conference, before the full preliminary proceedings.'

'I wonder if the defence will want their own autopsy?' said Pryor. 'That would be the third, but they're still entitled to one.'

Later that afternoon in the front laboratory, Sian was still excited about the increase in their workload.

'We've had a mass of stuff from Doctor Pryor's fortnight in Newport, as well as the Chepstow and Monmouth cases. I'll have to start a proper filing system for these microscope slides and tissue blocks. And now we've had two murders in the same week!'

Angela smiled at her enthusiasm. 'Hold on, we don't know what the Swansea case is going to turn out to be. The chap is only charged with a technical offence, not the violence.'

She relented when she saw that her technician looked a little crestfallen. 'But the Gloucester one is real gangster-style – and with the Gower body, you played an important part in making such nice sections for Richard to base his opinion on concerning those bruises.'

This cheered Sian up and she went off to her microtome humming happily. The mention of the shooting the other night brought back to Angela the image of Paul Vickers marching unexpectedly into the mortuary. Though she had firmly closed the door on that unpleasant episode, she was often depressed about the fact that life was passing her by when it came to romance – and yes, to her sex life, or rather lack of it.

The years were passing all too quickly and she wasn't getting any younger. Though she had no burning desire to jump into marriage and motherhood, she missed the social life she had with Paul, even though he turned out to be a rat. She determined to get about more, maybe join a golf club or go riding or do something to meet people. Yet she was enjoying this relaxed life in the Wye Valley and it would be an effort to start 'putting herself about' more. With a sigh, she rolled her laboratory stool nearer the bench and got down to more paternity tests, her trade having increased as the reputation of Garth House spread ever more widely.

Trevor Mitchell was right when he forecast that Richard would be required at a conference about Linda Prentice's death. Ben Evans phoned him the next day and more or less repeated what Trevor had revealed.

'You'll learn all the details next week, Doc,' said the superintendent. 'The prosecuting solicitor wants a meeting in his office in Swansea next Tuesday, as the case is coming before the magistrates again the following week and we want to oppose an extension of bail. I don't see why the bastard should be walking the streets when I'm sure he killed his wife.'

'Is he going to be charged with murder?' asked Richard

'I don't know, that's what's got to be discussed next week. It will need the consent of the DPP to send this to trial.'

The 'DPP' was the Director of Public Prosecutions and as he was in London, it was a cumbersome business dealing with major offences. The lesser cases were handled by local solicitors who acted as agents for the police, but the big stuff had to be considered by the famous offices in St Anne's Gate, Westminster.

At the urging of the three women in the house, Richard had gone to Cardiff and bought a ready-made suit in Evan Roberts, an outfitters opposite the castle. It was of dark grey flannel, double-breasted and with wide lapels. Though he preferred his 'big white hunter' outfits, which had served him well in the Singapore courts, he had to give into Angela's pleas for him to have more of the Spilsbury look when appearing professionally. He drew the line at the wide-brimmed trilbies favoured by police and newspaper men and instead decided on a smart Homburg with a rolled brim to go to the conference in Swansea.

As the solicitor's office was in a busy street, he again decided to use Jimmy Jenkins as a chauffeur and at two o'clock, he was dropped outside a large Edwardian house in St Helen's Road, near Swansea General Hospital. Jimmy promised to pick him up at four o'clock and to cruise around if he was later than that.

He was shown into a spacious upstairs room, where the prosecuting solicitor, Maldwyn Craddock, was presiding from behind a large desk. Craddock was a very fat man, his neck bulging over his collar and his pink face rounded by comfortable living. He had sparse silver hair parted in the middle above a misleadingly jovial face with blue eyes and a small purse-like mouth.

Already ranged before him on hard chairs were Ben Evans, Lewis Lewis, Dr O'Malley and the Gowerton coroner, Donald Moses. Richard took the empty seat next to the other pathologist and after being greeted cordially by Maldwyn Craddock, the lawyer got straight down to the main issues.

'Right, gentlemen, I need to know what we are charging Michael Prentice with next week. At the first hearing, it was only a charge of obstructing the coroner, but are we going to be able to improve on that, given that the DPP agrees?'

Donald Moses looked a little put out at this.

'It's not a trivial offence, Maldwyn, like riding a bike without lights!' he complained. 'For a start, it's made a nonsense of my original inquest verdict of accident. It will all have to be done again and the paperwork chased up to London and back.'

The fat lawyer held up a conciliatory hand. 'I wasn't belittling it, Donald. Just wanting to know if we can turn the screw a bit more, so to speak. Mr Evans, what's the position from where you're sitting?'

'I think Prentice is lying through his teeth, sir. Why would he carry the body all the way up one cliff, then drive half a mile and carry it down another? And this suicide note sounds phoney to me.'

'And why go to the trouble of wire-brushing his oil leak off the track?' added Lewis Lewis.

Craddock nodded benignly. 'But our problem is proof! We would need enough to convince the magistrates to send him for trial for murder or manslaughter – and to be frank, we haven't got there yet. Already he has to be committed to the assizes on the obstructing of the coroner's charge – and possibly the DPP might crank that up to 'perverting the course of justice', but homicide is a different kettle of fish! What about this suicide note, Superintendent?'

Evans shifted his bulk on the uncomfortable seat. 'Inspector Lewis has already taken it up to Cardiff. The lab there is the acknowledged document examination centre for the whole country. We want to know who typed the letter, the wife or the husband.'

'Will they be able to tell us?' asked the solicitor.

'The problem is that though there's no doubt that it was typed on the machine in the house, that's not the issue,' answered Lewis, who had spoken at length to the expert in Cardiff. 'I was told that differentiating between two typists is very difficult. It depends on things like the heaviness of keystrokes, the repetition of mistakes and the style of writing, but it's not an exact science, unlike comparing defects in the machine itself.'

Ben Evans nodded his agreement. 'We've got samples from both of them from typed documents we found in the house and Inspector Lewis has taken those, together with the actual typewriter, up to the laboratory. We now have to wait for their opinion.'

They discussed this for a while, Lewis pointing out that Linda had been a trained secretary before her marriage.

'It gives us a better chance of proving whether or not she wrote it, as she would have a more professional style, rather than the amateur two-finger bashing that someone like her husband would be likely to use.'

'What about fingerprints?' asked Craddock.

'Of no use, sir,' replied Ben Evans. 'Both the letter and the typewriter keys have got plenty of both their prints on them. They both used the machine in the house long before this affair, that's where we got these sample letters and carbons. And as for the actual suicide note, he admits having the body in the house, so he could just have pressed her fingers all over it.'

The prosecuting solicitor moved on to another aspect.

'Tell me about this oil business?' he asked.

The superintendent turned up his hands. 'It was a nice piece of detection, but now that Prentice has admitted driving to the place where his wife's body was recovered, it doesn't matter so much, except to raise the question of why he lied about it and why he felt so vulnerable that he went and tried to scrub it off.'

Craddock was making notes on a yellow legal pad in front of him.

'Yes, that's a very telling point, of course. Tied in with the fact that he moved the body from one bit of sea to another, it's so far the only hint we've got that he might have killed her. But it's still not proof and I'm damned if I can see why he did it!'

Richard Pryor sat quietly in his new suit, listening to the exchanges. This was police business and had nothing to do with him, but it was intriguing stuff, all the same.

Eventually, Craddock got around to the medical aspects. He turned to Patrick O'Malley first.

'Doctor, it seems there is absolutely no doubt that Linda Prentice drowned?'

The Irishman, who seemed to be trying to remain as inconspicuous as possible, hastily agreed.

'As far as I'm concerned, yes, she died of drowning. But I make no claims at being a forensic chap, that's Doctor Pryor's province.'

'You made no particular reference to the bruises on her body?' asked the lawyer, mildly.

O'Malley looked uncomfortable. 'Well, I knew she had been recovered from a rocky part of the coast and most of the injuries were scratches from that. I assumed the bruises were from the same cause.'

'But I understand that you can't bruise a dead body?'

'She would have been alive for a time in the water, until she drowned. She could bruise against the rocks then,' said the pathologist, rather evasively.

'You didn't carry out the tests under microscope that Dr Pryor did?' asked Craddock, smiling indulgently. 'You see, Doctor, I'm trying to anticipate the questions the defence will no doubt put to you, if the Director of Public Prosecutions decides to run this for murder.'

O'Malley admitted that he had not thought it necessary, given that he had been told the death was accidental, but he readily agreed with what he knew of Pryor's interpretation.

Craddock gave up tormenting O'Malley and turned to Richard.

'A rather unusual situation, Doctor Pryor! Here you are, a private expert retained by the family, yet now you may have been transformed into a prosecution witness.'

Richard matched his smile in return.

'That's how it goes, Mr Craddock. Facts are facts, whoever commissions me.'

The prosecuting solicitor then went through Richard's statement in minute detail, questioning every piece of evidence until he was sure he knew its significance. The bruises were the focus of his interest and especially the dating and location of these injuries.

'So in summary, they are a mixture of ages, Doctor, suggesting that they were inflicted over a period?'

'Certainly not in one episode,' replied Richard cautiously. 'I can't give you exact timings, but some were probably of the order of a week or two, others were more than a day or so – and a few were so fresh that they could have been inflicted during the previous day or as Dr O'Malley said, even in the water immediately before death.'

He added the last as a compassionate sop to reduce the other pathologist's discomfiture.

'And you are also quite happy that the cause of death was drowning?' was the final question, to which Pryor had no difficulty in giving a positive answer.

After some more general discussion, the lawyer laid down his pen and squared up the yellow pad on the desk in front of him.

'I'm not sure where this leaves us, gentlemen,' he said, his smile having vanished now. 'I'm not all that optimistic about being able to push the charges beyond obstructing the coroner and wasting police time. We might be able to jack it up to "perverting the course of justice" but as for murder, I can't see much hope of that.'

He fiddled with his pen again. 'It will be up to the DPP and no doubt he'll consider all the papers and perhaps brief Counsel to give an opinion. Even if the magistrates would wear it and commit him for trial, I can't see a judge letting that charge go to the jury as it stands, on the evidence we have so far.'

'What if the letter proves to have been written by Prentice?' growled Ben Evans, reluctant to let his instincts be confounded. 'What earthly reason would he have for writing a false suicide note, other than to cover up a homicide?'

Craddock bobbed his head in agreement.

'It would indeed be a telling point, but is it enough to send a man to the gallows? And Inspector Lewis told us that determining who typed a given document is not a straight-forward exercise, it has a lot of subjective opinion about it. Much would depend on the strength of the document examiner's evidence, as opposed to a defence expert, who I am sure would be called to challenge him.'

Richard Pryor sat listening to the lawyer demolishing his own case, but recognized that this was the sensible thing to do. It was no good going to court with flimsy evidence that a competent defence counsel could shoot down in flames. Maldwyn Craddock made one final resumé of the situation.

'We have a man who is having an affair with another woman. His wife finds out and they have a stormy period. He wants a divorce and she refuses so he becomes violent on at least one occasion, gripping her arms and probably her throat. This is corroborated by the letter she writes to her friend.'

He paused to drink from a glass of water on his desk.

'Then she is found dead in the sea, which is assumed to be an accident. After his car is proved to have been standing further along the cliff, the husband admits that he has suppressed a suicide note, which may or may not be genuine.'

He stopped and looked along the faces in front of him, his eyebrows raised in an invitation to comment.

The detective superintendent was the first to respond.

'That's about the measure of it, Mr Craddock. A lot will depend on the strength of the document examiner's opinion on who wrote that note.'

Donald Moses, the coroner who had been largely silent until now, agreed with Ben Evans. 'In my opinion, every-thing hangs on that note. If the death was an accident, why on earth try to make it look like a suicide? The only conclusion is that he's trying to cover up the fact that somehow he killed her.'

The prosecuting solicitor drummed his fingers restlessly on the edge of his desk.

'Agreed, but how did he kill her? Doctor Pryor, have you ever heard of someone being carried alive and then thrown into the sea to drown? Especially as it seems she was an experienced swimmer.'

Richard shook his head. 'It seems very improbable. The only way would be if she was drugged or drunk. We did an alcohol on her urine and it was negative. We still have a blood sample in our fridge, perhaps it had better go to the forensic laboratory in Cardiff for drugs screening.'

'What if she was knocked out first?' suggested Lewis Lewis. 'There was an injury to the back of her head, wasn't there?'

Richard nodded. 'There was a recent bruise under the back of the scalp, yes! Impossible to say whether or not it would have rendered her unconscious or not.'

'Remind me, was that a fresh injury, Doctor?' asked Craddock.

'Fresh, in the sense of being within a day before death,' replied Richard. 'We originally assumed that it was from being banged against the rocks, which in an accidental scenario, could account for a good swimmer being drowned.'

The solicitor nodded his fleshy head. 'That's certainly what any defence counsel would allege – and I presume you couldn't deny it?'

He did not wait for an answer but again surveyed the others in the room.

'So it looks as if we'll have to run with what we've got, unless something new turns up before the preliminary hearing. Prentice has confessed to the suppression of the letter, so he can't dodge that, but we may have to be content with whatever sentence that brings.'

EIGHTEEN

I t was the beginning of the following week before Garth
House heard anything from Gloucester about the shooting.
Brian Lane, the detective inspector they had met in the
woods, rang to say that they had made an arrest and that the
defence had requested a second post-mortem.

'We collared a villain from Bristol who admits shooting
Harry Haines, but he's claiming it was in self-defence. There
was a confrontation between a gang from Bristol, who reckon
they own the rights to bribery, corruption and protection
rackets in the South West, and Haines's mob from
Bermondsey, who want to take a share of the graft. They
were in the car park of a country pub near Gloucester that
afternoon when it got violent and they went chasing off into
the woods behind. This ruffian we've got locked up claims
Haines pulled a shooter on him, and he fired in self-defence.
Not clear about the range, but as you said, it wasn't close.
The London gang scarpered and a couple of the local thugs
drove Haines's body down to where we found him and stuck
him in his car. It was a half-hearted attempt to make it look
like a suicide, but none of them are bright enough to do it
properly.'

'So what about this second post-mortem?' asked Richard.

'His solicitor is getting Professor Millichamp down from
London on Wednesday afternoon,' replied the detective. 'So
would it be convenient for you to attend the mortuary then,
to represent the police?'

Though second autopsies were usually performed quite
amicably between the two pathologists, they always kept a
wary eye on each other's findings. Richard knew of Arnold
Millichamp by name, though he had never met him. He was
a pathologist of the old school, attached to St Bartholomew's
Hospital. Always sure of himself and never in doubt, he had
a reputation for dogmatic inflexibility, especially in the
witness box. Still, thought Pryor, there was not much he

could disagree about in this case – the chap was shot in the neck from a distance, end of story. But an hour later, he had a further surprise when Millichamp's secretary telephoned. Sian happened to take the call and instead of switching the phone through on their new GPO system, which had at last been installed, she hurried down the passage to his room and poked her head around the door.

'It's a lady from London,' she hissed, though the caller could not have heard her as Richard's phone was firmly in its cradle. 'A professor's personal assistant, she sounds very posh!'

When he spoke to her, he had to agree that her Thames Valley accent was a bit overpowering, but she was still very civil when speaking to the Welsh natives. She confirmed the time for Gloucester, but then explained that Professor Millichamp had also been asked to examine the body of Linda Prentice in Swansea and would it be convenient if they could do that on the following morning?

Rather taken aback by this sudden rush of business, Pryor agreed, but made sure that Millichamp's secretary, who identified herself as Prudence Mortimer, was aware that it was Patrick O'Malley who had performed the original examination and should also be present. She rather grandly informed Richard that she was aware of this and it was under control. He wondered whether he should offer to help them with their travel and accommodation requirements, but her super-efficient manner decided him to leave them to it. When she had rung off, he went in search of Angela to tell her of the developments.

'I know old Millichamp, he came into the Met Lab several times to look at material for the defence,' she said. 'He's one of the London grandees, like Simpson and Camps. Does a lot of civil and defence work, goes about with his secretary in a big chauffeur-driven Mercedes.'

Richard grinned. 'In that case, I'd better turn up to meet them in my chauffeur-driven second-hand Humber. I'll tell Jimmy to take off the cords around his trouser legs that day!'

The telephone was on overtime that day, as Ben Evans from Gowerton rang to confirm the time for the third post-mortem on poor Linda. 'The coroner has said that the burial must go ahead as soon as this is over, he's not going to delay any longer.'

'Any more news from the forensic laboratory?' asked Richard.

'They've screened Linda's blood and urine for drugs, nothing at all there. And as for the so-called suicide note, they are not very hopeful of deciding who typed it.'

'What's the problem, I wonder?'

'It seems to be that the message is so short that they've not got enough to work on as regards differences in style or even the opportunity for significant mistakes.'

'So it's a non-starter trying to accuse him of forging it?'

'One of the experts in Cardiff thinks it's a fake, but he reckons that his opinion wouldn't stand up against good cross-examination in court.'

The superintendent had no idea why they were getting a prominent pathologist from London to carry out yet another autopsy, but suspected that the solicitor representing Michael Prentice was covering all bases, with fees commensurate with his enthusiasm.

'The lawyer is from the same firm that does Prentice's motor company business. He's not a local guy, he comes from Slough. I hear they've briefed a barrister to come to the magistrates' hearing, no expense spared.'

'What about the father, Leonard Massey?' asked Richard. 'As a Queen's Counsel, I'll bet he'll want some big guns involved. A wonder he wasn't at that conference we had with Craddock.'

'If he hadn't been a potential witness, I expect he would have been there!' chortled Evans. 'I'll bet he's spitting tacks that he can't get involved professionally.'

The next call after Ben had rung off was Trevor Mitchell.

'As we expected, Agnes Oldfield is jumping up and down at the news of the blood group,' he groaned. 'Edward Lethbridge has tried to tell her that it takes us no further forward, other that not ruling out the remains could be either her nephew or about nine million other men in Britain!'

'She doesn't want another meeting, I hope,' said Pryor.

'No, but she's gone off on some other tack now, that I've got to follow up,' said Trevor. 'She found an old address

book of Anthony's amongst his stuff when she was searching
for a transfusion card. She's been phoning umpteen people,
making a nuisance of herself, but came across one who knew
him in Birmingham University when he was a student
umpteen years ago. This chap said that Anthony was in a
climbing club there and fell off some cliff in the Peak District
and had to go to hospital for a day or two. So now Agnes
wants me to find this chap and then scour the hospitals in
Derbyshire to see if they have any medical records or X-rays,
like we did for Albert Barnes.'

'The best of luck, Trevor!' said Richard. 'At least it's
good for trade, you should be raking it in with all these
fees and expenses.'

The investigator promised to let him know what happened
and Richard went back to work, looking at reports and microscope slides in a civil case where the family of a shipyard
worker was suing the employers for compensation for fatal
asbestosis.

At teatime, he regaled the team with the latest news. Angela
murmured that she didn't think she'd come with him to
Gloucester, as there was nothing she could contribute. Richard
suspected that she was afraid that her former fiancé might
turn up again, though that seemed unlikely.

When Wednesday came, he did not carry out his threat to
be driven to Gloucester by Jimmy, instead he left him cutting
down the undergrowth at the top of the plot with an Allen
scythe, a fearsome motorized device with large wheels that
took more energy to steer than the operator would have used
in cutting the weeds by hand.

It was now well into July and the capricious British weather
had turned wet and windy now that the school holiday season
was under way. He drove past Lydney and when going
through Newnham, was tempted to keep his head down in
case he was spotted by Mrs Oldfield. When he got to the
Royal Hospital, he found the fabled black Mercedes 170S
already outside the mortuary, a driver with a chauffeur's cap
busy polishing the chrome of the radiator. Inside the body-
store room, Detective Inspector Brian Lane, accompanied by
a photographer and the coroner's officer, was talking to
Arnold Millichamp and his personal secretary. The latter was

exactly as Richard had pictured her when on the telephone. A tall, thin woman with severely cropped grey hair, she had a long, intelligent face devoid of any make-up. A tan twinset and a long brown skirt surmounted sensible shoes and to complete the picture of an English lady, even in a mortuary she wore a single string of pearls. Her employer was also tall and thin, with a completely bald head and a large hooked nose. Dressed in legal garb of black jacket and striped grey trousers, he sported a blue bow tie.

Brian Lane introduced them and Millichamp shook hands and Miss Mortimer nodded gravely and murmured a greeting.

'Pryor, you were Professor in the University of Singapore, I recall,' said the London man, in a mellow voice that would have suited a bishop. 'You've given up the ivory towers of *académe*, then?'

Richard grinned. 'I didn't get much *académe* in Singapore, Professor, but plenty of experience. The local newspaper had a regular column called "Yesterday's Stabbings!"'

He handed Millichamp a carbon copy of his post-mortem report, which the pathologist gave to his secretary. She had a leather case under her arm and she slipped the report inside, as she took out a large notebook and a fountain pen, ready to record every pearl of wisdom that fell from her boss's lips.

They all moved into the post-mortem room next door, Prudence now also carrying a large case which she opened up on a table at the side. This was Arnold's tool kit and declining one of the red rubber aprons that the mortuary attendant offered, took a very new-looking yellow oilskin one from his case. Hanging the cords around his neck, he turned and with practised ease, Miss Mortimer tied the waist tapes around him. She then offered him a new pair of rubber gloves, which he snapped on with the flourish of a surgeon about to perform a craniotomy.

Pryor more humbly hung a rather frayed apron around his neck and followed Millichamp to the porcelain slab, where Harry Haines was already laid out. He summarized his findings for the defence pathologist, which was a short speech, as the only real area of interest was the neck wound and the damage inside the head.

'I excised the bullet entrance hole in case the police wanted to examine trace elements on the surrounding skin,' he explained, as Brian Lane displayed the photographs taken at the first autopsy. 'I've got the piece of skin intact here, fixed in formalin, if you'd like to see it.'

Millichamp rapidly reopened the stitches of the first post-mortem and made a quick but thorough examination of all the organs and the damaged skull and brain. For all his pomp and showmanship, he was an astute operator and though he worked with extraordinary speed, Richard saw that he missed nothing significant.

After he had finished, he rooted around in the jar that Pryor had brought and studied the small bullet wound, using a lens from his box to look at the edges of the hole.

Then, pulling off his gloves, he went to the table and rapidly read through Richard's report, handed to him by Prudence.

'Very good, very good!' he muttered, but somehow his tone was devoid of any condescension.

'A two-two pistol, I understand, Inspector?' he asked Lane.

'Yes, Professor, a Harrington and Richardson rim-fire job. The lab has already matched the weapon to the remains of the bullet that Doctor Pryor recovered. They're now doing some test-firings on it to check on range characteristics.'

As they washed up at the sink, Millichamp thawed a little and asked Richard about his new private venture. After hearing about their first few weeks, Millichamp nodded pontifically.

'You need to get yourself on the Home Office list, Pryor. I'll put in a word for you when I get the chance. We need all the experienced people we can get, especially now that universities are starting to close down their departments. Bloody short-sighted, but that's the government for you, can't see further than the end of their nose, if it'll save them a few pounds.'

Declining the offer of a mug of mortuary tea, the great man and his elegant assistant left, saying that they were staying that night near Swansea, at the Caswell Bay Hotel.

'That's only a few miles from where the lady we're seeing tomorrow was found,' said Richard.

Arnold Millichamp nodded. 'That's partly why we're going there. The defence solicitor wants us to see the scene, though as I gather that it's unlikely that a murder charge will materialize, I don't quite see the point.'

They went outside, where the chauffeur loaded their cases into the boot of the Mercedes and the two passengers sank into the back seats.

'I look forward to seeing you again in the morning, Professor,' called Millichamp before he closed the door.

As the car glided away Richard realized that he had been called 'Professor' by another of the same standing and felt an unreasonable pride in the title, in spite of having decided to abandon its use.

The more cynical Brian Lane watched the car out of sight. 'I wonder if there's anything going on between those two?' he muttered, with a policeman's suspicious mind.

Next morning, Pryor made an early start, again driving himself, as Jimmy was moonlighting somewhere down the valley, working on a vicar's garden.

He parked at the railway arch in Swansea's Strand before the black Mercedes arrived and had a chance to talk to Lewis Lewis and Dr O'Malley who were already there.

They stood drinking Camp coffee made by the attendant with water from a battered electric kettle, rendered almost palatable by milk powder which Richard suspected was actually from a baby-food tin.

'So the murder charge is a non-starter?' he asked the detective.

'Looks like it, the lawyers are not going to run with a charge that doesn't have a cat's chance in hell of succeeding,' said Lewis mournfully.

'So Arnold Millichamp is wasting his time coming here,' observed Pryor. 'Just like he did yesterday.' He told Lewis about the Gloucestershire shooting.

'Well, he's getting well paid for it, I'll bet. No one comes all the way from London for peanuts.'

The man in question arrived with his secretary a few moments later and as the attendant was ushering them in, Richard hoped that he would not offer them a mug of his peculiar brew. The look on Prudence Mortimer's face when she saw they had to work in a blocked-off railway arch was enough, without the offer of chicory extract mixed with Cow and Gate.

When they went into the inner sanctum and were kitted up, Richard could see that poor Linda was deteriorating. After two dissections and a third in the offing, it was high time that she was finally put to rest. He sometimes wondered at his own immunity to the horrors of death, presuming it was part predisposition and part familiarity. Pryor was often asked how he could possibly do such an awful job, but realized that he rarely thought about it. Those who could not handle the macabre job either never started or soon gave up. Not a few of his colleagues had become alcoholics and several had committed suicide, an occupational hazard which was more common amongst all doctors than the general public.

Shrugging off these morbid thoughts, he asked Miss Mortimer if they had had copies of his report.

'We have all the documents, thank you, Professor,' she said with a charming smile that made him feel that she was not such a cold fish as she was assumed to be. Prudence seemed indifferent to the proximity of a dead body in a poor state of preservation, looking more disconcerted by the strange building in which they had to work.

Once again, Richard went through his findings for Millichamp, several times emphasizing that Patrick O'Malley, who hardly uttered a word, was the primary pathologist.

'I'm afraid after the previous dissections and the passage of time, you won't have much to look at,' he said to the visitor. 'But no doubt your instructing solicitor will have given you copies of the photographs and I can give you a spare set of section of the bruises and the major organs.'

As before, Millichamp worked with considerable speed, not that there was much left to examine. The important bruises had been taken by Pryor for microscopic examination, though he had brought them all in their labelled jars of formaldehyde for the other pathologist to see.

'You are extremely thorough, Professor Pryor,' complimented Millichamp as he washed his hands in the porcelain tank that was the only sink. Patrick O'Malley again tried to make himself look invisible, as the two forensic pathologists launched into a discussion of recent research into new methods of dating injuries, both agreeing that the results were not all that helpful.

The two visitors left after delighting the mortuary attendant with a one pound tip for his help. Richard Pryor was left with something that was much more valuable to him, another assurance from the influential Londoner that he would 'have a word' with some unspecified authority about getting him onto the Home Office list – and an invitation to visit his department at 'Barts' any time he was in the big city.

A few weeks' routine work followed, Richard Pryor gradually building up his foundation of coroner's cases which brought in a modest, but steady income. Similarly, Angela Bray's reputation in the field of paternity testing steadily increased the number of blood tests she was called on to perform. Some of these came from far afield and in some instances, she was asked to go and actually obtain the samples from mother, child and putative father. This mean going off in her little Renault, with a consequent increase in the fee. Sometimes she took Sian with her on these jaunts, if the technician had time, though even here, the number of defence alcohol estimations was gradually increasing.

As well as physical work in the laboratory, both he and Angela began getting case papers for expert opinions on a variety of subjects, both criminal and civil. Lawyers were increasingly demanding a second opinion on autopsy reports, biological opinions and road and industrial accident claims. Even insurance companies were coming to the Garth House partnership, as it was coming to be known, when they wanted to confirm or contest some dubious claim for compensation. By the end of August, Richard and Angela felt confident that their bold venture to go private was going to succeed and decided that they could order some more equipment for the laboratory which would extend the range of investigations that they could offer.

They heard nothing from Agnes Oldfield or her solicitor and one further visit from Trevor Mitchell confirmed that he had been unable find any trace of Anthony being treated in hospital after a climbing accident.

The Gloucester shooting went before the magistrates and, as expected, the local gangster was committed for trial at the next assizes in several months' time. Richard was called to give evidence at the magistrates' preliminary hearing, but there was no cross-examination, this being reserved for the later trial. Arnold Millichamp was present in court, sitting behind the defence solicitor, but apart from leaning forwards a couple of times to whisper in the lawyer's ear while Richard was giving his evidence-in-chief, he seemed to have no contrary opinion.

Afterwards, Arnold waited outside the court with Prudence Mortimer to greet Richard affably and talk about the two cases in which they were involved. Though lawyers generally do not encourage prosecution and defence experts to confer, there was no potential conflict of opinion in either the shooting case or Michael Prentice's problems, especially as the latter was not facing any charges relating to his wife's death or injuries.

Even so, they both spoke circumspectly and most of their chat was about the forthcoming November conference in Cardiff, to which Millichamp expressed interest in attending. Before they parted, the London pathologist repeated his invitation to Pryor to visit his department – and also offered to have Sian there for a week or two, to get some experience of a bigger laboratory.

When he took this bit of news back to Garth House, the technician was wildly excited and almost ready to pack her bags for a visit to London, until he calmed her down.

'But it all helps to get us better known,' he said to Angela. 'If I can get onto this Home Office list, we can throw our net even wider.'

The magistrates' hearing in Gowerton had been a damp squib, as the prosecution wanted more time to prepare their evidence. Ben Evans said it was requested by the document examiners in Cardiff, who were seeking other opinions elsewhere, to decide if they could substantiate their suspicions that Linda had not written the suicide not.

In spite of the objections of the police, bail was extended

and Michael Prentice carried on living in Pennard and
working at the Jersey Marine premises, though what his
colleagues there thought of him, was unknown.

In the meantime, Brian Meredith, the Monmouth coroner,
had wrestled with the paperwork and the General Register
Office, to annul the death certificate issued for Albert Barnes.
Mrs Molly Barnes protested loud and long to him about what
she claimed was a 'denial of her rights' and threatened to
go to the newspapers about it, until Meredith pointed out to
her that she had given false evidence about the watch and
ring, which could get her into trouble.

He had taken legal advice and found that he needed to
hold another inquest, as the remains buried in a corner of
the Monmouth municipal cemetery were now of an uniden-
tified person, which required an inquest with a jury. This
was a formality, after all the futile efforts to establish to
whom they belonged had failed.

Richard Pryor and Angela were called as witnesses, merely
to get the physical facts and the blood group put on official
record, but the outcome was inevitably another open verdict.

In early September, the delayed court appearance of
Michael Prentice took place in Gowerton. The dreary magistrates' court was invaded by a clutch of lawyers and local
journalists, but as the charges had been reduced to
'obstructing the coroner in the pursuance of an inquest', it
was not a very newsworthy event. Linda's father, Leonard
Massey and his wife were there, as well as Marjorie
Elphington, the friend who set all this in motion. There was
no sign of the other woman, Daphne Squires and Ben Evans
suspected that she had rapidly distanced herself from her
former lover and his troubles.

In the entrance hall of the old building, where witnesses
congregated, Ben Evans was holding forth to his inspector.

'The bugger should be up on a murder charge, not this
piddling offence that will only get him a couple of months
in the nick and a big fine!' he growled. 'If only those forensic
people could have come down definitely on that letter and
said it's a fake, we'd have had him, because there's no other
reason for writing it unless he did her in.'

'Craddock's not calling either of the doctors,' said Lewis

Lewis. 'I suppose there's nothing useful they can say, as nobody denies it was drowning.'

'It's not part of the charge, anyway. Doesn't matter what she died of, as all Prentice is being done for is mucking up the coroner's inquest procedure.'

This is exactly what was presented in court. Though the defendant had a barrister to represent him, the prosecuting solicitor went at it alone, given the relatively minor nature of the offence, compared with assault or murder.

The committal proceedings were heard before three Justices of the Peace, as there was no stipendiary magistrate in that jurisdiction. One was a dour steelworks manager, another was a fat and florid butcher and the third, who sat in the middle and acted as chairwoman, was an angular female head teacher with a particularly ugly hat. They were guided – or rather harassed – by the Clerk of the Court, a sergeant-major figure who sat below them, but kept bobbing up and down to hiss instructions at them.

Michael Prentice appeared in the dock, his counsel's application to have him sit in the well of the court rejected. He was soberly dressed in a dark suit and appeared totally composed and in control of himself.

Somewhat to everyone's surprise, he pleaded guilty to the single charge against him. On his lawyer's advice, he knew that there was no chance of evading the fact that he had suppressed the existence of the note when called to the inquest.

Maldwyn Craddock had considered Ben Evans's contention that as Prentice had been on oath in the coroner's court, this amounted to perjury – but as Prentice had not said that there was no note, because there was no reason to ask him, the omission to mention it was probably not enough to succeed with the more serious charge.

Even though the defendant had pleaded guilty, the magistrates had no power to sentence him, as the offence was one which inevitably had to be committed to the Assizes, in a few months' time. There a judge would hear the guilty plea and be responsible for deciding on the sentence. No doubt the expensive defence counsel would then earn his fee by an impassioned address in mitigation. But at the Gowerton magistrates, he employed the same skills in seeking an extension of bail, to try to keep Michael Prentice out of prison until his appearance at the Assizes.

The barrister, a rather gaunt figure in the legal uniform of black jacket and striped trousers, waxed lyrical on behalf of his client, in front of the stony-faced trio of justices.

'Above all else, my client was anxious to avoid the stigma of suicide falling upon his much loved wife and saw no harm in allowing her memory to remain unsullied by the assumption that this was a tragic accident.'

In the public seats at the back of the court, Leonard Massey almost burst with indignation at the 'much-loved' reference, but there was nothing he could do about it. By the nature of the narrow charge against his hated son-in-law, none of the peripheral evidence was relevant; it would have been a very different matter if the alleged domestic violence or the death was in issue.

The barrister was an experienced man and played upon the distress, confusion and grief that had beset Michael on finding the note and then her body on the beach.

'It is evident that he hardly knew what he was doing, such was his mental state,' he pleaded before the stony-faced JPs. 'Why else would he have carried his wife's body in his arms up that difficult track – and why would a temporary dislocation of his behaviour cause him to put her back in the water at a different place?'

There was much more of this, sometimes repetitious. The butcher on the bench was anxious to get back to his shop and as the bloody defendant had pleaded guilty, grumbled under his breath as to why they had to hear 'all this stuff'.

Eventually, after pleading for an extension of bail, mainly on the grounds that this was a one-off lapse of behaviour which would – indeed, could – not be repeated, Prentice's barrister felt he had done enough to earn his fee and sat down.

The clerk bobbed up and said something and the three magistrates retired into their room behind for ten minutes. When they returned, the chairwoman put on her most severe face and addressed the defendant.

'Though what you did was foolish and has caused

considerable disruption and unnecessary work for the
coroner, his staff and the police, we accept that you were in
a highly emotional and confused state after finding your
wife's body. In addition, you tried to spare her family the
stigma of suicide – and you have not attempted to evade
your responsibility for this crime by pleading not guilty. As
you are an otherwise respectable member of the business
fraternity, with no previous convictions, we agree to continuation of your bail until you are dealt with at the Assize Court,
naturally with the proper restrictions on your movements and
the appropriate sureties.'

There were further details of the conditions of his bail,
then the magistrates filed out and the court broke up.

If Leonard Massey had not been a well-controlled lawyer,
this is where he would have stood up and accused his son-
in-law of being a murderer. As it was, he strode tight-lipped
from the court with his wife trailing behind him and marched
out into the street to find his car.

The two CID men trudged the short distance to the police
station, annoyed but not surprised at the outcome of the case.

'The bastard even got bail!' muttered Evans. 'And I expect
that barrister will get the trial judge weeping and just rap
his knuckles and tell him not to do it again!

'Something might turn up,' replied his inspector, though
he did not sound too confident about it.

'In future, every time I put oil in my car, I'll be reminded
of this sod getting away with it!' growled the superintendent.

NINETEEN

Three weeks later, a letter arrived at Garth House which caused a celebration, prompting Angela to fetch the bottle of Yugoslav Lutomer Riesling which she had in her room. The whole staff, including Jimmy Jenkins, gathered in the lounge to drink out of a mixed collection of glasses, toasting Richard's appointment to the Home Office list.

The letter from an under-secretary in the Home Office was terse and colourless, but the essence of it was that '*if he was so minded, they would look favourably upon any application to have his name added to the list circulated to Chief Constables, as being medical practitioners suitable to be recommended to coroners as proficient in dealing with deaths which require forensic expertise.*'

A retainer of one hundred and fifty pounds per annum would be offered on condition that the pathologist made himself available at all times or to arrange for another listed pathologist to act in his absence.

'On call twenty-four hours a day for a hundred-and-fifty quid!' exclaimed Sian. 'I should join a trade union if I were you, Doc! Chaps sweeping factory floors get more than that for a forty-hour week!'

Her socialist crusading spirit was aroused, but Richard calmed her down by pointing out that he doubted that he would be called on very often, as he did not have a specific area to cover, but was only going to act as a back-up for other pathologists, as he had done in the Gloucester shooting.

'I don't know who fixed this up,' he said ruminatively. 'Brian Meredith and his brother have friends at court, so to speak, but so does Arnold Millichamp. And, of course, the Gloucester CID may have passed the word up to their Chief Constable.'

Whoever it was, the welcome title all helped towards consolidating their venture's position in the forensic community.

Several weeks passed and he had no other calls on his new status, but Moira sensibly suggested that as the summer holiday season had finished, other pathologists were no longer in need of a locum.

'We'll have to wait for one to break a leg or come down with malaria or something!' suggested Sian, facetiously.

A few days later, the dangerous waters of the Severn estuary provided another body for Richard Pryor to examine at the Chepstow mortuary. Though badly decomposed, the police found a Seaman's Identity Card in the remnants of the clothing and the index number was traced through the Central Register of Seamen. The victim was identified as a deckhand who went missing off Lundy Island two months earlier from a tanker taking crude oil for the Llandarcy BP refinery at Swansea. Richard found the body too far gone for a diagnosis of drowning and thought it a good opportunity to try out the controversial diatom test once again.

In their laboratory next morning, Angela once more showed Sian each step of the process. Small pieces of the tissues were taken, with precautions to avoid surface contamination with body fluids.

'That's to eliminate false results from getting diatoms other than via the bloodstream,' she explained. 'It doesn't matter about the lung, because that's going to be contaminated anyway, down the windpipe.'

Sian watched as the tissues from each organ were heated in small beakers of concentrated nitric acid in the fume cupboard, a dangerous operation if not done with great care, as the brown fumes from the highly corrosive liquid spiralled up into the exhaust outlet.

It took a long time for the digestion to get rid of all the organic material, but when the extracts had cooled, Angela put a portion of each into conical-bottomed centrifuge tubes and diluted them with distilled water.

'Couldn't you use tap water?' asked Sian, always cost-conscious, but Angela shook her head.

'Not safe to do that,' she advised. 'It often contains diatoms that grow inside the pipes.'

The digests were centrifuged to throw what was left of

the solids down to the bottom of the tubes, then she repeated this twice more to dilute the acid to harmless proportions.

'Now let's have a look at those,' she said, taking the tubes over to the microscope.

Putting a drop of the final sludge on to a glass slide and dropping a coverslip on to it, she peered through the eyepieces for a few moments, twiddling the stage controls to move the slides around under the high-power lenses.

Then she leaned back to let Sian's glossy head take her place. 'Plenty in the lung! Have a squint at those. Good old Bristol Channel diatoms!'

When Sian had satisfied herself, Angela went through the extracts from brain, liver, bone marrow and kidney.

She was glued to the microscope much longer this time, but eventually got up and declared herself satisfied.

'Thought we were going to draw a blank, but the marrow has hit the jackpot,' she said. 'You need to find a reasonable number of diatoms, not just one or two – then hope the chap hadn't been eating cockles or oysters the night before!'

Her technician seemed very taken by the technique and wanted to practice for herself.

'I'll have a go at the next body from the water myself,' she promised. Angela, impressed by her keenness, had a suggestion.

'We kept some tissues from the Gower case. Why don't you use those, as Richard was convinced she was drowned, so it should be a good positive.'

Full of enthusiasm and without any other pressing work for the moment, Sian looked out the labelled pots and started on the digestions. Angela kept a motherly eye on her from a distance, but let her get on with the procedures herself. By the afternoon, the acid digestion was completed and Sian happily made up the slides from the various tissues.

She spent a long time staring at them down the microscope, while Angela was busy with a paternity test on another bench.

'Any joy, Sian?' called the biologist eventually.

'Plenty in the lungs, but of course, you said that's of no use in proving drowning,' she replied, sounding rather disappointed.

'Are there none in the other organs, then?'

'Yes, I've only found half a dozen in the kidney and another five in the marrow. Is that enough?'

Angela rose and came across the room.

'Let's have a look. Lung first, eh?'

Sian gave up her seat and stood alongside, while Angela peered down the instrument, then slid the other organ slides into place under the lenses. This seemed to go on for a long time and the technician became restless.

'Did I do it properly?' she asked anxiously.

Angela made no direct reply but asked her to hand down a book from a nearby shelf.

'The thin green one, on the end,' she said in a worried tone. She riffled through the pages and Sian saw dozens of photographs and drawings of diatoms, some boat-shaped, some circular, others like needles.

'Give me that lung slide we made this morning, please. The one from the oil tanker death.'

Still with no explanation, Angela changed the specimens on the microscope stage, then changed them back again.

When she looked up at her technician, her face was serious.

'Sian, can you give Richard a call, please? I think we've got a problem!'

'But that's bloody impossible!' he exclaimed. 'Linda's body was hauled out of the sea by the coastguards, so we know she was in there!'

Angela shook her head stubbornly.

'I'm not denying that she had been in the sea, there are plenty of marine diatoms in her lungs. But she didn't *die* in sea water. It was fresh!'

Richard stared down the microscope, though he was none the wiser until Angela pointed out various illustrations in the atlas of diatoms that was still open on the bench.

'The ones in the kidney and marrow are all freshwater species, no marine ones at all. There are stacks of them in the lungs as well, but of course they're mixed with marine diatoms, as she had been submerged later in the sea.'

Pryor jumped from the stool and paced back and forth.

'There's no possibility of some mistake?' he demanded. 'Could the samples have been mixed up?'

Angela was unruffled. She pointed to the bench top.

'There are the pots in front of you! You were the one who brought them back and it's your writing on the labels, as well as the signature of the DI who was there.'

Sian, who had been standing wide-eyed listening to this, decided to join in.

'I was the one who did the digestion, Doctor. I'll do it all over again, just to make sure.'

Moira came in with some forms to sign and immediately sensed that something was going on.

'What's happening?' she asked. 'Am I interrupting something?'

'These two ladies have thrown a great big spanner in the works!' said Richard. 'I suppose we should have looked for these blasted diatoms straight after I did the PM, but it just didn't seem necessary, it was so obvious that she had drowned.'

'And now you've discovered that she didn't?' gasped Moira, afraid that her perfect doctor had dropped a huge clanger.

'No, not at all,' said Richard. 'But she drowned in the wrong sort of water!'

Angela explained that diatoms in sea water were different from those in fresh water. 'Though there's an overlap, there is such a preponderance of some species that there's no doubt which water it was. In fact, it's said to be possible to tell whether someone drowned in the brackish waters of an estuary, if both sorts are found together.'

They all thought about this for a moment.

'So where did the poor woman drown?' asked the practical Moira.

'In almost any water but the sea,' sighed Angela. 'They're everywhere – rivers, streams, ponds, lakes, even puddles if they've been there long enough.'

'So you could even find them in the bird bath in your garden?' said Sian.

'Yes, but you have a job to drown in a bird bath,' objected Moira.

Richard was not so sure. 'There have been plenty of cases

of people drowning in only a few inches of water, like a big puddle or a bucket. Of course they'd either have to be drunk or drugged, unless someone was holding them so that their nose and mouth were covered.'

There was another pregnant silence at this.

'Holding her face under?' said Angela sepulchrally.

'But under what?'

Richard stopped pacing. 'That's for the police to discover. But could you identify a particular source of water by the type of diatoms, Angela?'

She shook her head. 'Not firmly enough to give in evidence. This diatom business is only now being considered as useful, even though it's been suggested on and off for ages. Many people are still too critical of it to use it routinely.'

'So you couldn't definitely identify any river or lake as being the place? Not that there seems to be any of those around Pennard, it's on top of the cliffs.'

'She could have been driven from anywhere,' pointed out Sian. 'You said this Prentice chap has got a big Jaguar, he could have brought her from Lake Windermere, for all we know!'

'When are you going to tell the CID, Richard?' asked Angela. 'I think we ought to repeat the tests, just to be on the safe side.'

'I'll work all night, if you want me to,' volunteered Sian, eagerly.

Angela tempered her enthusiasm a little. 'Let's get the digestions started now, then they can simmer all night, so that we can look at them first thing in the morning.'

Richard nodded his agreement. 'Then I'll ring Ben Evans and make his day! Angela, if he finds some suitable water in the district, we may have to go down there and sample it for diatoms.'

Detective Superintendent Evans slammed his phone down and gave a roar of delight.

'Lewis, come in here!' he yelled out of the door. As his inspector hurried in from the CID room outside, he gave him the news like a trumpet call.

'I reckon we may have got that swine Prentice! Doc Pryor

and his team have done some fancy tests and reckon Linda
didn't die in the bloody sea at all!'

He explained what he'd been told on the telephone and
though neither of them fully understood the technicalities,
they knew they had to find some fresh water that would fit
the bill.

'Are we going down there now?' asked Lewis. 'What are
we looking for?'

'I've arranged with the doctor to come down today, with
the lady scientist who discovered this. She was a forensic
expert from the Met Lab, so she must know what she's talking
about.'

'Where's Prentice now? Still working in that place of his
in Jersey Marine, I suppose.'

'To hell with him for the moment, we've got to find some
water around there. Apparently, this lady may want to take
some samples.'

By noon, Richard and Angela were on the road in the
Humber, with a cardboard box containing a dozen glass
sample jars on the back seat.

They reached Gowerton about three o'clock, after a quick
snack on the way – a sandwich, currant bun and cup of tea
at Saunders Refreshment hut on Stalling Down, near
Cowbridge. At the police station, they met Ben Evans and
Lewis Lewis to give them a detailed account of their recent
discovery, emphasizing that as far as they were concerned,
there could be no other explanation other than Linda Prentice
had drowned in fresh water, not the sea.

'Let's go and find some for you, then,' growled Evans. He
and the inspector climbed into a patrol car with a uniformed
driver and the Humber followed behind. They went out westwards into the country, through Penclawdd to Llanrhidian,
then back to join the secondary road that went up over Cefn
Bryn, the hilly spine of the Gower peninsula.

'Where the hell are they going?' asked Richard, but soon
it was made clear, as the black Wolseley in front pulled over
to the side of the road, in the middle of a large stretch of
moorland. They stopped behind it and saw that at the side
of the road was a large, sinister-looking pool, surrounded by
rushes. They got out and joined the two detectives, who wore

their habitual belted raincoats and trilbies, as it had been a day of typical Welsh drizzle. The four of them stood at the edge of the almost circular pool, which was about a hundred yards wide.

'We brought you here first, as it's about the largest pond in these parts,' said Evans. 'It's called the Broad Pool at Cilibion.'

He pointed at the ridge in the distance. 'Up there on Cefn Bryn is Arthur's Stone and there's a legend that this pond is where King Arthur chucked in his sword Excalibur. Lot of nonsense, that – but there's plenty of water to get drowned in, even though it's shallow.'

Angela dutifully filled one of her jars at the edge and agreed that it was murky enough to be full of diatoms. Then they moved on and went over the hill to Reynoldston and back to Pennard through Parkmill, where they stopped again to sample the small river that ran down from Ilston to Three Cliffs Bay.

'The seaward end of this stream is not all that far from Pennard,' said Lewis. 'But it would be a devil of a climb up and down, as well as being busy with trippers, except at dead of night.'

'We may as well get to the house and work out from there,' suggested Evans. They went on their way again and arrived at *Bella Capri*, getting some curious looks from a few walkers, as the two large black cars, one with a 'Police' sign, drew up outside the house.

'No sign of his Jaguar, guv,' murmured Lewis, as they looked over the gate at the silent bungalow.

'Where do we start?' asked Richard, turning to survey the rather arid cliff top, with its rocky ground and scraggy gorse. 'There doesn't seem to be any streams or ponds up here.'

'The nearest river is the one that comes down the Bishopston Valley and empties into the sea at Pwlldu,' said Lewis. 'More of a stream, really, it goes underground for part of the way.'

The superintendent pushed open the gate. 'Let's have a look around now we're here. I suppose he doesn't have a swimming pool around the back?'

As they walked up the drive, Angela pointed to the circular rockery in front of the bungalow. 'What's that? A fish pond?'

They quickened their pace and went to the rather neglected heap of large stones, with its central cement-lined hollow. Angela put her fingers into the murky water and pulled out some weed with green slime trailing from it. 'I'll bet this is rotten with diatoms,' she announced.

'Bit small to drown in, isn't it?' asked Lewis, dubiously.

'Let's try it and see!' said Ben Evans, suddenly grabbing the smaller man and pushing his head forwards over the outer ring of stones until his face was almost touching the water. Fortunately, he had left his hat in the police car or it would probably have fallen in.

'Hey, lay off, boss!' he complained, as the grinning superintendent pulled him back up. 'But you're right, it could be done.'

Angela had an objection. 'Surely she would struggle and then there would be signs of restraint! Wouldn't she show fresh bruises on her shoulders and arms if she was gripped to hold her under water for a few minutes?'

Richard pursed his lips in doubt.

'If she was thrashing about, yes – but what if she was unconscious, after a bang on the head?' he asked. 'There were certainly signs of a recent head injury, which could be put down to being bashed against rocks while still alive in the sea – but which we now suspect didn't happen!'

They were suddenly interrupted by a call from the police driver, who had been leaning on the bonnet of the big Wolseley, having a surreptitious smoke.

'Super! Does the chap you're interested in, drive a Mark Five Jaguar?' There was an unmistakable urgency in his voice, as he pointed an arm down the track towards Southgate.

Ben Evans's head snapped up as he replied. 'Yes, a black one! Why?'

'Because a car like that was driving right up here, when it suddenly reversed, turned in the bushes and has gone like a bat out of hell back down the road, sir!'

Lewis stared at his senior officer. 'He must have spotted us messing about here at the pond!'

The superintendent was already pounding down the path, moving very quickly for a man of his bulk, Lewis racing after him. They piled into the police car, the driver discarding his Woodbine and scrambling in to start the engine.

'Get after him, man! There's only one road out of this place,' snapped Lewis, who had taken the front passenger seat.

The driver did a neck-jolting two-point turn into the bracken and gorse at the side of the bumpy track, then shot off after the other car, which was already well out of sight. Angela and Richard were left staring after them, her diatom pot still in her hand.

'Never a dull moment in this job,' she said calmly.

In the police car, the driver was bemoaning his lack of acceleration.

'We'll never catch a big Jag like that,' he said bitterly. 'Why couldn't he have had a Standard Ten instead?'

Thankfully, unlike some of the CID cars, this one had radio and Lewis was already reaching for the handset. Calling up the Control Room, he requested interception on the most likely roads back towards Swansea, as westwards was a dead end at the end of the Gower peninsula, with only ocean between it and North America.

Their driver raced the Wolseley through Pennard, the chromed gong on the front bumper hammering out a warning as they went. The road branched at Pennard Church and Ben Evans yelled for the constable to take the left fork and go up to the next junction and then towards Fairwood Common, the road to the centre of Swansea.

'Where does he think he's going?' shouted Lewis. 'He can't get away, there's nowhere to go.'

'He's in a panic, that's what!' replied Evans. 'He saw us looking into that pond and realized the game was up.'

Lewis was on the radio again.

'They've got two traffic cars coming from Dunvant. If he's on this road, they should block him before he gets there.'

In a few moments, they were on an open road going across the moorland towards Upper Killay, the now-abandoned RAF fighter station on their left.

'That's them ahead,' shouted the driver, just as Lewis had a radio confirmation that the first traffic car had made contact. Peering down the long straight road, Lewis could see one

vehicle slewed across the road and another tilted on the verge
at the side. In a few more seconds, they were alongside
another police car, with the Jaguar half-toppled into a rush-
filled ditch, where it had attempted to squeeze past.

Two uniformed officers were pulling a dishevelled figure
out of the driver's door when the two detectives approached.
Shaken, but still defiant, he began blustering about illegal
harassment, but Ben Evans jerked his head at his inspector.
Lewis Lewis stepped forward and laid a hand on the man's
shoulder as he was held by the other officers.

'Michael Prentice, I'm arresting you for the murder of
your wife Linda. You need not say anything, but anything
you do say may be used in evidence.'

Ben Evans added his own unofficial rider.

'You'll hang for this, you callous bastard!'

The morning tea break at Garth House had become a regular
briefing session, where news of their cases was bandied
about. A week after their trip to Gower, Richard reported a
telephone conversation he had with Ben Evans in Gowerton,
who was officially ringing him to tell him that both he and
Angela would be required to give evidence at the magistrates' court in a few weeks' time.

'There's going to be a full hearing at new committal
proceedings against Prentice,' Ben had said. 'He's got another
high-powered barrister to represent him and it looks as if
they're trying to wangle a manslaughter verdict to save his
neck.'

The three women in the staff room all wanted to know if
Michael Prentice had confessed to what had happened.

'I can't see he can plead manslaughter if he held his wife's
head under water until she drowned!' objected Sian.

'Ben Evans told me that Prentice coughed to causing the
death when he saw us taking samples at the garden pool –
but he later retracted some of it to try to bolster his
manslaughter defence,' said Richard.

'So what did he say he did?' asked Sian, who had developed
a proprietorial interest after having prepared the diatom test.

'He claims they had a hell of a row again over his in-
fidelity with that blonde woman. She threatened him with a

carving knife and chased him out into the garden. They struggled against the rockery and some how she fell face forward into the water and drowned!'

'That sounds utter nonsense to me!' declared Moira.

Richard drank some tea, then agreed. 'Of course it is, but if the alternative is an eight o'clock walk in Swansea prison, he'll clutch at any lame excuse.'

Sian shuddered, suddenly less proud of her expertise in demonstrating diatoms.

'It's pretty horrible to think that what I did could lead to them hanging that man,' she murmured.

Angela put a reassuring arm around her shoulders.

'It's not what *you* did, Sian, it's what *he* did that matters,' she said softly. 'He killed her, then threw her into the sea as if he was getting rid of some inconvenient rubbish.'

The technician nodded. 'I suppose I'll get used to it, but I still think that this awful ritual of hanging is barbaric. The sooner it's abolished, the better!'

Privately, Richard Pryor agreed with her.

EPILOGUE

Edward Lethbridge sat in his office above the building society in Lydney, drafting another will for a client who seemed to change his mind about every six months. There was a tap on his door and one of the secretaries from the next room put her head in.

'There's a gentleman to see you, Mr Lethbridge. He doesn't have an appointment, but he said he won't keep you more than a few minutes.'

The solicitor sighed and pushed his papers aside.

'Very well, Mavis – show him in.'

A tall man entered, dressed rather foppishly in a velveteen jacket and a limp bow tie. He had wavy hair greying at the temples, framing a high forehead and a pointed jaw. Advancing to the desk, he thrust out a hand to Lethbridge.

'Jolly good of you to see me at such short notice,' he said with a slight lisp. 'I'm Anthony Oldfield, I gather you've been looking for me.'

Lethbridge had seen and heard many strange things during his professional life and he rose to the occasion well.

'Well, well, Mr Oldfield, this is a surprise.'

He motioned the visitor to the chair opposite. 'You aunt has been searching the country for you.'

'I realize that. I've been living in the Auvergne for a few years, a bit cut off from news, you know!'

He explained that a friend had sent him an old newspaper cutting with Trevor Mitchell's advertisement for information concerning his whereabouts, giving the solicitor's address for any reply.

'I decided to pop over and let you know that I was still alive and kicking. Put the old lady out of her misery!'

'But why did you just vanish like that?' asked the lawyer, secretly astonished at the man's nonchalance.

'Couldn't stand the old girl any longer!' replied Anthony. 'After giving up my flat, living in the same house with her was hell. The place was like a museum, couldn't smoke my pipe indoors, didn't like me drinking there, nag, nag, nag! So one day, I just decided to push off. Always liked France, so I stayed there.'

'And never let her know where you were?' asked Lethbridge.

'Never got around to it. I was afraid she'd want to come over and stay and talk about my bloody will again. But when I saw that I was assumed to be dead, I guessed she was after probate, so thought I'd better come and straighten things out. I haven't actually seen her yet, I came straight to you.'

They talked for a few more moments, then Anthony rose to leave.

'Mustn't keep you, I've imposed enough already.'

Before he reached the door, the solicitor had one more question.

'Do you by any chance have a depressed sternum, Mr Oldfield?' he asked with a mischievous look on his face.

Oldfield stared at Lethbridge in astonishment.

'How on earth did you know that?' he said.

AUTHOR'S NOTE

I n regard to the use of diatoms, the reliability of which is
still controversial, in the *Yacht Christine* case (R-v-Verrier,
1964), the body of a murdered man dropped off a yacht
off the English coast was recovered many weeks later in
Belgian waters. Forensic study of the diatoms established
that they were of a type found only off the Kent coast and
not on the opposite side of the Channel.